THE HAMMER THE SICKLE AND THE HEART

Trotsky and Kahlo in Mexico

ALSO BY C. P. ROSENTHAL

How the Animals Around You Think: The Semiotics of Animal Cognition (2019)

You Can Fly, A Sequel to the Peter Pan Tales (2018)

The Legend of La Diosa (2018)

The Shortest Farewells Are the Best (flash noir with Gail Wronsky, 2015)

Ten Thousand Heavens (2013)

Tomorrow You'll Be One Of Us (sci-fi poems with Gail Wronsky, 2013)

West of Eden: A Life in 21st Century Los Angeles (2012)

Coyote O'Donohughe's History of Texas (2010)

Are We Not There Yet?: Travels in Nepal, North India, and Bhutan (2009)

The Heart of Mars (2008)

The Loop Trilogy (author's original edition, 2007:
    Loop's Progress—Experiments With Life and Deaf—Loop's End)

Never Let Me Go: A Memoir (2004)

My Mistress, Humanity (2002)

Jack Kerouac's Avatar Angel: His Last Novel (2001)

Elena of the Stars (1995)

Loops End (1992)

Experiments With Life and Deaf (1987)

Loops Progress (1986)

THE HAMMER, THE SICKLE AND THE HEART

Trotsky and Kahlo in Mexico

A NOVEL

C. P. ROSENTHAL

LETTERSAT
3AMPRESS

Publisher's Cataloging-In-Publication Data
Names: Rosenthal, Chuck, 1951- author.
Title: The hammer, the sickle and the heart : Trotsky and Kahlo in Mexico : a novel / C.P. Rosenthal.
Description: Pacific Grove, CA : LettersAt3amPress, 2020.
Identifiers: ISBN 9781733378925 (paperback)
Subjects: LCSH: Trotsky, Leon, 1879-1940--Fiction. | Kahlo, Frida--Fiction. | Trotˊsˇkaiˊaˇ,
    Nataliiˊaˇ Ivanovna, 1882-1962--Fiction. | Rivera, Diego, 1886-1957--Fiction. |
    Revolutionaries--Soviet Union--20th century--Fiction. | Artists--Mexico--20th century--Fiction. |
    Man-woman relationships--Fiction.
Classification: LCC PS3568.O8368 H36 2020 | DDC 813/.6--dc23

Published in 2020 by LettersAt3amPress
680 Lighthouse Ave #397
Pacific Grove, CA 93950

Publisher/Editors: Jazmin Aminian Jordán, Michael Ventura
Book and Jacket Designer: Ash Goodwin, www.ashgood.com

LettersAt3amPress

For Gail,
as always

PUBLISHER'S PREFACE
Michael Ventura

MAYBE IT IS HEARTENING, maybe it is scary, maybe it's both, but history has proved this to be true: An *idea* in one century can become a *nation* in the next. That is the history of the United States and also of the Union of Soviet Socialist Republics—the Soviet Union, for short, which included Russia, the Ukraine, Chechnya, Byelorussia, and about 11 other countries unfortunate enough to border Russia. After the Second World War, the U.S.S.R. also controlled most of Eastern Europe, including Poland, and half of Germany. It seems that only an incredibly powerful idea, or core of ideas, can swell a nation into the size of a continent.

In the United States it has been bad political manners to notice out loud that the motivating ideas of the U.S. and the U.S.S.R are very much alike. C.P. Rosenthal begins *The Hammer, The Sickle, And The Heart—Trotsky and Kahlo in Mexico* with words that either nation could sign: *The desire for liberation lived in the heart and soul of every human being . . . Industry and technology had changed the world forever. Every human being could now share in technology and freedom.*

The next sentence would surprise many across the U.S.A. *He [Leon Trotsky] believed that this could begin in Russia and spread to the world. This was the dream.*

Sounds like the American dream. Yet it was the motivating dream of Marxist-Leninist Communism as well.

There are other parallels, if you are interested: both the U.S. and U.S.S.R. could resolve their internal contradictions only through civil war, and both expanded their territories through conquest and subjugation. But the U.S. was, of course, capitalist; the U.S.S.R., socialist. Whatever the moral values of each system, there is no doubt that capitalism facilitates production and distribution fantastically better than socialism. So the U.S.S.R. is no more. (As for justice . . . with these two nations justice, like beauty, is often in the eye of the beholder.)

There is, of course, another major difference: The U.S. has relied— sometimes more so and sometimes less so—on what it calls the *consent of the governed.* Not so the U.S.S.R. As Leon Trotsky says in C.P. Rosenthal's book, "People must be led"—though he also claims to be "ambivalent about democracy." Easy to sound gentle in Mexico, on the run from Stalin, hiding out in the home of Frida Kahlo and Diego Rivera; he wasn't so ambivalent when he and Lenin betrayed every guarantee in the original 1917 constitution of the Union Of Soviet Socialist Republics and ruthlessly maneuvered to consolidate Bolshevik power, with Lenin and Trotsky at the top.

I have come a roundabout way to the art and grace of C.P. Rosenthal's novel, in which the fugitive Trotsky lands (as he really did!) in the arms of Frida Kahlo. Stripped of his authority, with no one to command but himself, he can rely only on his humanity . . . an existential challenge he's hard put to meet.

Rosenthal has, in Trotsky, a rare character who reshaped history, but who then finds himself as vulnerable and as prey to chance as the most common, powerless person. Almost absurdly, Trotsky seeks protection from—artists! Frida Kahlo and Diego Rivera. Great artists, but the problem is: protection is not something artists are very good at.

Artists will not protect you from yourself, that's for sure.

Especially if the artist is Frida Kahlo. She painted only self-portraits because, as Rosenthal writes, "Kahlo had the world in her, dangerously so." Trotsky's remarkable wife Sedova tells him, "She's not seducing you, she's seducing the planet."

Enough of me. You will meet remarkable people in this book. You will listen in on the conversation of intellects you cannot help but envy. There are moments of grief that are hard to be in the same room with; there are funny passages where you may not expect them if you don't enjoy laughter in bed; here dreams turn into art, but also into nightmares, and nightmares turn into—history, I'm afraid. Out of which some amazing paintings get painted and a man—C.P. Rosenthal—makes from the weave of history a finely inflected, evocative, wonderfully written novel, dedicated on every page to our desire for liberation.

Michael Ventura
May 1, 2020

The novelist . . . must be forgiven for taking certain liberties . . .
not only because it is his right to invent, but also because he had to
fill in certain gaps so that the sacred coherence of the story was not lost.
It must be said that history is always selective, and discriminatory too,
selecting from life only what society deems to be historical and scorning
the rest, which is precisely where we might find the true explanation
of facts, of things, of wretched reality itself. In truth, I say to you, it
is better to be a novelist, a fiction writer, a liar.

—Jose Saramago

THE HAMMER, THE SICKLE AND THE HEART

Trotsky and Kahlo in Mexico

INVASION

THE DESIRE FOR LIBERATION lived in the heart and soul of every human being, in every worker, every farmer, every mother, father, even every child who worked in the factories, on farms, in the cities and on the steppes, in each person who toiled for their daily bread. Sweat was not the child of poverty but the birthright of every man and woman.

The human animal was the animal who worked, and work the badge of human equality. Leadership needn't imply wealth; intelligence and diligence lay in the capacity of each human being. Industry and technology had changed the world forever. Every human being could now share in technology and freedom. He believed that this could begin in Russia and spread to the world. This was the dream. That is why there must be revolution. And why the Russian Revolution succeeded. It was written in history and from history the future emerged.

He, Leon Trotsky, and Vladimir Lenin, did not invent communism. Communism invented them. But when Lenin died, Leon Trotsky found that iron fists were yet clenched around the desire for power. He'd miscalculated. Fear lay as deep in the human heart as liberation and liberation was the enemy of power.

He'd been expelled from Russia. Men and women he once led

watched passively or were blindly mowed down. He, Lev Davidovich, Leon Trotsky, was exiled by Joseph Stalin. He was exiled to Soviet Central Asia, Alma-Ata, where he unified a farmers' collective. With his ideas he made friends, with his friends he went hunting and fishing. He found that the idea of liberation wasn't dead, in fact there was no soul at all but for the yearning for liberation, even if those who yearned for it didn't understand this. He wrote tirelessly to the world. Too influential, even beyond the land where he once made war and saved the Bolshevik Revolution from the reactionaries, the Royalists, the Whites, in the new nation he'd created with his own heart, with his own bloodied fists, Stalin and the GPU exiled him again, farther away, this time to an isolated island in the Black Sea, Prinkipo. Because he was yet a hero to the people, yet immortal and dangerous, Stalin was afraid to kill him.

But if he wasn't afraid to die, others were. So they betrayed him, then confessed to crimes against the party and were murdered anyway.

In Mexico, he would have preferred the invasion route of Taylor or Cortez, landing in Veracruz, an army of ideas in his wake, but he landed in Tampico on the Norwegian tanker, *Ruth*. Three weeks crawling across the Atlantic. It only took Columbus five. Their departure had been a secret. His arrivals and departures, into exile, out of one exile and into another, were always secret, less to protect him than to quell his followers, of whom there were many. Even his presence on board the *Ruth* was kept secret from the crew. In the evening when he and his wife, Natalia Sedova, dined, they dined with the captain and their Norwegian assigned armed policeman, Jonas Lie. The captain spoke only of the cold, the winter weather, currents, fishing, the stars, and Lie, a quiet, bulky man who ate with his pistol on the table, talked of icebergs and sinking ships. Trotsky hated him, though by now he hated the Norwegian bureaucracy top to bottom. The captain gave them no access to electronic communication, not even the wireless. The boat rocked constantly over the rough seas. They were prisoners of Norway until they reached Mexico and during the early days of the voyage Trotsky was convinced that despite all assurances from the Norwegian government, Stalin had been tipped off and they would soon be intercepted by a Soviet gunboat, anonymously murdered, and reported lost at sea while trying to escape justice.

He and Natalia Sedova stayed in a tiny, windowless cabin, a storage room deep within the ship, with a bed, a chair and desk, a lamp. He wrote of Stalin's betrayal of the Revolution. She read and fretted. She read a play that Trotsky brought with him from Norway, Ibsen's *An Enemy of the People*, about a doctor who is vilified and stoned by his townspeople for exposing the civic and engineering corruption that has contaminated the town's water supply. Far too apropos. She was convinced, a Soviet interception aside, that this was not a deliverance, but a long ride to their last imprisonment. At night, he slipped from the room and walked the deck. Gazed out at the sea. Not to remember. Not to reminisce, but to plan.

"They'll recognize you and throw you over," Natalia said to him.

"If they recognize me, the seeds of revolution will be planted in them," he said.

"Corpses don't sow seeds."

"Revolution will spring from my corpse like grass. I'm more dangerous dead than alive." Had he read Whitman? Yes. And he believed what he said because he'd escaped death a hundred times. What indomitable will! And however great his ego, his will was greater, his dedication was greater.

This was the will that she'd fallen into the day they first met, by accident, in front of Baudelaire's tomb in Montparnasse, inseparable in revolution, the man she loved, married, fought next to, organizing women unionists into Communist cells, editing underground newspapers and journals, sneaking them into the hands of workers, for Communism, for Russia, from which they were now very far away.

"A Mexican prison if we're lucky," she said.

"Prison takes a thousand forms," he said. He spread his arms. "As you see. But inside or out, we'll fight with the pen."

So when they arrived in Mexico, she hesitated. The inevitable is often the hardest thing to face. She sat in the dim room deep inside the dark ship.

He took her hand. "Come, my love," he said. And she stood. They worked their way to the deck. Several of the deck hands saluted them as they made their way to the departure galley, but she hesitated again.

The captain rushed up to them. "You must debark!" he said. They knew enough Norwegian by then to understand.

"I must see allies, friends," Sedova said to Trotsky.

Lie stepped up, gun in hand. Trotsky stepped between him and Natalia.

"I'll kill you right here if I must," said Lie. "Debark."

"Kill me," Trotsky said.

Then a launch pulled beside the freighter and she saw American acquaintances, Max Schachtman and George Novak, both Trotskyites.

"President Cardenas has sent his train!" shouted Schachtman.

She stepped beside Trotsky and the two headed down for the plank.

On the plank, Trotsky was met by the famous painter, Frida Kahlo, wife of the muralist Diego Rivera who had negotiated Trotsky's amnesty with President Cardenas. Kahlo followed Trotsky and Sedova down the plank to the waiting train of the president of Mexico. Even so, Natalia didn't trust this group. In fact, she trusted no one. Why should she? But especially not this thin beauty who limped slightly, almost coyly, beneath her colorful native dress and scarves, a single eyebrow crossing her forehead, a wisp of dark fuzz over her lip. The brow was thick and full, but it didn't completely cross over her nose. It was enhanced with black mascara.

She was honored, Kahlo said in English when she came toward the boat to greet them, "honored to meet the man who had changed the world."

"Lenin changed it," Trotsky said. "I only saved it."

"Maybe," said Sedova.

Trotsky laughed and then everyone else did too.

And he was prepared to keep saving it, on the Russian steppes, in Turkey, in France, in Norway, and now in Mexico, even as Stalin lay in wait to pick off his allies, his friends, and even his family, the Soviet Union was yet worth saving; the peasants and workers of the world waited too, for a crack of light to explode over them into the brilliance of their own freedom. History demanded it. No one could stop it. Not even Stalin.

Kahlo escorted them to their train car. There, as she did when they were about to leave the boat, Natalia hesitated again. She couldn't separate the link between transportation and exile, exile and imprisonment, while he welcomed each or either as if they were new opportunities. Again Trotsky held her hand.

Natalia took the window. She gazed out at the plains stretching to the foothills of the Tamaulipas Mountains like the steppes that stretched to the Urals, though this was sunbaked country, scattered with palm trees and cacti. Ahead, the mountains blazed with splendor, all of it a relief from the dismal cold winter rain of southern Norway. Though she suddenly felt more assured she spoke softly to the window pane.

"We won't see Russia again," she said.

He turned to her. "Things could change," he said. He touched her knee lightly with his hand. "Persevere."

As if she hadn't already persevered. She thought of her sons, Sergei, a harmless engineer, who might be banished to Siberia, and Loyva, who ran a Marxist Socialist press in Paris. You raise them. They're boys. You think it will be that way for an eternity. Though sometimes, now, she regretted the years when she hid them while she and Trotsky were on the run, years when she left Trotsky for the boys, then the boys for Trotsky, fighting to bring them all together all too briefly. Now they were men. Gone. Stalin's shadow ever advancing.

Frida Kahlo sat at the other end of the car, alone, facing Novak and Schachtman. She looked across the way to Trotsky and Natalia, offered a relaxed smile apparently to the both of them, but it was obvious to

Sedova that her eyes were locked on Trotsky.

She was beautiful, petite, and young. So was Natalia thirty-five years ago in front of Baudelaire's tomb, in fact younger, barely twenty, and maybe more striking. Russian. In that soft, stark beauty of a young Russian woman. Even then, in the throes of love, the political world was foremost for her. And though Kahlo had faced horror, injuries and surgeries from which she could never recover, how did her martyrdom, her art, address the cause? Natalia Sedova, sitting next to Leon Trotsky, evaluated her own despair, an emotion Trotsky would never let himself feel. In that way he hadn't changed since 1902, almost manic with the fever of vision and hope in front of Baudelaire's tomb. Why there?

He'd been hungry to understand art. Devoured French novels. He even read them on the armored train as he launched his army across the plains a hundred times, thousands of miles. What had Baudelaire said? "To know, to kill, to create." Artists, like revolutionaries, perceived and portrayed realities that the masses could never understand, but could be raised up from their own ignorance against their own wills to satisfaction, to justice. Trotsky carried the copy of Ibsen's *An Enemy of the People* even now. Would Kahlo ever understand these complexities? And what of Rivera? Now their savior. Back from his dalliance with the Capitalists, the Fords and the Rockefellers who eventually rejected him. And now, in Mexico, expelled by the Communist Party for backing Trotsky and not Stalin. Is that what she and Trotsky had done with the Bolsheviks? Dallied? How many of Trotsky's allies were dying now for that dalliance?

The train stopped at a small station outside Mexico City. And though they were supposed to be traveling in secret they were greeted by a huge crowd of followers and journalists. Trotsky stood atop the train car stairs. He raised his arms and shouted in German, "Land! Bread! Peace!" The crowd roared and lunged toward him. But he loved this as much as she feared it. How many assassins were pushing through that mass? Police arrived and pushed back the crowd that parted when Kahlo appeared as the armed police led them toward waiting autos filled with more police.

The crowd roared, "Trotsky! Libertad!"

"Police cars," Natalia said to Trotsky. Everywhere, always, police and guards. She didn't need to say "prison."

"They're here to protect you," Frida Kahlo said. "Follow me."

And the frail woman led them to the middle automobile, a black Ford. A policeman opened the back door and Kahlo got in with them, Trotsky in the middle, Sedova to his right, Kahlo on his left. Natalia saw their legs touch. Their eyes met. For her part, Kahlo could meet the eyes, the mind, of anyone. She briefly smiled her legend into his.

Natalia, to his right, couldn't watch.

"Diego will join us when we reach Coyoacán," Frida Kahlo said, again in English, which she spoke as well as French.

Trotsky spoke French and English too, some German, but no Spanish. Natalia spoke neither Spanish nor English. Again, as in Norway and Turkey, they were in a land abuzz with alien signage and sound. But Spanish would come before they moved again, if ever they could move, and to where? He was feared everywhere, his presence a catalyst to the fears of the ruling bourgeoisie of the West because of what he meant, what he could mean, that the miracle he performed in Russia, a miracle of hope and justice would spread to the oppressed majority, in Mexico, in the United States yet mired in the Great Depression, the working poor all over the world.

"I can write anywhere," Trotsky said.

Kahlo's leg again touched his. There was electricity there. She said again, "Diego will meet us."

"Rivera will meet us in Coyoacán," Trotsky said to Natalia.

The car moved through the hills, beginning to wind its way into the sky toward the Aztec capital, 8,000 feet in the air. Clouds gathered and a storm unleashed.

"This won't last," Kahlo said. "January is a dry month."

Natalia lowered her window. The air was cold, mountain air.

"A cool month," said Kahlo, "but Mexico City is never cold. The hearts of her people are too warm for that."

"Heart," mumbled Trotsky to Natalia. "Herz," he said to her in German, and then in Russian, "Serdtse."

"Serdtse," Natalia repeated. The heart was trapped inside the body. You need only trap the body to trap the heart. "Everywhere we go we end up imprisoned."

"Not here," he said.

"Lev," she whispered. He would be wrong again, she was certain. She reached for his bicep with her right hand and pulled him toward her breasts. She looked across him to the confident Kahlo. The young don't believe they will age. And when they look at the old, they somehow believe they were born old, never strident, never beautiful. But when Trotsky met her, back from his first Siberian exile, he was twenty-three and she only nineteen, both young and strident. He was Bronstein then, Lev Davidovich Bronstein, already once divorced, with two daughters. His first wife, Alexandra Sokolovskaya, and the daughters, Zanaida and Nina, were dead now, official word on the daughters, both Bolsheviks, tuberculosis and suicide; that's how the powerless were murdered, by the official word. Their mother, who'd remained active in the party and in touch with Trotsky, simply disappeared.

Natalia's sons by Trotsky, Lyova, now Lev Sedov, and Sergei Sedov, were yet in Europe. Sergei, who'd married and become an engineer in Moscow, was never political, but was banished anyway. Lev, an active Bolshevik, was constantly on the run in France. They took her name, Sedov, not his, to obscure obvious detection. Even Trotsky used Sedov on his documents. But it didn't keep Sergei out of Siberian prison camp for being Trotsky's son. Soon he would be dead, she knew, and Lev, inevitably, until Trotsky stood alone, like a stump in a cleared forest.

"Not far from the city you can hunt and fish," Kahlo said to

Trotsky. "Even ride." Natalia arched an eyebrow and Frida spoke to her. "His reputation precedes him," she said to her, and though she didn't understand the words, she understood the tone.

Trotsky face broke into a relaxed smile, as if he were meditating.

"Here, in Mexico, we are yet wild," Kahlo said. "Yet tribal. Nothing could change that. Not the Spanish, not the French, not the Yankee gringos." She said, "You're not the only one who has fought." From her bag she removed a small, obsidian blade. Let her thumb run its edge.

As they swept north of Mexico City the sky opened into a valley, the mountains around spread out like sleeping gods. Kahlo pointed out the window, across his body, her finger almost touching Natalia's shoulder. As the car turned south she pointed to the west. "Teotihuacán," Kahlo said. "We'll go there. I'll find you one of these." She opened her palm to show him the shiny, black stone blade. "It was before the Aztecs, the Mexica. In its time it was bigger than Rome, bigger than London." She looked at Natalia. "Bigger than Moscow or Petrograd."

"Leningrad now," said Natalia Sedova, correcting her.

"Was a village of huts," said Kahlo.

"Does it matter now?" said Trotsky.

"Yes, it matters now," said Frida Kahlo. "You'll learn that. We'll show you."

He could wait to be shown. He was a student of history. History, the bowels of the future, he believed. Now he was in a land west of the West, in a nation conquered again and again, living as much as any nation under the bicep of imperialism, America, which would surpass France and Germany and England, where communism's last battle would take place.

They drove by a field where two white oxen pulled a plow. Passed oil wells and a refinery, its white silos billowing black smoke. He thought of the tractors he'd planned to be built in factories owned by the men and women who built them, fields of wheat plowed by peasants with the tractors, sharing bread with each other and with the workers in the factories and in the cities. He thought of libraries and playgrounds and hospitals surrounding Moscow, London, Berlin, Paris.

The car slowed as it passed through a village. Boys kicked a ball in the street. Then corn fields, agaves, a pulqueria, men under sombreros, women, their arms full of babies or wood. And then Coyoacán, a barely paved avenue, a blue house surrounded by an arroyo and a field of corn. Casa Azul.

CASA AZUL

POLICE GUARDS ESCORTED THEM from the car, through the gates and into the garden, which even in winter exploded with flowers and sweet smells. There were hairless dogs at their feet and big red and green parrots in two cages. A monkey ran to Frida Kahlo and jumped on her shoulder, wrapping his tail around her neck. Then Diego Rivera emerged, big-bellied, a floppy suit and a wide tie. He spread his arms. "Look at me!" he bellowed. "I bathed and dressed for the occasion! The revolution! The real revolution has come to Mexico!" He embraced Trotsky, then Sedova. Up close, he was not as big as he looked at a distance, and though bathed, he yet had paint under his fingernails.

He led them inside where a long table held plates of food, each dish of food either red, white, or green, the colors of the Mexican flag, the three colors of the Nopal cactus fruit, the colors of the landscape; the plates of food were laid out to spell TROTSKY.

Two young women, dressed more conventionally than Kahlo, stood near the table, Frida's sisters, Adriana and Christina. Chistina was thinner and prettier and gazed at Rivera furtively, it seemed to Natalia. Then a man and a woman, both dressed in white, brought out more plates and utensils. Frida dove under the resplendent Rivera's arm while with the other hand he began to pour out shots of tequila. The monkey, Fulang Chang, reached for a shot glass and when Diego gave him one the monkey threw back the tequila, made a face and put his glass out for more.

"Wait for the toast," Frida said to him, shaking a finger. "He never waits," Frida said to Trotsky.

The man and woman in white passed the tequila around.

"To permanent revolution!" shouted Diego Rivera.

"It's not vodka, but you'll learn to love it," Frida said to her guests.

"I drank Tequila in Paris once," said Sedova in French.

Trotsky savored it in his mouth. Pursed his lips. He felt the smokiness of the liquor in his nostrils.

"Mexico City has more cars than Moscow," Sedova said to Trotsky.

Trotsky repeated it to the group in English.

"We're closer to Detroit," said Diego.

Trotsky took more tequila when the bottle came to him again. He raised his shot glass. "Someday Americans will drive cars made here. To cars made in Mexico by Mexican hands!"

The sisters came to Sedova and Trotsky and introduced themselves.

"Are you painters, too?" asked Natalia in French.

Christina answered in Spanish. "I model," she said. "For Diego."

Suddenly the parrots were out of their cages and flapping through the room, squawking, though none of the hosts seemed startled at all. "Viva Mexico!" squawked one. "Viva revolucíon!" squawked the other. They settled down on opposite corners of the table.

"Careful what you say around them," Frida said to her guests in English. "They'll learn it."

"They'll learn it," said the first parrot and everyone laughed, even the other parrot.

The male servant came into the room with a tray of beer in bottles.

Diego grabbed two beers and gave one to Frida. "Let's eat," he said.

It was new food for the Russians, and Kahlo and Rivera didn't use silverware, which they thought bourgeois, using instead metal spoons coated in blue enamel and tortillas instead of forks. They ate peppers stuffed with pork, chicken, and cheese, corn tortillas with melted cheese covered in spicy, red sauce, fresh white cheeses and crisp, round rolls. The beer, Mexican beer, ranging from pilsners to dark lagers, was good.

After eating, Diego took Trotsky and Sedova aside. He reached inside his suit coat and removed a pack of cigarettes, shook it so one protruded and offered it to them. Trotsky seldom smoked and declined, but Natalia took one and Rivera struck a match and lit hers, then his own. Trotsky reconsidered and took one. Again Rivera lit.

"English?" he asked.

Trotsky nodded, but Sedova said, "Francaise, seulement."

"Francaise aussi," Trotsky said.

Rivera put his nose between his thick hands, then took a deep drag on his smoke. "I'll try," he said. "But soon, only Mexican, eh?"

"Si, pronto," said Sedova.

Rivera laughed. "Si, bueno," he said. "Did you have any communication aboard the ship?"

"Nothing," said Trotsky.

"How long?"

"Three weeks."

Diego Rivera sighed heavily. His brow furrowed.

"Best not wait," said Trotsky. "What's the bad news?"

"It's started," said Rivera. "There was a trial."

"Round one," said Trotsky.

"Zinoviev and Kamenev, eight more, I think, confessed to Trotskyism and conspiring with you to overthrow Stalin." Rivera inhaled his cigarette deeply, exhaled.

"There's no such thing as Trotskyism," said Sedova. Like Rivera she let her ashes fall to the dirt floor.

Trotsky, who'd been catching his ashes in his palm, let them drop. He touched Sedova and laughed slightly, wearily. He waited through a leaden pause. "They're dead," said Trotsky.

"Eight were shot. Your allies, Zinoviev and Kamenev, were each given ten years."

"When things first turned," said Leon, "after Lenin died, Zinoviev and Kamenev went over to Stalin. Not for long. They were intelligent men. They joined me then, the Bolshevik Opposition."

"They went back to Stalin," said Rivera.

"Ten years ago. He was winning. They were trying to save their lives."

"There's room for opposition in the party," said Sedova.

Trotsky stepped on his cigarette. "They chose stasis and bureaucracy. I told them they were dead men, anyway. Now they will be."

"He'll kill everyone," said Sedova. "You can't get close enough."

"There are plenty of Bolsheviks here," said Rivera.

"I am a Bolshevik," said Trotsky.

"But Stalinists," said Rivera.

"Stalinists who will try to kill you, Leon Davidovich," said Natalia Sedova.

"Us, my love," said Trotsky.

"We can protect you," Diego Rivera said.

Trotsky nodded his head skeptically. He tightened his lips.

"You can stay here until we find an even better place," said Diego.

Trotsky translated for Natalia Sedova.

"Et vous?" said Sedova. "And you?"

"We have other homes in San Angel, nearby."

"Merci," Sedova said. "Gracias."

"For now," Trotsky said.

Frida Kahlo came up behind the seated Diego and put her hands on his broad shoulders. He melted under them. His face softened. He reached back and touched her hand and tucked his head into her belly. "Mi amor," Diego said.

"Mi amor," said Frida Kahlo.

DANCE

TROTSKY LOOKED UP WHEN he heard the sound of a squeezebox. The man in white, his name was Chucho, began playing something that sounded like a cross between a jig and a German march. Kahlo spun away from Diego and took her sisters' hands and the three of them began to dance in a circle, Kahlo, visibly struggling, broke into a huge grin. She yipped and howled and her sisters laughed. Diego stood and clapped.

"Yet she's crying," Sedova whispered to Trotsky.

"Yes," Trotsky said.

Natalia Sedova got to her feet, squirmed past Rivera and joined the three sisters, skipping in circles, and shuffles, one, two, three, one, two, three. The parrots screamed, ahy-yiy-yiy-ahy-yiy-yiy!

Now Leon Trotsky stood and clapped too. Fulang Chang jumped into his arms and pulled on his tie. Trotsky lifted him, suddenly, surprising the monkey with his quickness, so it was easy for Trotsky to swing him into the air. "I've fought bigger and tougher than you," Trotsky said and Rivera laughed.

When the dance ended they drank more beer. Then Diego poured tequila again. "For the road," he said. Then Diego sang out, "I'm on my way to the port where a golden bark awaits to carry me away; I'm on my way, I've just come to say goodbye."

Kahlo leaned on Trotsky. "An old song," she said.

After that, the two Rivera's piled into the back of Diego's big Ford station wagon behind a chauffeur, Diego lifting the side of his coat to allow him to shift the big, holstered hand gun on his belt.

The woman servant, who said her name was Eulalia, led Trotsky and Sedova upstairs to a bedroom. There was another room that was Frida's alone. Natalia figured that if the crippled Kahlo could yet make love to Rivera, she couldn't share a bed all night with a man that size. This room had been Tina's when she lived there.

Trotsky nodded. Even as far away as Russia, the love lives of Kahlo and Rivera were notorious, though it was something the Russians had never said to each other. How much they had entered their intimacy already was odd, a surprise.

Trotsky watched Natalia undress. If her softness now sagged a little, he yet loved the way her body fell onto itself, her round breasts onto her small belly, the roundness of her behind and her still trim legs. He admired the grace with which she let her skirt and slip drop to the floor, then swept them up with one motion of her arm and hand.

"You're watching me, Leon," she said.

"I love to."

"Did you see the eyes of the attractive sister?"

He'd tried not to see the sisters as attractive. He was a guest. "The thinner one?"

"There's some trouble."

"It isn't our trouble."

"We're sleeping in her room, Leon Davidovich."

"Should I get a big gun, like his?"

"Your gun is big enough," she said and they laughed.

She slipped into her night gown. Came to him and undid his tie. "Let me undress you, generalissimo," she said softly. She kissed him on the lips. "Commander of the Train."

He did not believe in fate. He believed that men made fate and history made men, and women too, that history made war and love, and revolution, and that circumstance fell like rain, but that she mentioned the Train, after so long, that she mentioned it now, recalling the implicit and unspoken height of his power when he was far away from her, when men became an extension of his will as he raged between the Volga and the Urals inventing a new warfare. As the roads of Rome turned transportation and speed into empire, as trains and engineering brought the American Confederate rebels to their knees, he moved an army of men and machines overland with astonishing speed, notified by wireless or telegram of an amassing strike by the Cossacks or Whites, he traversed in a day what would take an army, or even a cavalry, men and machines, weeks to transport themselves. Train cars with mounted machine guns, train cars with cannons, horses, and automobiles, and soldiers clothed in menacing black leather, leapt from the bowels of the train and pounced upon their unsuspecting enemies. The dark train, soon became two trains; red flags flew from the engine cabs announcing the red army's arrival outside a village. There was no quarter. In war, men die. That's the only absolute law. Then he was as God or a lord, though he didn't believe in the former, and lived to destroy the latter. Yet revolution required the same faith as religious fervor. There could be no doubts, no second thoughts, no looking back, no fear of death. Zinoviev and Kamenev feared death.

Had she ever wondered then, in Paris, in Moscow, when he saved Kazan, saved Novogorad, which lay naked to the Whites under the bungling of Stalin, did she, as she should have, question his fidelity? It was solace, not love, not even infatuation. Could a kiss save the pillaging of town or village? In the end as in the beginning it never could. Yet the women appeared before him, kissed him, the commander of the great Train. Though they had been searched; he would never let a woman touch him, get in reach of him until she was naked. And when he slept, he slept alone with his gun.

Rivera's gun. Had he ever killed a man? Trotsky had killed thousands, saved thousands, both brave men and cowards, too, though he'd turned cowards into brave men with his heart and words.

He hung on a vortex of pity, violence, relief, as his wife, Natalia Sedova, naked, now undressed him and kissed him. For her part she knew more than she wanted to say. Did he guess it? Men are not so subtle. The whorl of their lives gets too big for them, swirls too fast. But when she saw Christina's eyes flash before Rivera, she saw a room full of salacious apprehension. Frida Kahlo was no innocent. But neither was Natalia Sedova.

They made love. It felt like sedition, but here, tonight, is where they lived. For so long they'd lived nowhere and now this nowhere, this Mexican nowhere of someone else's lives, felt right and wrong, maybe wrong enough to feel good. Afterwards, though they seldom smoked, they shared a cigarette.

"Did you like the tequila?" said Trotsky.

"I liked it well enough to get used to it," said Sedova.

There was a quiet knock on their door. They slipped into their robes and Natalia opened the door a crack. It was Eulalia, so Sedova opened up. Eulalia nodded and handed her a note, then left. It was in English, so Trotsky read.

"Tomorrow we're invited to help cook dinner," he said. "A kind of food festival where we can practice our Spanish." It was signed, Frida Kahlo.

Sedova took the note and held it. "It feels warm," she said. As Russians they were suspicious of intimacy. Then what? "We'll need to get some tequila for our room," she said.

MORNING

IN THE MORNING Eulalia brought them coffee and rolls. The coffee was strong but very smooth, the rolls thick and soft and slightly sweet. Sedova read. Trotsky walked in the garden, yet flowering in January, though not particularly aromatic. The cacti stood stubbornly, armed with needles. The ones that looked smooth were coated with what looked like soft fur and he assumed they were more poisonous than the large, spiked ones, the tiny needles invading your skin and impossible to remove. He had a literary mind. He saw parallels, metaphors, between people and cactuses. He examined the pre-Columbian statuary that sat on the ascending steps of a small stone pyramid in the center of the yard, squat, mostly seated effigies of myriad gods. He regretted the loss of polytheism with its layered, overlapping realities, one beneath, another above, one next to the other. Monotheism had got it wrong. It couldn't accommodate evil or choice, the primacy and subordination of the individual. But best, no gods at all. Gods reduced to statuary, decoration, metaphor, no more real than a banner, a medallion, a flag, though so very real to those who took them to heart or used them to manipulate minds and hearts. Admittedly, when he had to, he'd done that himself.

He went to the rabbit cages. Plucked some grass and offered it to the fattening hares. He once hunted them. He felt them now, hanging dead from their feet upon his back. Which was he? Which was better? Hunted and eaten? Fattened, then slain and eaten? Better not to be a hare at all. Or a man.

Out the gate and across the road, Allende Street, a young, pregnant woman named Micaela lived in a small hutch and tended a vegetable garden amidst the corn stalks. Besides the corn she grew squash blossoms, green chiles, and beans. He spotted her there and when he walked toward her she greeted him. She was obviously pregnant. He noticed then that there were a number of huts spread through the cornfield surrounded by clotheslines and earthen ovens. There was a small stream, drainage and irrigation ditches.

They introduced themselves and Micaela plucked some corn, a dozen cobs. "For your table," she said in Spanish. He understood and thanked her. "And for the little boss," she said.

"Frida?"

"Who else?" she said.

Then she went into her hutch and came out holding an orange kitten. She offered it to him to. "For your life," she said.

He pointed to the house. "Birds," he said.

"Chickens, parrots, are too big," she said.

"To eat?"

"Yes. Mice," she said. "Rats."

He recalled not seeing a cat in the Casa Azul and assumed the little hairless dogs ate the rodents. He figured, at worst, he could always return the cat.

He took the kitten and the corn and went back to the house.

Sedova, in the garden now, looked at him skeptically.

"Our contribution to the food and language festival," he said to her.

"The corn or the kitten?" she said. "They have dogs."

"Little dogs."

"You prefer dogs."

"Hunting dogs," he said.

"You'll name her Frida?"

"Don't be cruel, Natalia," said Trotsky. "Is it female?"

Sedova lifted the kitten's tail. "Yes," she said. "Conchita."

He followed her into the house and up to the room.

"Lorca?" he said.

"He is dead, my love. Among many others."

Trotsky breathed heavily. "Spain," he whispered.

"Another war you could turn around. But the Republicans are overwhelmed, outmanned, out gunned, disorganized, and someone on either side would kill you even if you could get in. You know all this."

"When it's over Hitler and Stalin will be allies," said Trotsky.

"So you've predicted. But not for long," she said.

They'd been over this before, but often you had to go over things again and again to make the real believable.

He put the kitten on the floor and she ran under the bed.

"Be safe, little one," Natalia said.

Later in the day, in the kitchen, Frida Kahlo thanked him for the corn. "From across the way?" she said. "When you can't get to the market or Xochimilco, she's good in a pinch."

The kitten had followed them downstairs and Frida broke into a quizzical smile when she spotted her. "You're quite the collector," she said to Trotsky. "Cats. Both predator and prey, that's the problem."

"Like me," said Trotsky.

Sedova took his arm.

"He has a bad attitude," Kahlo said to her. She poured three small glasses of brandy. Called for Eulalia. "Micaela will have that baby soon, so we can practice for two celebrations, the baptism feast and La Fiesta de le Virgen de la Candelaria."

"Catholicism," said Trotsky.

"Religion is everywhere in Mexico, Señor Comrade Trotsky. Nothing will end it, not science, not the State, not communism. Diego says its suppression is a Nineteenth Century anachronism. Spencer, no? He's dead. Religion goes on."

"Are you Catholic?" said Sedova.

Kahlo laughed. "No. But what would it matter?" She told them the story of the trapped miners who were led out of their collapsed cave by a woman who carried a baby in one arm and a candle in her other hand.

"Where was this?" said Leon Trotsky.

"Spain, Peru, Mexico, everywhere!" said Kahlo.

"Was she brown or white?" asked Natalia.

"Ha! You are a sociologist!" laughed Frida Kahlo. "Both brown and white, of course. It depends who's looking, who's telling, who's painting."

Trotsky broke into a wry smile.

"In Mexico we celebrate everything. In America they celebrate nothing," Kahlo said.

"I've been there," said Trotsky.

"Me too!" Kahlo said. She threw back her brandy and poured herself another, then turned to Eulalia who'd entered the kitchen. "Let's cook!" Frida Kahlo said.

The three of them sat down at the table and began peeling the corn. "Save the stalks, we'll use them," said Frida. Eulalia brought out fresh white cheese, masa harina, flour, beans, squash blossoms, different kinds of chiles, eggs, lard. Kahlo named the ingredients. She showed Trotsky and Sedova how to split the peppers, coat them, stuff them. They made tortillas, both flour and corn, while Eulalia heated the lard to fry the rellenos, enchiladas, and flautas.

Trotsky cut a pork loin into thin strips. They made a tomato sauce seasoned with onions and garlic, a salsa with chiles and oregano. They combined chicken broth, sugar, and lard with the masa harina and made a filling that they placed inside steamed corn husks to make tamales. If the work required standing, Kahlo didn't participate, but called out instructions from the table.

"I can't bend over the counter," she told them. "My back."

Later, Sedova and Trotsky walked in a nearby woods.

"Hired help," Trotsky said.

"We weren't hired," she said.

"She drinks a lot."

"She's in pain," said Sedova.

"You're oddly sympathetic today," he said.

"They don't live extravagantly, Leon," she said. "The help doesn't seem discontent. I assume they're paid well. Kahlo can't take care of the house. Or cook."

"Nor can Rivera?"

"You're not much for cooking or cleaning, my love."

"They have another house," said Trotsky.

"Two, in fact," said Sedova. "Studios. Connected. Though they can lock each other out. They're artists. This isn't Russia."

"I want to see his work," he said.

"And hers?"

He didn't respond because as much as he wanted to see Rivera's murals, he was in fact more riveted by Kahlo's painful self portraits and a little ashamed of his attraction to her, especially here, in front of Sedova.

"She's not seducing you," Sedova said to him, "she's seducing the planet."

"You're saying that if she were seducing me," he said, "then I shouldn't take it personally."

This time it was Natalia Sedova who didn't respond.

Trotsky said, "The G.P.U will locate us soon. I want to walk in Chapultepec Park before it becomes too dangerous."

"Too dangerous to take a walk." Sedova spoke in barely more than a whisper. "When that time comes, then what?"

"I should carry a gun."

"Like Diego."

"Men carry guns here," he said. "Even artists, like Rivera."

He took her hand as they walked under the pepper trees, the feathery leaves weeping down, the coral trees threatening to bloom, the scrub oaks with their majestic canopy, mesquite bushes at their feet. They turned back toward the house.

"Would you be killing your enemies now," said Natalia Sedova, "if you'd won?"

"My enemies were soldiers and reactionaries."

"But your enemies have changed. And now they're running Russia and want you dead."

"We've been through this many times. My differences with Stalin were philosophical," he said.

"And political. And now personal. If incompetent, he was clever. He smelled power everywhere," she said.

"I don't want power."

"No," she said, "you just want to change the world."

"The world will change," he said. "Inevitably. A victory for Stalin or even Capitalism won't stop it." He stopped and kissed her forehead. "And we will contribute until we're dead."

"Such a jubilant man you are," Natalia Sedova said.

He smiled. "I didn't lose," he said.

That night, they ate the food they'd prepared with Frida and Eulalia in the kitchen. At one point, on her way to relieve herself, Sedova examined the retablos that hung on the stairway wall, delicate, sometimes precise and sometimes primitive paintings on tin rectangles, some taller, some wider, often a supplicant praying to the Virgin or another saint, but usually the Virgin. Knowing French, she could decipher the Spanish, most often prayers for the sick or dying, especially children, but also for protection, safety, a placation, a boon. They covered the wall like colorful flags. She wondered if Frida's mutilated portraits weren't something of the same: Frida Kahlo, victim, virgin, saint, Mother of God, all in one. The reality was irrelevant. God, Christ, the Virgin, symbols, for Kahlo, deeper than religion.

When she got downstairs, Frida was putting on a shawl. "Come," she said. "I've called some friends, my sisters, we're going drinking and dancing!"

They piled into Diego's station wagon, a driver, General Wrong-Turn, Frida called him, at the wheel. Adriana and Christina, who Frida had telephoned, lived close by. The two of them dove into the front seat, leaving Kahlo, Trotsky and Sedova in the back. They headed to a club in the Zona Rosa. On the way, they passed a flat where Frida made General Wrong-Turn slow down to a stop and she pointed upward toward the second floor porch. "It's Tina Modotti's apartment," Kahlo said. "The photographer."

"With Weston?" said Natalia Sedova.

"Yes, Edward," said Kahlo, "and a son. Not hers. Modotti modeled for him. At first."

"I know the work," said Trotsky, though he didn't comment further. He hadn't made his mind up about photography yet, though he knew the work of Atget. He felt that Weston and Modotti both bent the real to a tipping point. He'd been through this with Stalin, who believed all art must portray the workers, the soldiers, the professions in heroic poses, working together, the rest be damned. Trotsky didn't necessarily find self expression bourgeois. At its best, it pointed to inner, universal humanity, and that freed the spirit and that spirit could only go one place, to freeing all humanity. Art could lend its hands to that.

"Leon knows about a lot of things," said Sedova. She took Trotsky's bicep in both her hands and squeezed it affectionately. "Not all of it revolutionary."

"Everyone is famous in Mexico City," said Frida Kahlo. "Everyone knows everybody. Everyone fucks everybody." She took both of them into her gaze. "I mean that in the most gentle way."

"Modotti is in Spain," said Trotsky.

"Yes, fighting," said Kahlo, "in Madrid. An impossible, horrible stand. Your friend, Stalin, is at least on the right side, if the losing side." She touched Trotsky's hand when she said this.

"Hitler has committed more money, more weapons, planes," said Trotsky.

"Lo siento, I'm sorry," Kahlo said.

He couldn't tell, precisely, what she was sorry about, but he felt, at that moment, true sorrow. Her dark eyes watered and she looked away. Sedova pressed harder on Leon's arm, his muscles tightening under her fingers. Kahlo had the world in her, dangerously so, you couldn't deny it.

Kahlo pointed again to the porch. "Anyway, Diego and I were married there. And a big party, of course."

They reached the night club where the three sisters drank tequila and beer and Sedova did the same, only more slowly. Trotsky held his beer on the table. When they arrived, a Mexican band had finished up and another band of black men took the stage with trumpet, saxophone, a bass, and piano. Sometimes the pianist sang.

"Americans," Frida said to the Russians, "the best kind of Americans."

They were soon joined by friends, painters, two men and two women, though they didn't seem to be couples. The music jumped, bounced, and Frida jumped to the dance floor, her arms above her head. She danced like a joyous puppet, both stiff and graceful.

Frida's sisters and guests joined her, bouncing, shouting, "Vamos! Vamos!" Go! Go!

Sedova got up to join them, and touch Lev's hand. "She grimaces," she said.

Spying Trotsky sitting alone, Tina left the group and sat across from him. "Are you enjoying my old room?" she said.

"I'm grateful," said Trotsky. "We're both grateful."

"Your Spanish is better already."

"My Mexican?" he said.

"In fact, yes," she said

He made a point to drink his beer heartily, then offered her a crooked smile. Her dark eyes twinkled as she grinned back.

Frida spun from the dance floor to the table.

"Are you seducing my sister?" she said to Leon.

"How could he not?" said Tina.

"Unavoidably," Trotsky said. "But not intentionally."

The band finished its tune and the dancers broke to the table. There was shouting and toasting. It was difficult to make out much of anything as the Spanish flew around them thick and quick. The Mexican band returned with trumpets, guitar, and accordion. Tina strode to the dance floor and Sedova sat down next to Lev again.

"You need an armed guard even here," she said to him.

"Are you armed?"

"Better than you think," said Sedova.

There was more dancing and on the dance floor people shouted and sang along; he could make out "revolution" and "roaches." Panting, Frida stepped away, limping, and sat down with the two Russians.

She looked at Trotsky, then Sedova, then back to Leon. "Tomorrow I'll go to San Angel to paint and leave you to get back to your work. Diego will secure the perimeter of the house. When I return we can go to the Zócalo, to Teotihuacan, and disappear in the crowds."

"While we still can?" said Natalia.

"It's that way with everything, isn't it?" said Kahlo. "There are still some things, some time to fall in love with Mexico."

When they returned to the house with Frida and her sisters Diego was waiting, his clothes smothered in paint. Fulang Chang was out and leapt to Frida, who nuzzled him. When they sat at the table, the dogs circled. The parrots squawked from their cages. Lorca appeared and leapt on the table but Trotsky immediately grabbed the kitten and held her on his lap.

"We'll have to get you a pet," Frida said to Sedova.

Natalia looked at Leon. "I have one," she said.

Trotsky grimaced, but everyone else laughed. Trotsky placed Lorca on the floor. She jumped back up. He put her down again.

"Remind you of anyone?" Frida said to him.

The kitten jumped up again and Trotsky cradled her in his palm.

"But I would change my tactics." He carried her to the kitchen and shut the door.

Fulang screeched. "She can get on the table, Lev," said Kahlo. "We don't care."

Natalie Sedova wondered if anyone else noticed that she'd used a more intimate name for him.

"She caught a mouse already," Diego said to Trotsky. He poured a round of tequila and raised his glass to Trotsky. "Permanent revolution," he said.

They drank, but the mood was somehow suddenly somber, if not tense.

"Let me take your sisters home," Rivera said to Frida.

"Please don't be too long," Kahlo said.

Rivera tilted his head. He put down his glass and rubbed his hands over his chest.

"My darling," he said. "Come along."

When they all left Leon and Natalia sat at the table alone. Sedova poured two glasses of tequila.

"Brest-Litovsk," said Sedova, raising her glass. Where he'd negotiated the Russian surrender to Germany. He was not a drinker by inclination, nor a smoker, but he could do both. This seemed to be an occasion, this falling, with gratitude, into someone else's mess. He touched his glass to hers.

"You see this as surrender," he said.

"You once said you were tired of it all."

"It was in the long winter night of Norway," he said. "Darkness and snow. Anyway, a man is permitted to get tired."

"And a woman, too."

"Yes," he said.

"You've escaped death a thousand times," she said.

"A thousand nights and one night," he said. He sipped. "A story."

"A hundred stories. I've read it, too."

"I know. So maybe only a hundred escapes."

"Maybe more," she said.

"It only takes once. A mistake, a misjudgment, bad luck, bad timing."

"You aren't a morbid man, Leon Trotsky."

He smiled at her, drank a little more.

"Did you like the music tonight?" she said to him.

"The accordion, like German polka."

"And the beer, too. It's said that India always conquers her conquerors. Maybe Mexico, as well."

"The black Americans," he said.

"Jazz. Peculiarly American, for now," Sedova said.

"Sometimes the piano displayed ambiguity, like Chopin."

She finished her tequila, put down her glass and took both his hands in hers. She said, "Lev Davidovich, we will not see Europe or Russia again."

LA GUERRA DE LAS FLORES

IN THE NEXT TWO WEEKS workers arrived to board up windows that faced a house across the way. Rivera had the wall surrounding Casa Azul raised and reinforced. He placed some young American volunteers, Trotskyists, to guard the gate and two more armed guards, these being Mexican, at the house's entryway. Kahlo came by only once, with Tina, for a cooking fest and Mexican speech lessons. Once again, Eulalia did much of the work, but she laughed and joked with Frida and Tina, and Sedova, too.

"The great man should go shoot us something to roast," said Tina.

Frida had found whisky and passed the bottle with a wink at Lev, but then twirled, passed and winked at Natalia and Tina, too. Eulalia said, no, she was working, they were playing.

By the end of the second week Trotsky mulled abandoning his biography of Lenin for a biography of Stalin, enraged by the most recent trial in Moscow where thirteen of Trotsky's original Bolshevik allies, men who were at his side in the failed revolution of 1905 and the successful one in 1917, confessed to plotting with Trotsky to assassinate Stalin. Again, Trotsky and his son, Lyova, were convicted *in abstentia*, this time of plotting with Hirohito and Hitler to overthrow Stalin and the Soviet.

Two of his oldest original, if at times embattling, associates, Bukharin and Rykov had been arrested and accused of training anti-Stalin terrorists.

A letter from Lyova arrived, full of despair. He confirmed that his brother, Sergei, and his wife had been arrested in Moscow. Sergei, convicted of poisoning his fellow workers, was sent to a Siberian work camp. There was no trace of his wife. "Father, it's pointless to continue," Lyova wrote.

Trotsky wrote back. "Continue or not, you'll be hunted down anyways. So fight! Send me the documents of the trials."

Sedova calmed him. "Sergei is alive," she said.

She obtained from Frida the location of a country home, owned by a friend, in a village nearby, Taxco, where they could walk; Leon could ride horses, hunt, and fish.

She said, "Even in Petrograd, in Moscow, you escaped to hunt and fish, to find the quiet."

"Yes," he said, but while she was making the arrangements, he took one of the guards and purchased a pistol and rounds.

They drove from the city, an armed guard driving, another in the passenger seat, Sedova and Trotsky sat together in the back. The cottage sat on the outskirts of the village and that evening they left the guards at the house and walked together, circling the town, through the mesquite and under the scrub oaks, the feathery coral trees and pepper trees. He held her hand.

The next morning at dawn he took a horse from the stable, sheathed a shotgun and rode toward the hills, following a stream until he found a swimming hole and swam. Then mounting again, he found a pond, followed its edge and found duck skate. Found shade and waited in there until the ducks flew in. He sat, slowly counting his breaths, the moments between their life and death. He waited for them to take flight. This was the dreadful peace of hunting, of waiting for your prey, watching them on the edge of their mortality and thus the edge of your own.

More mallards flew in, some females, too. They squabbled at each other. Fed in the shallows, ducking their bills. Bathed. Maybe they would sit together in the water until dark and escape him. He wouldn't frighten them, hasten them into the air. And it had been a while since he waited with a gun. Maybe they would move too quickly or wander away from where he sat, then begin their take off away from him and enter the sky too far away for him to take them down.

A mallard bit a female's neck. She squawked, protesting, and when he persisted she took flight. The group, disturbed, followed and with two quick shots he took two of them down. Having no dog, he waded in to get them. He hung them from the saddle by their feet, and still wet, he rode home.

To be racing on horseback again, the wind in his hair, the terrain whistling by in a blur, comforted him. There, for brief moments, there was nothing but that, the ancient mountains rising in the distance, a brace of rain, the moment of calm as he held the shotgun steady at the ducks' flight. Now the chill of the wind against his wet clothing. Two ducks on his saddle that they would dress and eat.

Together they de-feathered and dressed the fowl, roasted them with roots that Sedova foraged. They'd brought wine, and if Mexican wine was not the best, it was yet wine. It was a nice break from the liquor and beer.

"Eulalia would be proud of you," said Sedova.

"And Tina?"

"She's proud enough of herself, don't you think?"

"And what do you think?" he said. "That is what you think."

"There are too many capturing eyes. I'm uncomfortable."

"Would they harm you?" he said.

"Women age in ways that men don't," said Natalia Sedova.

"So you think I'm vulnerable."

"To youth. To a fascinating mind," she said.

"You are the most fascinating intellect, the most fascinating intellect of any woman I've known."

"But it isn't needed to make love."

He held his glass up to her and she spied it skeptically.

"I bought a gun, a pistol," Trotsky said.

"I'm stunned."

"It can only do damage in close quarters."

"You think they'll need to get close to you," said Sedova.

He brought down his glass. "It depends."

"It depends," she said.

She raised her glass now. He met it with his.

"Tomorrow fish," Trotsky said.

The next day he took the gelding back to the stream. He found a fallen tree that traversed it and observed the trout moving in the clear water. They were big and brown and moved comfortably and confidently in the current. He recalled his long days off the Prinkipo Islands fishing in the Sea of Mamara, thinking then that the better he fished the better he wrote, as he dashed off essays for the *Opposition Bulletin*. Now he watched the big brown trout in the shallows below him. One, in particular, held itself against the current with what looked like ease but must have taken tremendous power and skill. This was how he saw himself and so this one he would leave alone.

But before long he had enough of the fish for dinner and that night he and Sedova ate the trout fried. They even had enough food for the guards. The next day they returned to Casa Azul relaxed and tired. But waiting for them in the garden with Frida were two new guests, André Breton and his wife, Jacqueline Lamba. Breton wore a close fitting, dark suit, dark shirt and tie and thick, round spectacles. His thick hair was combed left to right. Lamba wore an extravagant sequined dress, heels, her wiry hair blasting out from her head. Kahlo wore her traditional Tehuana garb, her hair loose. Trotsky held two dead rabbits that he'd shot that morning, their hind feet in his left hand and their ears touching the ground. He held them out to Frida. "For your sister," he said.

Breton spread his arms. He spoke in French. "How can this moment be real!" he said.

Sedova spread her arms toward the other women. She said, "I feel underdressed."

And everyone laughed.

"Have we all been thrown out of the Communist Party?" said Lamba.

"I only attend parties," said Kahlo. "I never join them."

"Precluding your being thrown out," said Breton.

They had never met, though knew each other by reputation, and by the time Diego reached home, the five of them were in deep conversation around the dining table, drinking whisky and tequila, dark Mexican beer, sharing chips and fried nopales leaves. Breton agreed with Trotsky that the Stalinists were like the Thermadorian reactionaries of the French Revolution, so paranoid and bloodthirsty that when they were done killing their enemies they killed their allies. With luck no one would be left.

"But for Stalin," said Sedova.

Frida said to Lamba and Sedova, "Men and their prisons of ideas."

Breton pounded the table. "I love her!" he said.

"Me too!" said Rivera.

Breton followed Frida Kahlo's gaze that was now trained on Trotsky.

That night the three men hatched a plan to collaborate on an essay about art and communism, but Kahlo punctuated the evening by saying, "But not before we go tomorrow to Xochimilco!"

And so they did. At least the five of them. Diego stayed to paint.

"And your sister?" asked Trotsky.

"He's painting her," Kahlo said. She dipped her forehead demurely, then smiled, in his mind a bit too determinedly, too bravely.

They took an electric street car to the Tlalpan Road and at the San Fernando traffic circle caught the Xochimilco line, sitting in an open car. Frida leaned on a frail railing and lifted her face to the cool wind as cars and busses whizzed back and forth next to them. It was astounding to Natalia, knowing of the accident that almost killed Kahlo and left her hobbled for life, that Frida Kahlo would reiterate a situation so similar. Then Kahlo lowered her head and grinned wildly at them all and Sedova understood. It was defiance and bravado, intended for her audience, most notably Breton, and Trotsky, where her gaze lingered for a subtle, extra moment.

The line ended at the gardens of Xochimilco, where women sold dozens of different local vegetables piled on long tables and others prepared them in soups and stews of poblano pepper strips; tables overflowed with tomatoes, *huauzontles*, Creole squash, beans, corn, chiles, amaranth, lettuce and onions, radishes and carrots. Nearby, waterways dissected the thick foliage, and multicolored skiffs with painted figures and women's names atop their bows, carried parties of partiers; other boats sold fresh or prepared food, buckets of beer, still others were filled with mariachi or marimba bands.

"Once, all of Tenochtitlán was surrounded by gardens like this," Kahlo said. "They fed a city of Indians, the biggest city in the world." She chose a picnic boat, a *trajinera*, named Rosaria. "Only five of us will fit," she said. "We'll have to leave the guards."

"They can wait on the dock," said Trotsky.

Breton put a hand on Trotsky's shoulder and shook it slightly as they prepared to board the boat. "Don't you love her?" he said.

Trotsky chose to take it in a general way, a French way, and when Breton read Davidovich's silence as just that, he said, "No, I mean really love her, love her with all the madness of love."

Trotsky crossed his body with his right hand and touched Breton's right hand that still lingered on his shoulder. "What would be the point, comrade?" he said.

Breton laughed. The skiff pulled up. Breton jumped aboard first and put his hand out to Frida to guide her aboard, then Lamba, and then Sedova who touched Leon's hand as she took Breton's. Trotsky turned to the body guard and told them to wait there on the dock, then he leapt aboard the skiff.

Frida had brought a basket of carnitas, guacamole with chipotle chiles, and pork sandwiches, though she yet flagged down boats of *chalupa* merchants and bought fresh tortillas, nopales salad. From another she bought fresh sweet, maguey water, from another, tequila, and from yet another a bucket of cold beer. Surrounded by boats clunking against theirs and the shouts of merchants, they were a floating island of chaos and reverie, and Sedova, who sat across from Leon sought out his eyes.

"Don't worry, not like this, it's too chaotic," he said to her. "It would cause a great commotion. Others would get hurt. It would be suicide."

To add to it, a mariachi band approached and blasted into string and trumpet. Frida sang along. A marimba band pulled up now, too, beating on their hollow tubes and crooning with their wooden flutes. The mariachis quieted as the marimba group played the love song, *Maria Elena*, "Vengo a cantarte mujer, eres me fé, eres mi Dios, eres me amor." Kahlo knew every word of the soft, romantic melody.

In time the vendors dropped away, then the marimbas, and only the mariachi band remained. From his end seat Trotsky gazed out the back of the skiff where amidst all of the floating color a man launched a small rowboat. He watched as the lone boatman swung the prow of his boat toward them, rowing, his back to them, dipping the oars with increasing rhythm. When Frida thanked and paid the mariachis, Trotsky stood and said, "Please ask them to stay a bit longer." Then he stepped to the back of the skiff. Breton stepped next to him. The other picnic *trajineras* had followed the main channel while the pole man of the Rosaria guided their skiff to a slightly narrower bend to the left, a place where Kahlo had indicated she wanted to take them. Trotsky nodded at the rowboat.

"He seems to know what he's doing."

"Do you think?" said Breton.

"It won't hurt to be ready," Leon Trotsky said.

"We artists only commit suicide," said Breton.

Trotsky laughed. He turned to the three women who were staring at him. "When that boat draws near, have the band strike up very loud," he said to Kahlo.

"Muy riudosa," said Kahlo.

"Y rápido," Trotsky said.

The rower moved determinedly now, glancing once over his shoulder to guide the rowboat toward the skiff, Rosaria. "Step back, comrade," Leon said to Breton and raised his hand to the women. The band struck up as the rowboat met the skiff and the rower raised his arm for a lift aboard. Trotsky casually offered him his wrist and lifted him as the women began to sing and scream to "La Cucaracha." The boatman, now aboard, quickly reached to his belt and pulled out a knife. Trotsky pulled his .22 pistol from his belt and plunged it into the man's stomach. There were two quick reports muffled by the music, song, and the attacker's stomach, like the sound of two small firecrackers. Trotsky shoved the man back into his boat and pushed the rowboat away from the skiff with his foot. Kahlo quieted the band. "Gracias," she said to them and paid them again. Trotsky raised his palms and said, "A man taking a nap in his boat on a beautiful day," though before he could finish his sentence a bouquet of flowers fell from the air and landed in the rowboat.

Flowers falling from the sky. Then the air was filled with flowers, falling around them into the skiff. From the shore, and from some small skiffs poled by boys, girls flung armfuls of flowers and bouquets, pelting all of them. The rowboat filled with flowers, burying the assassin while Frida began gathering flowers, laughing and flinging them into the air, carnations, roses, marguerites, lilies, and more bouquets. "The Children's Battle of the Flowers!" yelled Frida Kahlo. Sedova, Lamba, and André Breton joined in, flinging flowers at each other. A rose struck Trotsky. "Struck by a rose!" Frida yelled, and threw another one, hitting his chest. A lily floated through the air and fell on the enflowered rowboat. Sedova pointed at it. Trotsky smiled wryly. The air was filled with shouts of children and the soft cascade of flowers.

TRIAL

ANDRÉ BRETON LEFT for New York and Paris the next week where he planned to promote one woman shows for Frida Kahlo. He pulled Trotsky aside before he left to plan the collaboration on their essay on art and communism that they'd work on when Breton returned to Mexico. They shared a bottle of cool red wine in the garden. They spoke French.

"We don't cool our red wine," Breton said.

"I'm aware," Leon said, "but for Mexican wine it takes the edge off."

Breton nodded, sipped. "Has your wife witnessed an event like the one that happened?"

"An event?" said Trotsky.

"On the boat."

Leon Trotsky sipped, then put down his glass. "A man jumped on our boat, then fell off," he said.

Breton nodded.

"Do you know Modotti?" said Trotsky.

"I met her up north, with Weston."

"So you know about her trial."

Modotti's boyfriend, a Cuban, had been a communist agitator. He was shot dead by fascists while walking with her down the street. The

Mexican authorities put her on trial for the murder. Though they couldn't generate a case against her the trial went on a long time. As for Sedova, her life and Trotsky's life had been threatened many times. In this case, if anything, the less said between them, then the less she'd have to lie about in any investigation. In this, their lives were well practiced. A man jumped on the back of the skiff and fell off. They could live, work, love without talking about it. Yet she was tired of being elusive, tired of being brave. This she told him. When would it end? How could it end?

"What's in the papers?" asked Trotsky.

"Nothing," said Breton. "Frida said Xochimilco is a land of witches."

"Brujas. I hope it is," said Trotsky.

Breton sat back. The sun danced in the garden. The wind danced. "You liked Paris?" he said.

"Of course, like everyone."

"Were you faithful?"

"In Paris?" said Leon Trotsky. "Yes."

"But not always, everywhere," said Breton.

Trotsky rolled his wine in his glass. He grimaced. "War changes everything," he said. "Who you kill. Who you love."

"And your wife?"

"Monsieur Breton," said Trotsky.

"I see," said Breton. He crossed his right leg over his left knee. He leaned forward. "We French see things a little differently. To make love, even to fall in love for a little while, doesn't necessarily break one's faith."

"And Mexicans?" said Leon Trotsky.

"You move directly and quickly, my friend," said Breton. "Diego sleeps with all his models."

"Tina," Trotsky said.

"Yes," said Breton. "Obviously."

"And you and Frida?"

Breton lowered his voice. "I would not confess to it, were it true, or false." He leaned back again. "She's not interested in me."

Trotsky rolled his wine again. Sipped.

Breton said, "She wants you."

The following week they learned of another trial in Moscow, the consequent confessions and the subsequent executions. Trotsky was accused of collaborating with secret agents while he was in Norway on a plot to assassinate Stalin. Several of those agents, in particular, Yury Pyatakov, confessed to traveling with a false passport from Berlin to Oslo in December 1935, to meeting Trotsky and deputy Führer Rudolf Hess to begin a wave of terror and sabotage in the Soviet Union. A dozen old Bolsheviks who fought with Trotsky in the October Revolution were tried, cornered into confessions with bribes of pardons, and then executed. In all, seventeen were killed. Eighty-three Trotskyites in the Far East were shot.

In an office just down the road from Casa Azul, Trotsky was at work for a response in the *Opposition Bulletin* to Stalin's accumulating accusations of conspiracy. He saw Diego Rivera moving with an uncommonly quick gate toward the office. Rivera burst in, panting, and said, "Your son, Sergei Sedov has been shot and killed!"

The men stood, staring at each other. Lev Davidovich lowered his head and said, "I am sorry to be alive."

He had to be the one to break it to Sedova. He brought the last letter they'd received from him, dated December 12, 1936, sent from Krasnoyarsk in Siberia where he was working as a factory engineer. He wrote, "My general situation is extremely grave – graver than one could imagine . . ."

Then, Natalia Sedov had whispered, "At least he is alive."

Trotsky held the letter to his chest when he entered the room. She recognized it.

"Sergei," she said.

"Yes," said Leon Trotsky. "Perhaps my death would have saved him."

She found it unimaginable. Her son. And she couldn't go to him. Couldn't kiss his forehead. Couldn't bury him. They held each other. After they finished a bottle of tequila, they lay in bed, each on their back. Tears poured down Leon Trotsky's cheeks. He remembered the lullaby they used to sing to Sergei when he was a child, as they put him to bed and he began to hum it. Sedova turned to him, touched his cheek, said the words, "Go to sleep, my child, go to sleep. Dream sweet dreams. Dream sweet dreams. Go to sleep."

They stayed in their room. Eulalia brought them bread and soup, water, tea, tequila. They mourned Sergei, talked of his love of music, literature, sports. If he didn't join the *Komsomol* in school, he yet loved Russia and loved the workers, men and women. But his passions were mathematics and engineering. They knew he would never have betrayed them, never have confessed to conspiracy in order to save his own skin. Besides, he was too smart. He knew that once the accusations started, he was a dead man. He would have been defiant, even scornful. So they shot him, far off in Krosmoyarsk, for being Trotsky's son.

They wrote a long letter to Lyova, pleading with him to flee Paris for Mexico before the Nazi's attacked France or the Soviet GPU tracked him down, though before the letter was complete Leon already hedged.

"He couldn't get the same work done from here," he said. "French communism will fall apart."

"Then he will be dead, too," said Sedova. "There's nothing left of the party but criminal insanity."

It had been eight days now. They had wept and mourned. Sedova began an essay entitled, *To the Conscience of the World* to vindicate her son. Trotsky put on a jacket and left the room, sneaked past his bodyguards and headed down the street for the woods. But on the street a black car drove up to him. A window at the back rolled down and he fingered his gun. A face appeared. Frida Kahlo's.

"Come here, Lev," she said. "Let's get lost somewhere."

General Wrong Turn at the wheel, they wended their way toward the teeming city, skirting the Churubusco, a giant monastery where the San Patricios, the Irish Americans who deserted the U.S. army to fight for Mexico, made their last stand against the Yankee invasion of Mexico City. Kahlo called it a fabricated war in order to precipitate the land grab of what is now Texas, New Mexico, Arizona, California, and the southern parts of Utah and Nevada. "They were Catholics," said Kahlo. "And unlike the States, Mexico had outlawed slavery."

"They died," Trotsky said.

"They were artillery men. But we ran out of ammunition. They surrendered and were hung."

"We," said Trotksy.

"Yes, we."

Into the city she pointed north toward Chapultepec Park, talked of the young cadets who threw themselves from the parapets of the castle rather than surrender to the North Americans. "Teenagers," she said. "Just boys."

After some silence she said, "I lost two babies in childbirth."

After more silence he finally said to her, "I know what you're saying." That he was not alone in his world of loss, of sorrow and pain.

She put a hand lightly on his knee. "Your kitten needs you."

He lowered his brow and turned to her. He felt as if on some brink of something frightening. Something he didn't want to broach. Desire.

"Your real kitten," she said. "I've been feeding her. She's yours. She's your obligation." She touched General Wrong Turn's shoulder. "El Zócalo," she said. And to Trotsky, following a little laugh, "He's a bad driver, but even so, if I told him where we were going at the start, he might have been too directional. After all, we're getting lost."

"I'll feed Lorca when we get back," said Trotksy.

They wended their way through El Centro to the great Aztec square that sat before the grand Cathedral. She had Trotsky get out, then offered her hand. He took it and she debarked as well. Under the massive church, the Zócalo expanded around them, filled with people and venders selling food, jewelry, and sundries on blankets spread out on the stone pavement.

"In five hundred years, the pavement is the same, the market hasn't changed," Frida said. "And we are anonymous here." She put her arm through his as they began to walk. "And you will see that I'm no nihilist."

"I thought you a pluralist," said Leon, "if a faithless one."

She laughed. "I was waiting for your sense of humor," she said.

They walked together that way, Frida limping slightly.

"Frida Kahlo and Leon Trotsky are walking arm in arm in the center of Mexico City," said Frida Kahlo, "and nobody in the world knows."

"Not even Diego and Natalia," said Trotsky.

Frida punched his shoulder. "Not even!" she said.

She pointed to her left at a huge, broad building with a gated archway through which he could see an open courtyard. Armed soldiers stood at attention in front of the gates. "Diego will paint the history of Mexico on the courtyard walls," she said.

"Will Lenin be in it?" said Trotsky.

"Likely," she said. "Rockefeller isn't paying for it."

Diego had been commissioned by John D. Rockefeller, Jr., in 1932 to paint a visionary mural about modern technology for the Rockefeller Center in Manhattan. He did. But it included a portrait of Lenin. Rockefeller insisted the portrait be removed. Rivera refused and Rockefeller had the wall destroyed in early 1934. Diego repainted it for the Palacio de Bellas Artes in Mexico City, adding a portrait of Trotsky standing next to Marx and Engels. He knew this.

"Do you want to see the one that you're in?"

"I needn't," he said.

"Don't be a grouch," said Kahlo.

"You met Rockefeller," said Trotsky.

"I did," Kahlo said.

She led him to the Cathedral. Talked about Tenochtitlan and the blood sacrifices atop the Templo Mayor. How the Cathedral was built by Aztec-Mexica slaves from the very stones of their temple that the Spaniards destroyed. "Look closely," she said, "and you'll see portraits of Aztec gods sneaked into the architecture."

Inside the gigantic church they walked among altar after altar set inside porticos with statuary depicting the bloody torture of martyr after martyr.

"Blood for blood," said Kahlo. "You can't explain it with words."

"But with paint," said Leon Trotsky.

"Yet neither can that be explained," she said.

They looked at a pieta, then a statue of the Virgin, her open chest exposing a bleeding heart wrapped in thorns.

"That is my heart," said Kahlo.

He knew enough of her work. He whispered, "I know."

They exited to a side street that opened to the jewelry district. Kahlo took him into a shop, found a thick, antique silver bracelet. She fingered it, slipped her wrist through where its circle opened, tried it on, then took it off and handed it to him. It was smooth and rich like metal silk. "The finest silver in the world," she said. "Buy it."

He stood, silently, holding the bracelet. Suddenly everything was crashing again.

"Buy it," she said, "for Natalia." And he did.

She asked for a piece of paper and a pencil, wrote down "Sergei" and handed it to the jeweler who took the bracelet to a back room and engraved "Sergei" on it.

Mysteriously, when they left the shop General Wrong Turn was there with the car. When they reached Casa Azul they stopped a half-block away. Kahlo kissed Trotsky lightly on the cheek and said, "Better if you go in alone."

Natalia Sedova was reading and drinking a cup of tea. There was opera on the radio. She looked up when he came in.

"Long walk," she said.

He didn't hesitate. He said, "Frida picked me up in a car. We went to the Zócalo."

"Without guards?"

"It was very crowded. I got a tour. She's very proud of Mexico."

"Just you and her?" she said.

"General Wrong Turn."

She held back. She didn't want to point out that it wasn't something one would do in Russia, spend an afternoon with a young, married woman. She was hurt. Should she tell him she was jealous? What would it accomplish?

He reached in his pocket and handed her the bracelet. She stood. He took it from her and placed it on her wrist.

They made love that night. There are ways that passion changes, with time, with age, with the simplicity of familiarity, almost like making love to a memory. He placed her beside him and held her face to face. He removed himself, went down on her. She quivered, finally pushed him away, and he came inside her again. There was nothing that they hadn't done before. She thought of the sons that this act had created, when it was an act of hope not despair. When she held his face between her hands, she saw the bracelet, a gift for her, but not for her. Had Kahlo tried it on? Of course. How did the French say it? You seduced one woman while making love to another. A woman could do it, too.

Now as they made love, or even just kissed or touched, she wondered how many more times there would be. How long before they finally killed him. She hoped that when they did, they would kill her, too. She hoped he wouldn't annihilate these last days by falling in love with a woman half his age. How did Kahlo manage to find him alone after eight days? How closely had she watched? Did he wonder at all?

When they were done they lay on their backs and smoked.

"We should find our own place," Sedova said.

"Yes," he said, "in time we will." But his mind had wandered to a stroll arm in arm on the Zócalo, to a quiet moment before a sacred burning heart.

The Moscow trials created some stir in the world, particularly in the United States and in France where Lyova Sedov published the *Red Book*, a collection of documents and facts attacking the forgeries of Soviet prosecutor Vyshinsky and the GPU. Trotsky pleaded for a trial, he wrote articles for the *New York Times* and the *Opposition Bulletin* saying that if any of the accusations against him could be proven he would voluntarily surrender himself for prosecution by the GPU in Russia. In the States, dozens of artists and intellectuals formed the American Defense Committee to investigate the accusations against Trotsky and in New York, a committee led by John Dewey and Suzanne La Follette, an anti-communist, agreed to come to Coyoacán to interrogate Leon Davidovich Trotsky.

Eminently prepared, Trotsky was excited and afraid. The Soviet ambassador refused to attend, as well the leaders of several Mexican communist and socialist organizations. Diego transformed the Casa Azul's study into a courtroom. A six-foot wall of sandbags and bricks was built around it, the house surrounded by armed police. People who wished to attend as spectators were searched for concealed weapons. Trotsky sat before the panel, Diego off the right side of the wide table, facing Leon's left shoulder, wearing a large sombrero with a peacock feather. And though Sedova sat behind Leon, nearby, Frida Kahlo, wearing Tarascan jewelry and dressed in a Tehuano blouse and skirt, sat near him at an angle to his right. Trotsky would conduct his defense in English, but if he struggled to understand a question, Kahlo was there to translate or re-explain.

"I am not a fan of communism nor your particular philosophy concerning it," John Dewey began, "but I believe in justice, education, and public disclosure. If you are found innocent, I will not be afraid to say so, nor shall I shrink from condemning you if you are guilty. Our mission here is to find the truth."

Trotsky said, "I have requested international reviews of my actions and my dedication to the revolution since my banishment. I've offered myself to the Soviet for extradition to be tried in public. What do they fear? I welcome this opportunity."

He documented his early, 1904, disagreements with Lenin concerning socialist democracy. It was an open, and temporary, disagreement, not a plot to unseat Lenin. He documented through timetables and letters that he was not in Oslo meeting with Hess and Pyatakov. He refuted each of his former, condemned allies' confessions. He responded to some pointed questions regarding the accusations of Mikhali Borodin that Trotsky sent him to Mexico in 1919 or 1920 and purportedly used stolen Tsarist treasures, given to him by Trotsky, to bribe Mexican officials toward creating a Mexican Communist Party.

"1919 or 1920?" asked Trotsky. "Which year? Who were the officials? Where are the letters? The jewels?" Though he admitted meeting Borodin briefly in China. "In 1919 and 1920 I was on the eastern front on my train."

A commissioner whispered in Dewey's ear and Dewey said, "Letters, documents, passports, can all be falsified."

"Then where are they?" He produced copies of all his correspondence within Russia since 1930. It went on for seven days.

During the meetings, Kahlo passed him notes. "Bravo!" or "Well said," or "Are you holding up?" or "You will be fine." Sometimes he turned the note over and, in pencil, thanked her.

Rivera gathered Sedova, Trotsky, Kahlo, and himself in the kitchen the evening after the first hearing. He served whiskey and beer.

"You will be exonerated!" he said to Trotsky.

"We will return to our Mexican language and cooking lessons," said Frida.

Yet that night, in their room, Sedova gazed in a mirror. She looked more tired and worn than Trotsky himself, which only reminded her of how young and beautiful Kahlo looked as she sat near Leon, her face bracing for every question from the panel, her visible relief when Trotsky calmly fielded the questions. Now, as Sedova turned from the mirror to look at her husband, he saw her consternation. He reached into his jacket pocket where he still held several of Frida's notes, pulled them out.

"They're nothing," he said.

"They're in Spanish."

"Simple Spanish. You can read them." He showed her.

"Are those all of them? I don't want to see them," she said. "The truth can be worse than a lie."

"You'd prefer she didn't help me?"

"Why are you on the defensive?" said Sedova. "Is there reason to be on the defensive?"

"I'll tell her no more notes."

"What will be the difference?"

He took her hand. "Please," he said. "One trial at a time."

The next morning, before things started up, he took Kahlo aside and spoke to her.

"We must stop the notes," he said. "It disturbs Natalia."

"It doesn't disturb Diego," said Kahlo. "And he is a jealous man."

"It could be seen as a public display," he said.

"Of what?" She stood on her toes and whispered in his ear, "You'd prefer this?"

He stepped back.

"It's my house. I'll pass notes to whomever I want to, whenever I want to," she said.

There was no way out now, not in any direction. He'd been too busy, too preoccupied, to have thought this through ahead of time. Natalia was right, after the trial maybe they should find another place. Though Diego, and Frida too, were important allies. He didn't wish to spurn their hospitality after all they had done for them, helping to place his work so they'd have money, feeding them, fortifying Casa Azul from attack.

Frida spun in front of him, skirt furling, stopped and met his eyes. "And I'll sit wherever I want to. You're the great advocate of letting the truth win out. There is nothing between us, no matter how much you wish that weren't so." Yet however defiant her words, her eyes were soft; she relaxed her shoulders as if yielding to him, then smiled slightly, not showing her teeth; she glanced downward, displaying her vulnerability.

That next day, in fact, she helped him field several questions regarding the confessions of his former allies. And though now bothered by anxiety, headaches, and dizziness, he endured it. Kahlo endured. Sedova endured. At the end, he spoke for hours, then his knees buckled and Kahlo caught him, held him up, and led him to Sedova. "I've arranged a place in the country for you recover and relax," she said to Natalia. "This is done."

TEOTIHUACÁN

IN TLAXCO THEY WERE both exhausted. He'd thought of a return to hunting, fishing, and horseback riding, but he was too tired and weak, still suffering from dizziness and headaches. They took short walks to get groceries, always followed by their guards. It was difficult to find something they could turn into Russian food: sausage, cabbage, rye, beef. Coffee was scarce. They settled on rice, beans, pork, water, tea, tequila and beer.

In the calm of dusk Sedova talked of their first days impoverished in Paris. How one night in a snowstorm he showed up at her door and when he stepped in she brought him to her, pulled him to the floor and made love to him. In the morning they walked in the uncommon snow, even a city like Paris quieted by the white blanket. Then, at the turn of the century, there was still the soft clopping of horses' hooves and the churn of spoked wheels over the cobblestone. They stopped for coffee, walked back to her flat and made love again. That's when he first called her Tasha, in intimacy, and she first called him Lev.

"An island," he said.

"In the snow."

"In Paris."

She said, "I thought it would last forever."

"One always does," he said.

Almost alone in a valley above Mexico City, surrounded by mountains, they made love again, and as he rocked with her he thought, will this be the last woman I make love to? will this be the last time I make love? Death felt close. Something else lay just beyond his sight. And Sedova, in the arms of something bigger than a man, even a great man, even if he believed that great men did not exist, only great causes, inevitable historical outcomes, she was married to that man and those causes, married to communism, Bolshevism.

She faced him when they were done, yet barely panting from the throes of love, of passion. Could she still call it passion? She wondered if she were driven to him now under the shadow of Frida Kahlo's fascination with him, the general of the victorious Red Army, the savior of Petrograd, the man who guided Lenin to form the first Workers' State. She lay next to him again. In her passion to share his vision, his work, his children, had she failed to appreciate the love, or did he? It was hard to know what they had let pass by them as they'd found their way to this, alone in the hills of Mexico with wo armed guards, waiting to return to their work? with voices brave? plaintive? speaking to the world? to history? to the Void? Maybe Lyova, alone in Paris, was right. It was over. Then came death. And then nothing.

"Would you ever leave me?" she said to him. When he said nothing, she said, "if I made love to another?"

"Another man?" he said. "Another cause?'

"You speak with Kahlo. I've never spoken to Diego."

"He stays busy," Trotsky said.

"Very busy," she said.

"You mean the sister?" he said to her. "She's an even bigger flirt."

"More than a flirt it would seem," Natalia said.

"Did you like Dewey?" he said to her.

She laughed. "He's too old."

He laughed too because it was not what he meant and she knew it, but he said, "A man is never too old."

And beneath the jest this is exactly what she feared.

"I meant as a fair man, a judicious intellect," he said.

"As Diego said, you will be exonerated, dear Lev."

He touched her cheek, which was softer now than when she was young, her hair, once wavy, now a little kinky and gray. When she was tired, like tonight, her cheeks sagged slightly and bags formed under her eyes, though when revived her face tightened and the lines disappeared, her dark eyes brightened and he was reminded of the girl he loved. But he was growing gray too. "Tasha, my Tasha," said Trotsky.

They returned to Coyoacán somewhat refreshed, and hopeful, even confident that in Leon's showing in front of the commission he flashed the brilliance that once led men, who in the first days of the civil war rallied the deserting troops at Svyazhk who were yelling "Death to Trotsky." And alone, without a weapon, he'd jumped on the roof of his car and spoke to them of their place in history and how the workers of the future would stand on their shoulders. He gave them back their rifles. "You are the only line between chaos and Moscow! Between the old days of subservience and poverty and the new days of merit and hope!" He rallied the Latvian Rifles, too, and there, on the Volga, stopped Kappel's monarchists and the Whites and retook Kazan. He did it again, at Kharkov. He never punished a deserter who returned (though he might execute their leaders), always re-armed and recruited any enemy who surrendered and was willing to fight for him. Dewey could see it. Sedova knew this, and said it to Rivera when she sought him out at his studio in San Angel on her and Trotsky's return.

He came down from his scaffolding, glanced back at Tina, and walked to the diminutive Russian who stood with an air of defiance before him.

He rubbed his paint smothered hands with a rag, put the rag in his pocket and then rubbed his hands on his overhauls. "Your Mexican is much improved," he said.

"How is your Russian?" said Sedova.

He laughed. "I have no plans." Though in the future he would retrun to Moscow as a guest of Stalin. Best that the shadow of the future is so dark.

"I would take your hand," he said, but he turned his soiled palms up. She took his hand anyways. He smiled. "I brought him here," Rivera said. "I protect you. I've been thrown out of the party for it. I let the commission meet at my house." He paused, put his hands in his pockets. "So I'm puzzled."

"We've never talked," she said. Now she didn't know why she was there either. To talk, though not about Frida Kahlo. Maybe she simply wanted to leave Leon alone at Casa Azul. Maybe this was how she could somehow save the fragile balance.

"I am a painter," said Rivera. "I live to paint. Then love." Tina got up from her seat but Rivera raised his hand to stop her advance. "Let's sit," he said to Sedova and motioned to a small wooden table where he held a chair for her, then sat across. "Tina," he said, "bring us some beer."

They sat quietly while Tina retrieved two beers from an icebox and brought them, setting one down before each of them. "Por favor, uno momento, Tina."

"Would you like a glass?" he said to Sedova. She raised her bottle, touched the tip of hers to his, then drank.

"You are a great woman of powerful intellect," said Rivera.

"Your praise is welcome," said Sedova. "But of course I didn't come here for it."

"Then?"

"Forbearance?" she said.

"Do you control Leon Trotsky?" said Diego Rivera. "He changed the world."

"And now he is paying the price," Sedova said.

"And you, as well. Married to greatness."

"To Trotsky," she said.

"To greatness," he said. "Have you seen Orozco's work? You should go to Guadalajara. The government ceilings. His fire and passion. Like me, he's a communist. It's a great time for Mexican painting. Siqueiros might be the best of us all, but he is lost in communism. Politics cannot precede art. I paint with my hands. I change the world with my hands."

"That wasn't good enough for Siqueiros?" Sedova said.

"And so he had me expelled from the party. For the Mexican Bolsheviks, Leon Trotsky is a Fascist."

"You know better."

"That's why I'm expelled. I'm a Trotskyist."

"For now," said Sedova.

"You're too smart for me, Natalia Sedova," said Diego Rivera. "Everything is for now." He took her hand. "Too beautiful and too smart."

She almost blushed. Now she knew that this is why she'd come, to find this out.

"Great men are powerless, too," he said. "Pushed witlessly by destiny."

"By historical forces. Leon believes that if he never existed someone else would have done his work."

"An artist can't believe that," Rivera said. "Great art makes destiny makes great art. Made by great artists."

"You believe you're unique," said Sedova.

"Yes," he said. "Maybe unfortunately, but yes."

So these were the lines. At least she could see the lines now. And how ironic it was that Trotsky's vision for the workers, the world, and how and why it would come about, how it should come about, was so unique.

So they were both dreamers, Diego and Leon. But dreams inevitably collide. Men put their work first, deluded by their dreams. Women bore and raised children, like Sergei, like Lyova, who would live in the ruins of those dreams. Did Stalin dream? One day, he would have nightmares too.

It was still morning when she arrived back at Casa Azul where she found Leon and Frida sitting in the garden. The dogs sprawled in a patch of sunlight. Lorca stretched, stomach exposed, across Trotsky's lap. Trotsky put out his hand for Sedova and they touched fingers lightly.

"They're not like dogs," he said,

"I have to remind him to feed her," Frida said to Natalia. "And we'll have to reinforce the rabbit cages or soon she'll be eating baby bunnies."

"And the chicks?" said Trotsky.

"Igual," said Frida. "Until they're big enough." She got up and walked to the parrot cages, muttering, cooing quietly to the birds. "Hello Frida. Hello Frida," the parrots said.

"She'll learn to leave them alone," said Trotsky. "Meanwhile I'll help with the cages."

"Cats are always a mistake," Frida Kahlo said to Natalia. "You turn him loose for a minute and he comes back with a cat."

"Then you've learned one thing about him," said Sedova.

"Watch the cat! Watch the cat!" said the parrots.

"We'll watch her," Frida said to them.

"We'll watch! We'll watch!" they said.

"Where's Fulang?" said Sedova.

"Too smart for this," said Kahlo. "Maybe he's painting, like I should be doing."

"But not today," said Lev Davidovich.

Kahlo spun quickly to look at him, then spoke to Sedova. "Does he already know me so well?"

"A student of human behavior. Always," said Sedova.

Trotsky placed his hand on Lorca who spun, clawed and bit his arm and then sprung from his lap. He wagged his wrist. "Less so with cats," he said and laughed.

"An excursion, yes," said Frida Kahlo. "Before we all go back to our work, more Mexico. Teotihuacán."

They took a black Ford sedan, one guard driving and the other in the front passenger seat, both armed with Colt 45's. In the back seat Sedova graciously took the middle, sitting between Trotsky and Kahlo. Frida undoubtedly understood the gesture and touched Sedova's shoulder with her fingertips, in sympathy? condescension? both? Once again they traveled without Diego and without Tina. How deadly the obvious had become.

"It's so good to have you here," said Frida. "There are things you don't do on your own and you forget how magnificent your life is until you can show these things to someone else." She leaned forward and wagged a finger at Trotsky. "But no melodramaticos this time," she said in Mexican.

"I thought I'd been rather stoic," he said.

"*You* maybe were stoic. The rest of us were jumping in our skins." She raised her double brows at Sedova. "No?"

Against her inclinations, Natalia was charmed. "I don't always get to see him risk his life," she said.

"And ours!" said Kahlo. "Behave," she said to Trotsky, "or we will stop hanging out with you." She laughed, which allowed them all to laugh. "I suppose you have your little gun," she said to Leon, who simply tilted his head toward her and smiled slightly. "All these big men have guns," she said to Sedova. "Why don't we little women have guns?"

"No one wants to kill us?" said Natalia.

"I've done too good a job of almost killing myself," said Frida Kahlo. She directed the driver to a parking lot beneath a small basilica. "Tepeyac Hill," she said. "Once the temple of Tonontzin, the mother goddess." She told them the story of Juan Diego, how in 1531, ten years after Cortez' conquest, the Virgin appeared to Juan Diego atop the hill and told him to have the bishop build a church to her there. When the bishop responded incredulously, the virgin appeared to Diego again, brought him to the hilltop and had him fill his cactus cloth *tilma* with roses. When the peasant returned to the bishop and dumped the roses at his feet, an image of the Virgin, now the Virgin of Guadalupe, remained.

The bishop built this basilica to house it.

"Smart bishop," said Trotsky. "Did he invent the story and hire the painter?"

"Is this the same woman who saved the miners?" Sedova said.

"The same and not the same," said Kahlo. "The Catholics steal the peoples' gods and goddesses and then steal the feast days. But it doesn't have to be a fact to be true. This is yet the most important goddess in Mexico, because there are no women ruling in heaven," she said.

"No mothers," said Sedova.

"You're right" said Kahlo.

Inside the crowded church people knelt in front of the image of the dark virgin standing on a crescent moon, her head radiating golden rays. Many of them fell to their knees when they entered the basilica and crawled toward the painting, stopping to touch their heads to the ground before inching forward.

"Like this," said Kahlo, "for four hundred years."

"Assuredly," Leon said, "it is guarded all night and no one slips in to retouch it or replace it anew."

"Like Lenin's grave?" said Frida Kahlo.

"I'm skeptical and admiring of such reverence," said Trotsky. "If it could only be turned toward each other; the material world, concrete reality, the workers' plight."

"In Russia this was investigated by the *Cheka*. They concluded that Juan Diego was an agent of the Pope," Sedova said.

"The *Cheka*?" said Leon. "Haven't they better things to do?"

"Besides chasing you around?" Sedova said to him. "I don't tell you everything I hear."

"You Russians and your agents," said Frida Kahlo. "I prefer angels, if they are equally surreptitious." She led them to a side altar where a large, silver crucifix, battered and bent, lay enshrined. In 1921 an anarchist had tried to dynamite the Virgin's image, but the crucifix fell on the bomb and saved it.

"You needn't comment," said Kahlo. "The church and state will never be reconciled."

Back in the car they passed under the twin volcanoes of Iztac ihuatl, *La Mujer Dormida*, and her lover, Popocatépetl. When the lowly Popo fell in love with the princess, Izta, her father sent him off to war and reported that he'd been killed. Izta killed herself in grief, as did Popo when he returned to find her dead. The people rose up and murdered their king and buried the lovers under these mountains where even today they yet erupt in volcanic rage.

"Romeo and Juliet," said Leon Trotsky.

"If it never happened, it's true a million times," said Frida. "Before Shakespeare, before Christ."

"Before the *Cheka* could find out what really happened," said Sedova, laughing.

Kahlo laughed, too.

"Stalin invented baseball while vacationing on the Black Sea," said Trotsky.

"Before he was alive," said Natalia.

"If I were smarter I'd think you two were making fun of me," said Frida Kahlo. She looked at Leon. "Blind rage at the loss of a beloved," she said.

"Faith breeds madness," said Trotsky.

"And madness, insight," said Frida.

"And the other way around, as well," said Natalia Sedova.

"I'm learning too much, too fast," said Kahlo and led them back to the car.

When they reached the pyramids of Teotihuacán the sun was low, its glancing light sliding across the temple of the plumed serpent, Quetzacoatl, giant effigies of his fierce head grimacing at the corners of his pyramid, almost as if yawning at the sunset. When the gods convened here at the end of the world, sacrificing themselves to create a new one, Quetzacoatl put the sun and moon in motion with his breath. Each solstice, at dawn, you can see his shadow crawling up the steps of his temple. Under the immense pyramids of the sun and moon, vendors, like ants, gathered up their ponchos and blankets, Mexican flags, silver jewelry and obsidian statues.

"When the Mexica arrived at Tenochtitlan, all this had been abandoned for a thousand years," Kahlo said. "They believed the gods built it. Who else?"

Trotsky knew of this place, yet its vastness and intricacy was incomprehensible; its walls, coated with obsidian and stucco, glistened in the late sunlight, the impossible work of ancient humanity. Who were they, these Indians? No one knew.

They walked to the ball court behind Quetzacoatl's pyramid, where men once played a game in which, not using their hands, they'd tried to knock a ball through stone circles on the walls.

"For fun?" said Trotsky. "What was at stake?"

"Their lives," said Frida Kahlo. "The losers had their hearts torn out, up there." She pointed to the top of the Sun Temple. "Or maybe it was the winners. They were eaten. A great honor."

They wandered back to the main causeway, *La Avenida de los Muertos*, oddly named, said Kahlo, because no bodies had ever been found there. "I'll leave you for a little while," she said, "and meet you here when the sun is down." Then she walked away toward the Temple of the Moon.

"Place to ourselves," said Natalia Sedova.

"Such timing," said Trotsky. He gazed at the top of the Temple of the Sun. "What to believe here in Mexico."

"Belief has nothing to do with any of it," said Sedova.

"Or everything," said Leon.

"That's what I meant," Sedova said.

"I'm going up," he said to her.

"Then I'll meet you here, sun god. Keep your heart in your chest."

Trotsky kissed her forehead, turned, and began the arduous climb up the steep, inexplicably tall steps of the pyramid. It was difficult, but the exertion felt good. With each step his mind cleared, envisioning the labor, the arms and legs and hands that laid these stones. He loved thinking of the world, this world, before it was Christian, how men and women yet worked, made laws, saw the firmament and sky filled with the thoughts of gods, the lovemaking of gods, their battles and squabbles as multifarious as humanity itself, just as infested with love, with greed, with glory. He could feel the ghosts of the prisoners as they were led up these steps to have their hearts shown to them before they died, each one as real, as sentient as he, each one born of a woman, his life filled with intention, with misery.

From atop the temple he followed the Avenida with his eyes and spied the complex of buildings beneath the Temple of the Moon, then looked beyond to the valley that spread out to the ring of mountains surrounding Teotihuacán, and in the distance, the lovers, Popo and Izta, now dozing volcanoes. He sat. He breathed, alone in his exile. He heard someone. Turned. It was Kahlo who sat down next to him.

"Those troughs are for the blood that ran down from the sacrifices," said Frida Kahlo. She pointed to the narrow spillways that ran from the top of pyramid to the ground.

"History is written in blood," he said.

"Women's blood," she said. "Forgotten blood. Unwritten history."

"That blood makes men, so men make war?" he said.

"That is your revenge. Because you cannot make children on your own, you kill each other, our children. These men pretended they were feeding the gods to keep the sun burning. But all life is sacrifice. I paint myself as a sacrifice. I paint myself sacrificed."

"To yourself," he said.

"To everyone. I didn't choose it," she said.

"History chooses," said Trotsky.

"Maybe," said Kahlo. "Maybe not."

He admired her aggression. That she was so vulnerable and indomitable both, that she was intellectually lithe, fascinating, determined to pry open the world with contradiction.

"How did you make this climb?" he said to her.

"Very slowly," said Kahlo. "But I was motivated."

"To see something?"

"You," she said. "Alone."

He felt the tremor of desire, something he hadn't felt in a long time.

"We could do it right here," said Kahlo.

"But what would that start?" said Trotsky. "And how would it end?"

"If you're going to take a risk, why not risk everything?" she said.

"Consequences," he said.

"You're already drowning in consequences. Do you think you'll be the first man I ever loved? I've loved every man and every woman. I've loved no one else but you." She kissed his cheek. She touched his chin and turned his head with her fingertips, kissed his lips, a kiss that he returned. "I will have you, Lev Davidovich. I will eat your heart because there is no one in the world like me."

And then she left him.

At the foot of the pyramid when he returned, Natalia Sedova could sense something in him, a change. His hands trembled. She'd seen him face death and not tremble.

"Flirting with the gods up there?" she said.

"Worse than gods," he said to her.

But those were inner recesses where she chose not to go. And for him, how could he not tell her, the woman he'd told everything to for thirty years? But he couldn't. He could yet tell himself that there was nothing to tell. Yet if he had not transgressed at all, everything inside him had already transgressed. He'd climbed the sacrificial pyramid. His heart was torn out.

MISERY

WHEN THEY RETURNED there was a letter waiting from Lyova.

"He's still alive," said Sedova. "In Paris."

But their old Bolshevik comrade, Kretinsky, who had fought for the Revolution with Trotsky as early as 1902, had been put on trial. Thinking it would be best for the party if he confessed to treason and present the Soviet as unified, he confessed to a conspiracy with Trotsky against Stalin and the Soviet. But the next day he reversed his position and said that he and the other defendants had lied. They'd broken from Trotsky in 1927. Other defendants began admitting that they'd lied. There was no conspiracy. A day later Kretinsky reversed his position again. They were all executed.

"Tortured into insanity," said Leon.

Even worse, Stalin's Soviet prosecutor, Vyshinsky, had begun interrogating former generals who fought with Trotsky during the Civil War, in the Urals and at Petrograd, and then against the 1921 sailors' rebellion in Kronstadt. The Kronstadt rebellion was yet a sore point for Trotsky because the sailors were communists petitioning for free elections, recognition of all Soviet political parties, economic freedom for small traders, the end of rationing, and the release of political prisoners.

Both Lenin and Trotsky feared they had been prompted by Mensheviks and anarchists backed by Finland and Estonia. The sailors, if left alone, would control the Kronstadt Fortress, the arsenal, and the Baltic fleet and, unwittingly or not, could spearhead an invasion of Petrograd by reactionaries in Finland and Estonia. The revolution was still young and Moscow was surrounded by drought, famine, and discontent that yet fueled Czarist, Menshevik, and anarchist groups in the countryside.

It was one of the most difficult decisions of his life, but Leon eventually agreed with Lenin and ordered the rebellion repressed. He sent a young general, M. N. Tukhachevsky, who at age twenty-six had become Trotsky's most valuable and loyal general during the Civil War, to quell the rebellion. The sailors fought him fiercely on the frozen Gulf of Finland and into the town. They went down fighting almost to a man. Tukhachevsky had been tied to crushing the revolt, now portrayed by Stalin as a Bolshevik rebellion against Fascism, and Tukhachevsky indicted as a Trotskyite.

Dropping Lenin out of the equation, at Field Marshal Tukhachevsky's trial the Kronstadt sailors were portrayed by Vyshinsky as Bolsheviks who Trotsky had massacred. As well, Tukhachevsky, who commandeered the failed Soviet invasion of Poland in 1920, was accused of going into that war under the hand of Trotsky, who'd convinced Lenin that taking Warsaw would lead to the liberation of Poland and its workers and incite the workers of Berlin and Paris into Bolshevik revolt, i.e. "Permanent International Revolution," an anathema to Stalin's current policy of "Socialism in One Nation," (though a year after the failure in Poland it was Stalin who engineered the invasion of Georgia). Trotsky, it was argued, knew full well that the Red army could not win the Polish war and its defeat would result in the fall of Moscow and Bolshevism to the Poles, leaving Trotsky in charge of Russia. Tukhachevsky's invasion and retreat were guided by Leon Trotsky's conspiracy to take power.

Trotsky remembered having opposed the invasion of Poland (and

Georgia) and arguing heatedly with Lenin about it. When the Poles, under Marshal Jozef Pilsudski, pushed the Red Army back to the Russian border, it was Trotsky who negotiated the treaty to end the war and the Polish advance. He said all this in his *My Life: An Attempt at an Autobiography*. Though it hardly mattered, now that book didn't exist and Lenin was dead.

Tukhachevsky could not refute that he'd been Trotsky's leading general and led the crushing of the Kronstadt rebellion and the invasion of Poland. The rest was Stalinist polemics. He was found guilty and executed.

"This ends it for all of them," Leon said to Sedova. "All the generals. And if he kills all the generals, who will fight Hitler?" In fact, in the next eighteen months, all the generals who once fought for Trotsky were dead. Stalin signed a non-aggression pact with Hitler and the Germans, divided up Poland with them, then fell under a traitorous German *Blitzkrieg*. The Germans were in eyesight of Moscow before Zhukov, miraculously under Stalin's radar during his anti-Trotsky military pogrom, saved the war for the Soviets.

Lyova closed his letter by saying that Sergei's wife had committed suicide, leaving their son, Seva, Leon and Natalia's grandson, an orphan. He said that he had passed beyond his despair, though he could feel the net tightening around him. "If I am found dead," he said, "it will not be by my own hand, but Stalin's"

"We must bring Seva here," she said to Trotsky.

"I am overwhelmed," said Leon, murmuring now.

"He must kill them all," Sedova said to Leon. "Stalin must wipe out all memory of you and murder anyone who might be sympathetic to a military coup."

"And when there is no one left?" said Leon Trotsky. "We should write Llyova immediately. Find out what they're saying in *Pravda*."

"What's the point?" said Sedova. "They simply reiterate Stalin. Write

Lyova and tell him to come here."

Trotsky hesitated. He had never accepted defeat. He could not. He would finish his biography of Stalin. Publish it in New York. The world would know. "How long have you believed it was over?" he said to Sedova. "It is never over. There is yet work to do."

"When have I stopped working?"

"But if your heart has given up," he said.

"Lev," she said. "Paris will be in flames. Or under Hitler's heel. It can't be saved for itself, let alone true Bolshevism. Bring our child home to us."

"The *Bulletin*," said Trotsky. "Each of these coming trials must be exposed as they occur."

"His assistant, Mark, can work in what's left of Europe," she said. "Lyova can guide him from here or New York. Mark Zborowski can work in Paris."

"It can't be done by telephone," Trotsky said.

"Lev, he is the last of all we have. Write Lyova and bring him."

He stared at her. She went to the end table near their bed, poured herself tequila. Drank it.

"I won't," he said.

"Then I will," said Natalia Sedova.

This is how it began. Or ended. Or almost ended. When he doubted her years of devotion to him. Years of work, years of dedication, time in prison. When he questioned all those years. Though neither of them could say it, even to themselves.

As she poured him a glass of tequila, and herself another, he took it, though he told himself that he shouldn't, that he should do something, some work, something to stop the flood. Would everyone he had ever touched die? Had he led a legion of dead men and women, all doomed? Was this the inevitable path of history's torrent? They didn't touch glasses. He sipped. He recalled Petrograd.

In 1919 the Red army was under pressure from the French in Crimea and the Ukraine. Czechoslovak rebels were on the march in the Urals and Siberia, allied to Admiral Kolchak who had declared himself loyal to the Bolsheviks only to turn on the Reds and proclaim himself the Supreme Governor of Russia. He had begun to move west toward Moscow. A Cossack army was on the Don. Another rebel army of 150,000, under A. I. Denikin, backed by the French, had swept through the Ukraine and was on the attack south of Moscow. Poland was belligerent. Around Petrograd, the Finns advanced from the north backed by a fleet of British war ships. From the Estonian frontier, an army under General Yudenich, supplied by the British with machine guns and six tanks and backed by Kolchak, was sweeping south in an attempt to envelope Petrograd, cutting the rail route to Moscow. The ancient Russian capital where the Revolution had its roots was home to a million people, many of them workers and communists. But convinced he could not hold Petrograd and that defending it would be a waste of lives on a doomed engagement, Lenin decided to surrender the surrounded city to the Whites in order to tighten the lines of defense around Moscow. In London, British newspapers declared that the Bolshevik revolution was doomed.

Trotsky raced to Moscow to convince Lenin that the only solution was to quickly attack. To surrender the city would leave the workers and communists there defenseless to White slaughter. Under the possibility that Finland and Estonia might commit their militaries to the invasion, he agreed to prepare an evacuation of the army and workers to the southeast, but he believed that if he moved quickly he could win the day before that. Remarkably, he was backed by Stalin. Lenin fought with him briefly before giving his consent and Trotsky quickly returned to his Train and swept away Kolchak and the Cossacks. Then he took his Train and raced to Petrograd where, confronted by 25,000 of Yudenich's troops and dozens of British tanks, he found the city in despair and the army in disarray.

He searched the government offices for Zinoviev who was supposed to be in charge. He found him lying on a couch, complaining of a migraine. There, he left him to begin his own defense of Petrograd

He dispatched the train soldiers to organize the defense, traveling from one part of the city to another giving rallying speeches to the populace. Workers, both men and women, filed out of the mills and factories to hear Trotsky promise that Petrograd would not be surrendered to the Whites. "We are a million strong!" he told them. "If they are unlucky enough to penetrate our outer defenses, we will be waiting for them on every street corner with machine guns and wrath!"

Along with men and boys, women, wives and daughters took up spades and began digging trenches along the Seva River. Trotsky had city blocks strewn with barbed wire, built barricades along the street corners as men and women took up rifles and manned some sixty machine guns to cover the corners in angles of crossfire. By car he rushed to the front, only fifteen miles from the city where the Whites had captured Krasnaya Gorka, The Red Hill fort from where only two years earlier he'd launched the Revolution. He found his soldiers in full retreat, throwing down their guns and running. There, he jumped on a horse and began rounding up the men, pushing them back to the battle. "I will lead you!" he cried over the tumult and rode ahead of them into the oncoming troops and tanks. Bullets flew past him with their sweet, nauseating whistle, but he rode forward and his troops rallied, driving the Whites back. It was the difference between warriors who had everything to fight for, and mercenaries who did not.

Retaking and entrenching the Red Hill, he took a car back to Petrograd. He set up the cannons, released the students of the military schools and sent them to the front. As the British warships thundered off the coast, he rallied the men and women, students and workers with speeches that praised their courage and heroism. They moved forward to fight, even as the tanks drove forward against them. Against this fury and frenzy, the tank commanders abandoned their tanks and ran.

Then Trotsky wired Lenin for reinforcements and in three days he had them. A Bashkir cavalry division, guns and food, another army, the Fifteenth, arrived and set up against Yudenich south of the city on his right flank. Yudenich was stopped and a day later the Reds were on the offensive. Yudenich left his army on the field and fled to Estonia. "Remember," Trotsky told the citizens of Petrograd, "the tanks and guns that you turned back were the pawns of English capitalism. You fought not only for yourselves, but for the workers and laborers of England, your brothers and sisters."

This is the man who stood in front of Natalia Sedova now in a small bedroom in Mexico City, feeling the nauseating whistle of her resistance.

She saw his gaze. She knew that clamping of his jaws when Petrograd washed over him, a man at the peak of his power, never dreaming, how could he? It was impossible to imagine that it could come to this.

From Petrograd, Trotsky rode his train into Moscow, stopping briefly to receive the Order of the Red Banner, along with the city of Petrograd itself, and Josef Stalin. That Stalin, who played little or no role in the defense of the city, received the award, angered Leon, but he was too busy hurrying east, back to the war on the Volga and Urals, and to the Ukraine to take on Denikin, to take much notice of how much power Stalin wielded in the Politburo. He took more consolation that Stalin didn't show up at the Bolshoy Theater to receive the award. This was the crack in the wall behind his back. On to his next battle, he never turned around to notice. Did he take time then, any time, to make love to his wife or kiss his sons? She'd married into his great dream, his historical, history-changing dream, and this impossible destiny.

"If you write Lyova and tell him to come here," he said, "I will write him and tell him to stay."

"You would have him choose between his father and his mother," she said.

"Between his own safety and the future of the world," he said.

"Then you'd better start your letter," Sedova said.

That day Natalia Sedova wrote to her son.

My dearest son, Lyova:

Read me gently but soberly, a mother always fears the worst.

When Mikhail Tukhachevsky was sent into Poland in response to Pilsudki's invasion of Kiev, he was only twenty-seven years old. Your father was against it, arguing to Lenin that the Red army was already overextended fighting the Whites along the Volga and the Urals. Nonetheless, Mikhail's mistake at the gates of Warsaw was tactical, not even strategic let alone diabolical. He overextended his lines and Pilsudski broke through the middle and pushed him back to the Russian border. It was there that you father negotiated the truce and treaty. Tukhachevsky was very young, a half-decade younger than you are now. Too young to lead armies. He proved himself more stalwart and cautious a year later at Kronstadt, however sadly one chooses to regard that unfortunate, though necessary, affair. Your father was Commissar of War then. He had seen horror again and again.

He sees it now, but the guns of time have turned on him. Permanent revolution, however much we conceived it and fought for it, has been suspended, by circumstance, by history, what does it matter now? And however much I might choose to continue to fight alongside your father for its legacy, I have already given my life to it. Were we in the streets of Moscow or Petrograd, we could join the ranks and ride behind your father's steed into battle. But our war against the GPU and the Politburo is now not even a war of words.

At this moment, your father is writing you, too, to urge you to stay in Paris and fight on. This will mean your death. This, you must already know. What little there is that remains for us to do can be done here or anywhere. Come home to us. Come home to me, your mother.

There is no dishonor. Lev Davidovich will forgive you in time, won over by your dedication and his love, and Leon Trotsky shall too.

We will contact you about arrangements to have Seva sent here. Help us follow through with this, and then follow him.

As always, keep my love within you.

Your mother,

Natalia Sedova

Trotsky, as he said he would, wrote him as well:

Lyova, son and comrade:

The last we heard from you, you were on the brink of despair. Now, on hearing from you again, we are beyond that boundary. I shall not waste the time of a man who is as busy as you are, as busy as you must be. The opposition must stay in Europe, led by you, the son of Leon Trotsky. However your mother might protest, this is not a death sentence. A life sentence, possibly, but not a death sentence. I have been sentenced to death a hundred times and now live in exile under its specter, as does your mother, though she seems not to recognize it. Whether the war against Stalin and injustice has already been lost, it doesn't matter. The words that we write now will last until the Revolution rises again, and if it fails again, then rises again, and again. Stay in Paris and do your duty, my son. We, as individuals, mean nothing to the world. Our place and time mean everything. I do not need you cowering by my side, however much I love you.

Your father,

Leon Davidovich/Trotsky

Neither of these letters quite reached Lyova Sedov. They were intercepted by his secretary, Mark 'Etienne' Zborowski. "Anything new?" Lyova asked. He knew what his father would have to say. At the moment he didn't need it drummed in. Etienne didn't think Lyova needed to hear what Natalia Sedova said at all. "Arrange to send Seva to Mexico," said Mark. "Continue to fight on." Who could suspect that Lyova Sedov's closest friend and editor of the *Opposition Bulletin* was a spy for the Soviet GPU. If the *Bulletin* was powerless, even harmless, better to have Lyova in Paris where he could be more easily followed and Mark's own cards left unexposed. Worse, what would Zborowski be worth to the GPU without Lyova there? In fact, he'd become acutely aware how closely his own demise would likely follow Lyova's. If the *Bulletin* had taught him anything it was that anyone even vaguely or briefly tied to Trotsky ended up exterminated. Given the information he had, and now, over time, even some sympathy, the easiest thing for the GPU to do, in Stalin's path toward rubbing out all memory of Trotsky, was to get rid of the memory. He would be ready, in a moment, to flee to Germany.

André Breton arrived in Mexico City again, determined to bring Frida Kahlo to New York and Paris. Diego had told him that things were not so good with the Sedova/Trotskys. Trotsky was planning to go to Veracruz alone with his guards where he could distract himself with the buzz of the city and fishing from the wharfs. They'd never had this kind of disagreement. If the children were hers, the sons were his, an implicit contract, a division between the domestic and the political that had gone unquestioned for decades, though clearly Sergei's death had brought it to the fore.

Breton caught him in the garden, petting Lorca who rubbed on his shins while he reinforced the rabbit cages. He liked Breton who was quick witted and unafraid to challenge him.

"Keeping the enemies close to each other," said Breton.

"I don't even think she could hurt the big ones," said Leon.

"None of us can hurt the big ones," said Breton.

They both laughed, but Trotsky said, "I don't like the parallels."

Breton left and brought back two cold bottles of beer. "Mexico is a land of beer like France is a land of wine," he said. "Though I love the agaves, the way they spread their flightless wings."

"Too many wings to fly," said Trotsky.

"I love your mind. To think, cloth and liquor, clothing and drunkenness." Lorca came to him. "She has bad taste. My kind of sentience," he said.

They drank dark beer, cold, biting, bitter. "Good," said Trotsky.

"This trouble with Natalia. Is it over Frida?" said Breton.

"No."

"Not yet," said Breton.

"Everyone knows there's trouble?" said Trotsky.

"In paradise there is always trouble. You said something to Diego."

"I'm writing about him for the *Partisan Review*."

"'Arts and Politics,' yes," said Breton. "I saw a draft. 'The greatest interpreter of the October Revolution.'"

"You're jealous," said Trotsky.

"Of many, many things," said André Breton. "Of the earth and sky. But I'm not a revolutionary."

"You're communist."

"Socialism in one country. Surrealism in one person."

"A poor joke, comrade," said Leon Trotsky.

"But it was the only one I had that worked," said Breton. "I know this. You seduce the wife by endearing the husband."

"Not my intent," said Trotsky.

"Intent is meaningless. No one is innocent, though I don't believe in innocence either. Did you try to seduce Tina?"

"She isn't busy enough?" Leon said.

"She has said you faked a fire drill and cornered her outside."

"That sounds just like me," said Leon Trotsky. "Doesn't it?"

"I'm a surrealist. Anything sounds like everything."

"Doesn't she flirt with you, as well?"

"American baseball has a metaphor for everything," said Breton. "How shall I say it? Hitting for the cycle."

"Stalin invented baseball. Before he was born. You should know that," Trotsky said.

"That just makes too much sense," said Breton.

They both laughed again. Trotsky thought of his flirtations with Tina and would have thought them too obvious, too out in the open, for anyone to think it could go beyond that, though in this salacious enclave maybe the opposite should always be considered plausible. But if so, wouldn't what was considered plausible become immediately unlikely? He found it interesting that they weren't talking about the one affair that everyone knew to be fact, Diego and Tina, which if anything explained all the more the rumors about himself. He wished for the larger world, a bigger stage, but that being gone, than at least a much smaller, simpler one, like reinforcing rabbit cages.

"Rumor flies, the truth walks," said Leon.

"Or crawls very slowly," said Breton.

Breton put his hand on Trotsky's forearm. "Remember, you are a great man, mon ami."

"No longer."

"Greater than ever. The Dewey Commission will affirm it." Lorca surprisingly jumped on Breton's lap. "A ghost," said Breton. "What a loss." Referring to García Lorca's recent death by Fascist firing squad. The cat leapt down and meowed at Trotsky. "All art is political," Breton said. "How many have died under Stalin's insipid social realism."

"Mayakovski," said Trotsky. "Gorky."

"Others, too. Death by drivel. I would kill myself, too."

"Regrettable, but it's yet the wrong choice. You wouldn't kill yourself. You'd keep producing art until they executed you."

"And your son?'

"We've finally come to why you're here," said Trotsky. "To die for a cause is not suicide. But he isn't dead."

"For a dialectical materialist you're extremely resistant to the inevitable," said Breton.

"A bad pun," said Trotsky.

"It's good we aren't afraid to fight with each other," said Breton. "So, our manifesto?"

"I'll begin work on it in Veracruz," Trotsky said. "You can have at it when I return."

When Leon Trotsky left for Veracruz, Natalia Sedova, noticing that Frida had returned to Casa Azul, found her in her in-house studio, sitting at a small, wooden table with Jacqueline Lamba and another woman who turned out to be Diego's second wife, the one before Kahlo, Lupe Marin Rivera. Paintings spread across the walls, stood propped on easels, leaned against chairs. A good many were self portraits of Kahlo, of those, several were grotesque, her body wounded, her heart exposed and bleeding, her womb and sex distorted in macabre poses of giving birth to herself.

Natalia couldn't remember the last time she'd been alone with three women, having arrived, she told herself, for the sole purpose of seeing Frida alone, without the tension, the confusion, of Leon's presence. Now she felt both comforted and disconcerted. They were here. The men were off somewhere. None of them were following a man, not their own husband nor someone else's. "I'm sorry," she said, "I didn't mean to interrupt."

"Not at all," Frida said. She introduced Lupe. Lupe and Lamba turned toward her and said hello. They sat, drinking coffee with cognac. They'd been laughing.

"We might be celebrating," Frida said. "Modotti is back from Spain."

"Whatever that means," said Lamba.

"Whatever that means," Frida said. She poured a cup of coffee and cognac for Natalia. Lamba pulled a chair to the table.

"Did you ever drink this in France?" Lamba asked.

"I spent six months in a Paris prison," said Natalia. "Even there we drank it." They were speaking Spanish and though Sedova had picked up enough to plan, in the moment, what to say, or translate what was said to her, it took her a little time to do that. She'd miss a word here and there, mostly verbs where she struggled with subject-verb agreement, though she knew enough Spanish to have caught Frida's terms of endearment for Leon during the commission's investigation.

"I've spent six months in a body cast," said Frida.

"I'd prefer prison," said Sedova.

"You would," Kahlo said. "I would."

"Is Lyova your only child?" asked Lupe.

"The only one left," said Sedova.

"I have two daughters," said Lupe, "by Diego."

"I've lost two in birth," said Frida Kahlo. "Two more before birth."

"Maybe better," Lamba said to her. "I have two daughters as well. Men want boys, but for too many reasons they're more trouble."

"There is no better to any of it," Natalia said.

Frida clinked Sedova's cup, poured more coffee around and pushed the cognac bottle to the middle of the table. "Diego mentioned your disagreement with Leon," she said. As usual, she'd moved quickly to the point.

Of course, how could everyone not know everything. Despite the comforting glances around her, Natalia almost wept.

Lupe touched Sedova's hand. "We were talking about Xochimilco," Lupe said to Natalia. "Were you frightened?"

"There wasn't time to be frightened," Sedova said. "Were you?" she said to Frida and Lamba.

"Diego fired his gun at Isama Noguchi," said Frida. "The sculptor. But Diego always misses."

"She slept with him," Lupe said to Sedova, pointing at Frida.

"A fling," said Kahlo.

"Have you been in that situation before?" said Lamba.

"Which one," said Sedova, "flings or guns?"

"Maybe they can't be separated," said Frida.

"Maybe for men," said Lupe.

"Let's leave the flings for now," said Lamba. "Guns."

"Around guns, yes, plenty of times," Natalia said. "But usually none go off."

"Do you have a gun?" said Lamba.

"Not on me," said Natalia Sedova and they all laughed. "Till then, Lev believed he was too powerful for Stalin to risk assassinating him. So it's more frightening now, thinking back. We haven't really talked of it, though maybe it's time."

"Give him this little trip," said Lupe. "He'll change his mind about Lyova."

"It will get crowded here," said Frida. She drank and laughed. "Is it afternoon yet? I'm going to need a real drink."

"My daughters are at school," Lupe said to Natalia, then she nodded slightly at Kahlo.

"Wrong Turn can get them," Frida said. "Or better, we could all go. Get away from my dreary paintings. Take in a comida corrida, be back for siesta."

"Far from dreary, your paintings are threatening and most unique," said Sedova. "You paint, yes?" she said to Lamba.

"Yes, but I deplore reality," said Jacqueline Lamba, "interior as well as exterior."

"I hope my daughters write cook books," said Lupe. "No politics, no art." Not knowing that her eldest, Guadalupe, would become a lawyer, and marry a lawyer who would become president of Mexico, then she'd write a cook book.

Sedova scanned the room again, less than the surfeit of sexuality, both symbolic and actual, the paintings were profound expressions of Frida's solitude and pain.

Frida stood. "Let's go!" she said.

They piled into Diego's Ford station wagon, picked up Lupe's daughters, Guadalupe and Ruth, and drove to Chapultepec Park. Jacqueline's daughters were in the states. Lupe's girls immediately wanted to hop on the riding ponies and Lupe and Lamba hitched up their skirts and rode off with them into the park.

"Do you ride?" said Kahlo to Sedova.

"Not those things," said Natalia and laughed. "Besides, I'm inappropriately dressed." She wore a straight black skirt that she couldn't pull up. Thinking she might find something out about what was going on she said, "I don't see Jacqueline in any of Diego's murals."

"She didn't sleep with Diego," said Kahlo, "she slept with me."

"An historical mistake if not an aesthetic one," said Sedova.

"We'll see about that," said Frida. She led Natalia to a fruit stand and bought two mangos, each perched atop a stick. The vendor had sliced them like a pine cone, then rolled them in hot red pepper. "These are amazing," Kahlo said.

In fact, they were. The thick sweet juice of the ripe mango along with the fast heat of the red pepper both ignited and soothed the palate. It ignited more than that, too. "But we'll need a bathroom right away," Frida said. Pointing to the nearby public restrooms, she whisked Natalia off to the women's room, Frida giving an elderly woman at the door a peso for toilet paper. In adjoining stalls, Frida's laughter was contagious. But if it was a joke, it was as sympathetic as it was audacious and Sedova willingly played her role in it. When they emerged, Frida pointed at the mango vendor and yelled "Excellent location!" He grinned and waved.

They didn't spy the pony riders.

"Diego is in favor of lesbian love," Frida said. "Men have but one sexual organ, a woman's whole body is sensual and sexual. Besides, he isn't jealous of women. He's jealous of men."

"Noguchi," said Natalia.

Frida only tilted her head and raised one eyebrow, then offered an impish, if not impudent smile. Now the pony riders came around the bend, yelping like campañeros. They dismounted and Frida led them down the walk of poets, the girls demonstrably moaning and yawning, until they reached the statue of Sor Juana de la Cruz.

"Do you know her?" Frida asked Natalia.

Sedova did not.

"A nun. Sixteenth Century," said Kahlo. "Her convent still stands. You can see her room. She praised the workers and the Indians, worked among the sick and poor, had many suitors and wrote love poems for them, or for God, or gods, she was ambiguous. But the bishop censored and silenced her, banished her to the lepers where she died. She's as famous as the Virgin of Guadalupe."

"And who's next?" shouted little Lupe.

"Frida Kahlo!" shouted Ruth. They both shouted, "Frida Kahlo! Frida Kahlo!"

"Excellent, my good little parrots," said Frida. "For that you get a Coca Cola."

Jacqueline whispered to Sedova, "I'm French. In France there are more women artists to go around."

"I heard that," Frida said to Lamba.

"Cook books," Lupe said to her girls. "Cook books."

"There is plenty rivalry in cook book writing," Frida said. "Besides, you have your own literary aspirations."

"Novels," said Lupe. "Not painting, not poetry. No backbiting masquerading as socializing."

"My heart," said Frida. "Put a pistol to my heart!"

"A Mexican cliché," Lamba said to Sedova, again in a whisper meant to be heard.

Sedova could tell this was not banter erupting for the first time, but a game they played again and again.

The girls, who clearly had taken this tour before, ran off to the fountain of Montezuma Llhuicanima, the Aztec Emperor who built the aqueduct that carried fresh water from Chapultepec to Tenochtitlan. He vacationed where the park was now and kept a zoo here, maybe the first in the world. The girls took off their shoes and socks and frolicked in the pool beneath the fountain. Frida pulled off her stockings, lifted her skirt and put her feet in, too. In this, Sedova joined her, as now did Lupe and Lamba. They relaxed there under the cool shade of the Cypress and *ahuahuete* trees, originally planted by Montezuma as well.

"It was all a woman's idea," Natalia Sedova said and the women laughed.

"At least he listened," said Frida.

From there they wandered through the grassy park, past the lake where boaters rowed in canoes or foot-peddled paddle boats shaped like white swans around an island of grass and trees. Of course the girls campaigned for a ride in the swan boats. Frida declined on account of her leg. Lamba said, "The stinky old ponies were enough for me."

"I'll take them," said Natalia Sedova.

"They won't peddle," Lupe said. "They'll just shout at boys."

"I've handled worse," said Natalia.

"You think so now," said Lupe.

They rented a swan and Lupe purchased some bread crumbs so the girls could feed the fish and ducks that pestered the boaters, then the girls followed Natalia onto the swan boat.

Lupe gave the bags of bread crumbs to Sedova as she pushed off. "Don't let them eat them or throw them away all at once," Lupe said.

"Mama has rules, rules, rules!" said little Lupe. She was a little more flamboyant than the younger Ruth, though both, through luck or fate, had the more gentle features of their beautiful mother.

"Society runs because of rules," said Natalia.

"How horrible!" said little Lupe.

Sedova handed Ruth one of the bags while looking at Lupe. "And changes by breaking them."

The girls immediately stuffed their mouths with handfuls of crumbs and cast the rest into the water where droves of mallards and ducks swarmed to the side of the boat while huge carp and even a few turtles dodged between, stealing bread chunks. As Sedova steered for the island a few real swans took notice of the feast and began to paddle toward them. Young boys, pre-teens, began to shout and wave from the shore in a pantomime of courtship that none of the children, boys or girls, were really ready for.

Near the island, Sedova doled out the rest of the bread, and there, on the shore, even squirrels and iguanas took notice of the floating party, but soon the bread was gone and fish, fowl, reptiles, and squirrels lost interest and set out for other donors as Natalia circled the island and headed back. The sisters, now dragging their hands in the water, settled down, too. In that brief, quiet span, Sedova's thoughts ran to her sons, and times like this, on the water or in the snow, tobogganing, playing soldier while their father was at war. She knew the war would end, whatever its outcome, but your children, that they would grow up and move away, how can you believe that? How could you believe that it would end?

"You were in a revolution," Lupe said to Natalia Sedova.

Sedova looked at the girls, pausing, wondering. Finally she said, "To help the people."

"Of Russia," said Ruth.

"Of the world, really," said Natalia Sedova.

"The whole world?" said Lupe.

"Did it help kids, too?" said Ruth.

Sedova paused again. "I don't know," she said. "We tried."

"Do you have kids?" said Lupe.

"Two boys, grown up," Natalia said, "but one died."

"In the revolution?"

"Because of it. It's a difficult thing to explain."

"Papa says we've had many revolutions in Mexico," said Ruth.

"They succeed and nothing happens," said Lupe.

Sedova turned the paddle swan toward the dock where the other women were waiting. She said nothing.

"Mr. Trotsky is a big revolutionary," Lupe said.

"Yes," Sedova said.

"Are you?"

"Not so big," said Natalia Sedova.

"Was your boy young like us?" said Ruth.

"Not so young," Natalia said.

"Boys died here fighting the gringos," said Lupe. "They wouldn't give up. They dove from the walls of the castle."

"The gringos are powerful," said Sedova. "For now."

"For now," said little Lupe

"For now!" said Ruth. "Are you a gringo?"

Natalia laughed. "No, I'm Russian," she said. "But Mr. Trotsky and I are fighting for all workers and farmers, Russian, French, Mexican, even gringos."

They reached the shore and the dock man pulled the swan to the wooden dock and Sedvoa followed the girls to the lawn.

"A good time?" said Guadalupe Rivera.

"We solved the world's problems," Sedova said.

"Then it's time for a Coca Cola," said Frida Kahlo.

They passed under Grasshopper Hill where the Toltecs first settled in the region before the Aztecs. Chapultepec was Toltec for grasshopper, a staple for the Toltecs, which they ate fried. Frida was limping demonstrably now as they made their way to a little open-air café that sold ice cream, Coke, candies, and beer. A woman tended the counter and a little hammock swung between two support poles with a baby wrapped up inside. Frida bought two small bottles of Coke for the girls and brought tequila and limes for the women.

"Tequila?" said Lamba.

Frida nodded toward the woman at the counter. "We're friends," she said.

The woman brought cheese quesadillas to the table on paper plates with a jar of pickled jalapeños and carrots.

"Can we go past the boy heroes?" asked little Lupe.

"On the way out," said Frida

Little Lupe looked at her mother. "We talked about them on the swan," she said.

"They have golden statues on top of tall poles," she said to Sedova.

"Do you want to be a dead hero or alive?" Jacqueline Lamba said to little Lupe.

"I can't be both?" little Lupe said.

Their laughter woke the baby who began to cry. The vender exchanged glances with Frida who smiled and went to the hammock. She pushed it, rocking it gently.

"The motion quiets them," Lupe said to Natalia.

As Frida sang softly to the quieting child, Sedova again thought of Sergei and Lyova. Heroes die, but innocents do, too. From her angle, she could see Kahlo's right cheek where a tear formed in the corner of her eye, then ran down her cheek and landed in the dust.

The road from Mexico City to Veracruz followed the invasion route taken by Cortez in the early 16th Century and the Americans in the middle of the 19th. Since arriving, Trotsky had studied both wars, though Mexico's wars didn't always end in defeat; they'd expelled both the Spanish and the French. The American land grab was no different than any other. In the last century the Ukraine, where he was born, had been conquered nineteen times without any regard for the Ukrainian populace. For the

States, the land war with Mexico was not about Mexico at all, but about the resources in what was now the western states, particularly gold, a substance that the native Indians didn't even value. Across the ocean, Stalin bought time by backing the Republic in Spain, while at the same time courting Hitler who backed Franco, hoping that when the inevitable conflict with Germany came the Russian expanse and the Eurasian winter would stop the next invasion. Trotsky wondered if he would live long enough to see it unfold.

Fishing off the docks of Veracruz reminded him of his days in Prinkipo when his friend, the Greek fisherman, Karolambos, taught him how to sprinkle oil to clarify murky water and throw stones to steer fish into his nets. Neither of them shared a word of language in common. In Veracruz he left his guards at the hotel and wandered, fishing pole in hand, to the fishing piers. The words of the Mexican fishermen, broken by bursts of excitement and laughter, over their catch, comforted him. Now, as on the Sea of Marmora, he was away from Natalia, though then she had Lyova bedside her. Of the things he'd felt for her over the years, he'd never felt estranged. They were united by love and cause, or had she given her life to him by giving her life to that cause?

He took pleasure in the sunrise. On Prinkipo, there'd been burning sunset after sunset over the Black Sea. Was there more hope in the dawn? He returned to his hotel in the afternoon and began work on his essay on art and revolution. His contact with Rivera and Breton turned his pen as he wrote, meandering toward the necessary freedom of the imagination, he now found that art couldn't serve ideology, that the art of the communist revolution would flower from the new human freedom, the relief from pain and labor. He contemplated Frida Kahlo, beauty and pain, her bleeding heart, his own burning heart. Briefly, his resentment of Natalia took refuge there. Breton's joke was no joke. Surrealism in one person was historical reality, fracturing bourgeois social alignment, transcending nationalism and war by seeking the elemental interior of what it meant to be human, to be any human, to envision humanity.

The cook at the hotel prepared the fish that he'd caught in the morning, then, at night, he reclused in a nearby bodega, tequila and beer. A juke box—he seldom saw them in Russia—played jumpy tunes of accordion, guitar, and fiddle. Smoke floated among the men who smoked cigarettes and talked about a recent strike of trainmen and bus drivers. There had been no women in the establishment until tonight. A woman with curly dark hair and glasses, a white blouse and black pants, laced boots, sat at the end of the bar with a brown drink on ice. You seldom saw ice in Mexico. The expense aside, people didn't drink water. You didn't drink what hadn't been fermented or boiled. The woman's features were angular and striking, stern, like a face in a Rivera mural. She watched him. He supposed that if her intentions were malicious she wouldn't let it be apparent that she was watching him. Yet when she got up from her stool, he let his hand slip inside his suit jacket to the inner pocket where he carried his gun. Half way to his table, she spun and stood sideways, exposing her own pistol tucked in her belt. "I'm going to put it on the table," she said in Spanish, but her accent was American. She walked over to him, lifted the pistol by the handle with her index finger and thumb, and set it down.

When he remained motionless and said nothing she said, "How many guns does a woman need?"

"Two?" he said. He let his hands drop to the table top.

"You'd be dead already," she said.

She looked at the chair across from him and he nodded at it.

"My English is better than my Mexican," Trotsky said.

"They let you go out alone?" she said in English.

"Should I be afraid of something?"

"Mr. Trotsky," she said, putting out her hand. "Comrade. Tina Modotti."

Trotsky shook her hand. Her grip was firm, confident, and sensuous.

Close up, he saw that she was older than Frida or Lamba, more womanly, if that can be said. She took off her glasses and put them next to the gun that was a little bigger than his, likely a thirty caliber. Her eyes were the color and texture of steel. He took off his glasses as well.

"I didn't expect you to look so human," Modotti said. She motioned to the bartender who brought her another drink, barely glancing at the guns. "I was expelled from the party before I left for Spain."

"Then who did you fight for?"

"Against," she said. "Franco. Hitler. But we had nothing to fight against tanks, planes, machine guns. We were all suspicious of each other. A tenth of us were GPU agents. They watched us closer than they watched the fascists."

"That's why I'm ambivalent about democracy. People must be led."

She looked away from him, then back. "Then where were you?"

"On the planet without a visa," Trotsky said. "I'm barely here."

Modotti sipped her drink. She moved confidently, strong and almost seductive. It distracted him. The women of this hemisphere had piqued his sexuality, or maybe he'd been too idle, away from conflict for too long, living in the claustrophobia of ideas.

"I worked for Red Aid in France. Undercover. But now I'm neither Trotskyite nor Stalinist," Modotti said. "Neither is Rivera. You should know that."

"I'm not a Trotskyite either," he said. "I've never been. Trotsky is a fascist, isn't he?"

"Frida owns a portrait of Stalin."

"I do, too," Trotsky said. The conversation had turned into a dance and he wasn't a dancer. She'd recognized him. For now, she didn't want to kill him. She'd been to Russia. Worked for Stalin. But she'd put her life on the line in Spain.

"I was cross-examined in Moscow," Modotti said. "About you."

"That I'm a traitor, plotting with Hitler and Hirohito to murder Stalin."

"I believed that, but I had nothing to tell them."

"But you think I'm a traitor."

She said nothing. Sipped her drink.

"So you fell out with Rivera and Kahlo, and Cardenas, because they helped me."

"I believed in Stalin. I thought him a visionary."

"Who executed all the revolutionaries who put him in power."

"I wanted the Soviet Union to succeed," she said. "I still do."

"Even with Stalin's coming alliance with Hitler?"

"That's why I resigned from the party. I went to New York but they threw me out of the States. So I'm here again. You find me confused? I'm confused."

Well, he'd cleared the air. He'd sat across the table from purported allies as well as enemies. She was straightforward. Despite herself, fearless.

"I'm warning you not to trust Rivera," Modotti said. "His friend, Siqueiros, is a Stalinist."

"His friend, Siqueiros, threw him out of the party," he said. "*El Popular, Bandera Roja, La Voz*, all supported Siqueiros. They still support Stalin and demand my deportation."

"That's nothing I don't know," she said.

"Rivera is sincere, but sincerity can't be trusted. I understand, but I must rely on mistrust now." He downed his tequila and followed it with beer. "You modeled for him."

"For Weston, too," she said. "So I know. Did you model for your portrait in the Palacio?"

He laughed.

"You have blue eyes," she said.

"You expected black."

"It's been said."

He ordered another round for himself.

"You're traveling alone?" she said to him.

"You are, too? I have guards at the hotel."

"I meant without your wife."

"I'm working on an essay about revolution and art with Breton."

"I know him," said Modotti. "Only too well. I'm through with art, and revolution, too. When I get back to the city I'm going underground for good."

"I don't have that choice," Trotsky said to her.

"Your son is still in Paris," she said.

"The *Bulletin*," he said to her.

"His secretary, Zborowski, Etienne, is a GPU agent, code named Cupid."

He wasn't shocked, but he was surprised. He'd heard from Victor Serge, in Paris, that a GPU agent with various code names, Cupid, Tulip, Mack, had engineered the assassination of his associate, Rudolf Klement, found decapitated in the Seine. He knew Zborowski. But he'd known Zinoviev and Kamenev. He'd worked with Stalin. Betrayal was more common in the world than loyalty and friends could be more dangerous than enemies.

"How do you know?" he said.

"The GPU was all over Spain," Modotti said. "I escaped to France over the Pyrenees. Went to Paris. The French are bastards and cowards."

"The British, too," he said. "But their workers are not."

"You wish," she said.

"After Hitler and Stalin carve up Poland, Hitler will turn on France, then Russia. Despite Stalin, I hope Russia, and the Soviet Union, can survive."

"What can any of us do?" Modotti said. "Nothing."

"Fight on. There is yet hope if the workers unite."

"You've spent too much time in exile, Comrade Trotsky. There's not a chance."

"Not a choice?" he said.

She sat back, held his intense stare. "There was a time I wanted you dead," she said to him.

"It will happen soon enough," he said.

She finished her drink and stood. "Tell your son to be cautious," she said. She offered her hand and he took it. "You must give Frida my best," she said and left him.

He returned to Casa Azul the next day, seeking out Natalia Sedova. The first thing he said was, "We must bring Lyova here."

He explained what Modotti had told him.

Sedova wept. "Etienne is his best friend," she said.

"All the more likely then," Leon said.

"He's trapped."

"No," said Trotsky.

He said they should tell Lyova to take Seva to Switzerland where a couple named Rosmer could care for him. He'd have a letter waiting for him there, instructing all of them to come to Mexico, and to tell no one, not even and especially Zborowski.

"Lyova's girlfriend," said Sedova.

"Which one? Lyova is sophisticated. He'll know how to deal with it."

"Will he believe you about Etienne?"

"It's a precaution. Time will tell," Leon said.

They held each other. It came to Leon now that the last year of Lyova's depression and despair might have been spurred by this very inclination, that his work in the *Bulletin of the Opposition* had been anticipated in Moscow and cut off in the pages of *Pravda* by rebuttals that occurred weeks before the *Bulletin* was published. Lyova's and Trotsky's arguments against the trials and executions were denied in the news before the opposition could even make them public. Trotsky had been a fool. How much of Lyova's despair was folded into his suspicion, his knowledge, that he was cornered in Paris, something he couldn't have written to his father. But it wasn't too late to save him.

"I was wrong," he said.

"He knew he was risking his life. But no longer," she said.

That evening they dined in Casa Azul with Diego and Frida. The Dewey Commission had released their findings. Trotsky was innocent of all accusations against him. Nonetheless, both he and Natalia were subdued by thoughts of Lyova. About the Commission, they felt more relieved than celebratory.

Frida was excited about her upcoming show in New York, though no dates had been set.

"I don't know if Breton has the savvy to pull it off," she said.

"He has the power to pull it off," said Leon.

"He has Frida Kahlo, the greatest artist in Mexico!" said Rivera, raising his glass.

They toasted. They ate red snapper soup, chiles in walnut sauce, poblano chiles stuffed with picadillo.

"Art and Revolution is ready for Breton," Trotsky said. "And you," he said to Rivera.

"Breton is a lucky poet," said Diego, "to have landed in Mexico, in Casa Azul now. With Frida Kahlo and Leon Trotsky. But he has a draft, as well."

"You'll contribute," Trotsky said to him.

"My signature," said Diego.

"And yours, Lev?" said Sedova to Leon.

Across from Trotsky, Kahlo let out a soft hum and smiled at him, then at Natalia, as if surprised that the formal Sedova would use an endearment for Leon in public, even if she, herself had done so.

"No, not for now," Leon said. "I'm not an artist. It will carry more weight with just Diego and André."

"And appear less dangerous?" said Sedova.

"You won't fool anyone," Kahlo said. "They'll see your paw prints."

"Not his hoof prints?" said Sedova.

They laughed.

"But not my signature," he said.

"He thinks signatures are bourgeois," laughed Rivera.

"Everything I do is my signature," said Frida Kahlo. "I only paint me!"

"Which is the opposite in a way," Sedova said.

"From Diego," said Kahlo, "who paints whole worlds?"

"You portray the pain of the world," Natalia said to her in Mexican, then in Russian, said, "Universal pain, the sacrifice of the self, even if to the self, the subversion of self, the obliteration of self inside the body, a dialectic, the sacrifice of self to essence."

Trotsky tried to translate, abandoned Spanish, did a little better in English, then said, "Natalia, you should have written my essay!"

"And signed it?" Sedova said.

They all laughed again.

"And now it's *your* essay, is it?" said Frida.

"To one of the great intellects of the world," said Trotsky. He stood and toasted Sedova. Diego stood, too, and Frida raised her glass but did not quite stand, her face twisting with pain as she lurched forward, then sat back down.

When Trotsky and Rivera settled down again Leon said, "I saw Modotti in Veracruz."

"She didn't try to kill you?" said Diego.

"Gun on the table. She sent her regards."

"To me?" said Diego.

"Well, to Frida," Leon said.

Rivera laughed. "She wasn't happy we took you in. She's partial to Stalin."

"Less now, since Spain. She's dropping politics, going underground," said Trotsky.

"We'll see how long that lasts!" said Rivera.

"One can work from underground," said Frida. "I still admire her."

Trotsky hesitated to talk about Lyova's peril and decided it was best not divulged, but he said, "I've changed my mind about Lyova. I'll ask him to come to Mexico, to bring our grandson, then we'll have to find our own place."

"That will take time," Frida said.

"There's time, I hope," said Sedova.

"Duty and work versus love, those are hard choices," said Rivera.

"You choose between them?" Frida said to him.

"Not unless I must," said Diego.

"Or I must," said Kahlo. "I congratulate you on changing a hard mind," she said to Natalia.

"He did it on his own," Sedova said.

Diego got up and poured more tequila, sliced lime. "Best we drink a little more," he said.

"I'll read Breton's draft, then type up the essay and get it to you and Breton," Trotsky said.

It wasn't a position he would have taken ten years ago when he, like Stalin, and Lenin, too, would have subordinated all intellectual activity, all self expression, to the dictatorship of the proletariat. Whatever his commitment to permanent revolution, he was less sure of himself now, now that he saw how it could be misdirected to the rule of a single tyrannical dictator. It was Trotsky and Lenin who rationalized skipping over an essential step in Marx's dialectic, industrial capitalism, and seized necessity where it seemed most unlikely, in an impoverished populace under the heel of an autocratic czar. They'd steered a proletariat and peasant revolution around the purportedly inevitable path of historical materialism and bourgeois capitalist industrialism to achieve communist equality. Yet now, under Stalin's autocratic bureaucracy, despite emphatic proclamations by *Pravda* to the contrary, Russia was worse off than even before the Czar. Industrial production down, trains and tractors broke down and went unrepaired, farm production was reduced to potatoes and rye; the populace was on the verge of starvation. Communism had been crushed in a Germany on a collision course with western democracy and communism both. He thought then of the possibility of a Fourth International, bringing the workers of the planet together to stop a world lurching toward catastrophic war. Ten years ago he would have denied that art could play any role in that. But living in Mexico at Casa Azul had changed his mind.

Sedova was right. There was essence in the individual protest against reality, an essence that all true art engendered. Consciously or unconsciously the independent artist waged war against the false art of Fascist Germany and the Soviet Union that demanded that art serve the vision of the state, a vision that excluded and condemned free expression. But art, by its very nature, could not be confined. Free expression was endemically revolutionary and the independent artist, sculpted by the forces of history, even in bourgeois societies, was essentially challenging and critical. Art must be free from constraints. To pose the problem correctly, he wrote, in art humanity expresses its need for harmony and full existence, which class society denies. Thus, any genuine artistic creation implies a conscious or unconscious protest against that reality. Art alone could not find a way out of this impasse because it was dependent on society, and society could only be saved by revolution. The struggle for revolutionary ideas in art begins with the struggle for artistic truth, conceived not as obedience to this or that school but as the artist's inflexible fidelity to his inner self. "The independence of art -- for the revolution. The revolution—for the definitive liberation of art." This was his statement for *A Manifesto for an Independent Revolutionary Art*. But there was more work to be done.

Still, Breton was delighted. Rivera grabbed Leon by the arms and kissed him on both cheeks. Sedova said, "I couldn't have written it better."

"You came out my hands," Trotsky said to her.

Trotsky and Sedova let the guards follow them to a nearby café that served rich coffee and dark, Viennese chocolates. The walls were yellow and the tablecloths perfectly white, the flatware gleamed in the sunlight that poured through the windows.

The Dewey Commission had exonerated him. In New York City,

Trotsky's *The Revolution Betrayed*, his explanation of Stalin's consolidation of autocratic bureaucracy in the Kremlin, was published by Doubleday.

"There is some hope," Sedova said.

He said, "Sometimes there is some."

They went back to work. At Casa Azul she started an essay on the necessity of opening professional occupations to women. He went back to his office off Chapultepec.

And back to his biography of Stalin for which Harpers had given him a sizable advance. With his guards near him, one walking in front and the other behind, he strolled in the park and contemplated a Fourth International.

It was during a moment of confidence and peace, writing again with a view of the tree filled park, that Diego Rivera appeared at his door. "My friend, my friend," Rivera shouted, "your son, Lyova Sedov is dead!"

"What are you saying?"

"Appendicitis," said Rivera. He put his hands to his face.

"No one dies of appendicitis!" shouted Trotsky. "Not in the 20th Century!"

"Complications, afterwards," said Rivera. "A fever, coma. I'm so sorry."

"Why are you telling me this? Why is it you always delivering this misery?" screamed Leon.

Rivera moaned. He spread his arms. "But who else?"

"Anyone! Anyone else!" Trotsky screamed. "Get out of here! Get away from me!"

He staggered from the office to Casa Azul where he found Sedova working. "My love," he said. "My love. It's Lyova. We were too late."

He fell to his knees and she met him there. Again they wept.

"He has taken them all. He has taken them from us one by one," Sedova whispered. "And made us watch. Now we are alone."

BETRAYAL

BUT FOR SEDOVA, all his friends, his allies, his family, had been murdered. But for his own records, all of his work, all of his transactions since the revolution had been destroyed. Lyova's girlfriend, Jeanne, had disappeared with Trotsky's grandson, Seva, and all of Lyova's and Leon's papers. Leon Trotsky had been rubbed out of institutional memory in Russia. What remained was propaganda: a plot to assassinate Stalin and his attempted conspiracy with Germany and Japan to destroy the Soviet Union. Even in the newspapers of the United States and Mexico, Stalin controlled all of the information disseminated about Leon Trotsky. The Mexican Bolshevik papers, *La Voz, Bandera Rosa,* and *El Popular* called him a fascist and screamed for his deportation. In the States, some of his old allies, like Max Eastman, began to look at him askance. In Russia there was no one left to remember him or defend him. There was nothing the population could read or hear that didn't decry him as a traitor.

In the Soviet Union, his oldest and dearest ally, Nikolay Bukharin, was put on trial. Calmly he'd confronted Vyshinsky by pleading guilty in general to all of the accusations of conspiracy with Trotsky, "irrespective," he said, "of whether or not I knew of, whether or not I took part in, any particular act." Ignorant of it all, he took full responsibility. "I am speaking," he said, "not to this court, but to history." He was murdered in the cellars of Lubyanka prison.

In their room in Casa Azul, Trotsky and Sedova wept and mourned. There is nothing more grievous than the death of one's child. Now he'd lost four, two of them Sedova's. They'd given Sergei eight days of mourning and so they did with Lyova. In that time Victor Serge wrote them from Paris. Whatever the facts about Lyova's appendicitis, Etienne Zborowski, the agent Cupid, had notified the GPU that Lyova had been admitted to a White Russian clinic in Paris on the rue Narcisse-Diaz. There he was poisoned and murdered.

Again, Sedova had lost a son to the revolution gone bad. Now there was no more to lose. The battle that Trotsky waged was now fought on the dark side of the moon. She'd followed him there when it seemed there was no choice but that choice. And while he rode the horse of rational argument against the tanks of reality, she'd manned the barricades behind him. Real battle was simpler. You placed your body in front of the enemy. Better to die like that, then, in the fury of a cause. Now, could the cause even be named? Leon was right, they were too late. She was too late. The stand she made to bring Lyova to Mexico was made too late. Did Trotsky's letter even reach him? What was left inside her but emptiness?

She didn't have to insinuate that he'd killed his own sons. Had he died in the Urals or on the Volga, been blown up on his train, he wouldn't have faced Stalin's torturous revenge, and neither would his first wife, their daughters, and now Sedova's sons. When had permanent revolution become permanent exile? He'd always believed that somehow he would return to Russia. He wouldn't have to plot a coup. Stalin's madness would have its run. The skeleton of the Soviet Union, if barely surviving him, might stagger, but wouldn't fall, and cooler minds would bring Trotsky home to lead, to rebuild a true dictatorship of the proletariat. The odds of that now, if not almost totally diminished, were impossible. Once his defeat was unimaginable. Now there was nothing but total defeat. Not even noble defeat, but ignoble. He was no longer waiting for those impossible dreams, he was waiting for death. "Is it all over?" he said to her.

"Much of it is all over," she said. "If there is any victory it's far beyond our lives."

He clutched at her. Would they kill her first?

She'd known him for too long. She knew he was thinking it. "I don't think I'm important enough. I'm not Krupskaya or Rosa Luxemborg."

He didn't believe that. They could murder her in front of his face. She was at least that important. "I'm sorry," he said to her.

"I've been quite wide-eyed," she said.

"Though it's gone far beyond what we could have imagined."

"I couldn't have foreseen it. I'm in despair. I'm torn in sorrow, but not regret."

"Not regret," he whispered. For the first time he understood suicide. Would that be enough to convince them to leave her alone? And, like Lyova, though he was not suicidal, his extinction opened in front of him like a crack of light. Under the cascading realizations that rise with the foam of despair, he felt burdened by Sedova and, as well, for a moment, absolutely free. "You must leave me," he said to her.

"For what?" she said.

"For your life."

"You are my life. Evermore so."

"You will die for me?"

"I have a hundred times. Maybe I've died every moment, everyday."

"While I lived."

"Your life isn't over," she said to him. "Nor mine. It doesn't matter whether that is fortunate or unfortunate."

The next day he wrote an obituary for his son. It was, without irony, full of optimism for the workers' fight for liberation. "All of us must die. How and when we cannot choose. But why and for whom we lay down our lives moves the world forward. Let Lyova Sedov live in your hearts and point to a future of freedom from oppression for your children and their children. Destiny has denied him a living victory. Let his death unfold your destiny and your victory."

He also wrote a suicide note. He thought that with luck his increasingly high blood pressure would kill him, but he was prepared, if his suffering was too much, to do it himself. It would not be an outburst of despair or hopelessness; he would die with unshaken faith in the communist future. He wrote, "This faith in humanity and the future gives me even now such power of resistance as cannot be given by any religion."

When he showed the note to Sedova, she nodded. "Revise it," she said. "Include me."

He said, "I was afraid you would agree."

The next day he emerged from their room with a Spanish translation of *The Communist Manifesto*. He stopped at the rabbit cages. The rabbits knew him and came to his fingers. It gave him pleasure. He mumbled to them, on the verge of stupidity, "It's good to be alive." Then he went to the kitchen and sat with a cup of coffee. He added cognac. He'd placed a note inside the book that said, "We cannot meet." He waited until Frida Kahlo came down the stairs holding Lorca. Like a female cat, she always knew where everyone was in Casa Azul. She poured herself coffee. He gave her the book.

"You're a bad cat owner," she said.

"And so, people will one day say I loved dogs." He poured brandy into her coffee cup. "If I am remembered at all."

"And one day, following your beloved pet down a garden path, you run into your assassin."

"He should be so unlucky," Trotsky said.

Kahlo put Lorca on the table. The animal watched the motionless Trotsky, then came to him. He let her rub on the knuckle that held his cup.

"You can't seduce a cat," Frida said.

"Who would want to seduce a cat?"

She opened the book and looked at his note. "From each . . ." she said, "to each . . ." She looked up. "I'm sorry about Lyova."

He only nodded. "I'm going north to San Miguel Regla, to hunt and fish. Clear my mind."

She said, "You're fearless."

He said, "What's left to fear?"

"Everything," she said. "Every moment."

"Then that's the same," said Leon Trotsky.

Frida glanced again at the note inside the *Manifesto*. She reached inside her sleeve and brought out a small piece of canvas, a reiteration of her self portrait with Fulang Chang draped over her shoulder. "There's a note on the back," she said. "Read it later." She sipped her coffee, then added more cognac to both their cups. "You're not taking Natalia?" she said.

"She's sending me alone," he said.

"Have you heard of Karma, comrade Trotsky?" said Frida Kahlo. "Does life reward virtue?"

"All karma is bad karma, dear Frida. It clings to life and life to it."

She watched him intensely, held his eyes. "Without my suffering, Lev Davidovich, I'd be nothing."

He touched her hand. "The world will disagree," he said.

She stood and kissed his forehead. She said, "Then bring on the world."

He took one guard with him to San Miguel Regla. He had his pistol and a shot gun. He carried the painting of Frida and Fulang Chang. On the back it said, "I'll find you."

He'd not been completely honest about Natalia's sending him out alone. Natalia planned to join him later in the week. Casually, Frida spoke to her of coming along. Maybe they could get Adriana's husband to drive them out. The offer disconcerted Natalia. "I don't know," she said. But when Natalia delayed, Kahlo immediately found a driver and left for San Miguel Regla alone.

When Leon arrived at the cottage he promptly sheathed the shotgun and jumped on a young gray stallion. Riding out, he recalled the days when he hunted deer, sometimes even bear. But this time he didn't try to hunt. He only wanted the wind, the sweating horse; he wanted, if for only a moment, to dream of another time. He found a small river—in Russia they would have called it a stream—and dismounted; the reflections of the surrounding woods danced in the ripples that rose with the breeze; nearer shore, rivulets clattered and gurgled over rocks; the mix of colors and movement reminded him of watching from a hill as his troops moved through terrain, paths found and followed in a kind of regulated chaos, the movement of an army. He thought of his recruiting for the Red Army, arming and training peasants and workers, deserters and vagabonds, ragtag remnants from the Great War, thousands of them, who moved at his command, his train passing through the regained villages and towns where workers and soldiers lined up to cheer his name. "Trotsky! Trotsky!" In a few months, a quiet, Jewish intellectual now sat at the right hand of Lenin and commanded the largest army in the world.

Then, he could have any woman he wanted. Sedova and his two sons were far away, in Petrograd. Yet he was careful. If he took a woman, he took her only once, after she'd been searched, and he with a gun nearby. But for one. A girl in Kazan, the daughter of a Kulak mother and a Cossack, she rejected them to join the revolution. She showed up in front if him in a long line of men, waiting for her boots and rifle, her strawberry blonde hair on her shoulders, her green eyes glaring and determined. He didn't discriminate, women could work the lines, women could fight. Outside that city, when her comrades had been thrown into retreat, she dropped behind a machine gun and held a hill until he arrived and rallied a counterattack in which she jumped on an abandoned horse and rode beside him. When they'd retaken their original line, he saluted her.

"You ride well, comrade," he said.

"My father is a Cossack, Comrade Trotsky," she said.

Two things happened then. Word came from Petrograd, where

Natalia ran the Soviet Museum of Education, that a young assistant with pale brown eyes and flaxen hair, who ran messages and packages to and from the museum, had fallen for her. He brought her small presents, flowers, stayed after work when she worked late. She was still young, in fact at the point in a woman's life when the facets of attractiveness matured into true, powerful beauty. They'd been spotted together after work, as well, and once rode bicycles together in the park.

Trotsky wrote to her, chiding her for embarrassing him, and what about the boys? She wrote, "He is a companion during hard times. If I were behaving illicitly, wouldn't I be less transparent? The children are well taken care of."

He had the boy transferred to Tsaritsin, on the embattled edge of the southeastern frontier. Later, when he himself rode his train down there to relieve Stalin of command, he looked for the boy, but he never found him. He told himself then that it was merely curiosity.

A week later an airplane bombed the iron train, hitting Trotsky's command car. He escaped by jumping out the window as the car tipped onto its side and jammed shut the entry doors. Seven other train cars were destroyed. It seemed he'd already faced death a dozen times, but in reality, facing it was easier than having it sneak up on him from the sky. Now he felt it all around him, though he wouldn't show it, wouldn't change. Yet the iron train now felt more like a slack rope hung between trees. When his office train car was rebuilt, he called for Maria Sizskaya, the young woman who'd helped him rally his troops. In the meantime, she'd helped lead a riverboat attack to the rear of the White lines. Flanked and almost surrounded, the Whites fled Kazan. Sizskaya was on the crew that saved an artillery barge that had gone aground beneath enemy shore batteries and whose remnants were withering under severe fire. They dislodged the boat and returned to the fray.

She stood before his desk, her hair tied back, her ragged jacket buttoned, where there were buttons. She saluted him. He stood. She was tall and easily looked him in the eyes. When he looked at her eyes, he thought, sylvan.

"You should have a better uniform, comrade Sizskaya," he said.

"No favors, comrade," said Sizskaya.

He stepped from behind his desk. "Your heroism is well noted."

She nodded toward his book shelf. "You're reading Mallarmé," she said.

"Among others," he said. "Do you read poetry?"

"And write it," she said.

"I prefer fiction," he said. "Balzac and Zola, for their hard realism. Even Poe."

"Poe isn't realistic," said Sizskaya.

"For his psychology of torture," said Trotsky.

"He's a lousy poet," she said.

Trotksy laughed. "I'm easy prey to intelligence," he said. "You deserve a command."

"You can't give a woman command."

He admired her quick wit and hard minded, realistic logic. He'd been holding his hands behind his back, but now he released them, placing his left hand on his chest and rubbing his chin with his right. "Are you bothered by any of the troops?"

"Of course," she said. "Sometimes. But not compromised."

He stood before her. "Not yet," he said. "Because of your skills, and for your safety, would you accept a position as one of my assistants?"

"I want to fight," she said. "For the Revolution."

"Please relax," he said. "You can fight with me when I fight."

She relaxed her shoulders. Stepping slightly to her right he studied her profile, definitive cheeks, straight nose, soft lips neither thin nor full. How old could she have been? Certainly no more than her early twenties.

"Are you married, comrade Sizskaya?" he asked.

"No, comrade."

"Children?"

"No, comrade."

"No lover?"

"I was engaged to the son of a wealthy Kulak. I loved him, but I didn't want to be a rich peasant's wife."

He chuckled. "You could never be a Kulak's wife."

And with this, she smiled.

He faced her again and when he stepped closer she didn't back away. "Are you bothering me now, comrade?" she said.

"Yes," he said, and they kissed.

She was quite literate and often worked in the printing car, editing the train's newspaper, *En Route*. When the train stopped on the steppes to launch mobilized machine gun attacks from its automobiles, she rode next to him in his open car, machine gun ready. It was a quietly and quickly acknowledged union, implicitly accepted by the train's workers and troops because it both distracted him and softened him. It was simply another magical secret of the iron train.

Now, standing next to the river, he remembered her white skin, her hands almost too delicate to bear. He wished he might have seen her in a dress.

They tried not to talk about the future. Talk of the future brought on personal intimacy and love. They could only have one future, the future of the Revolution. So as they made love, they told themselves this lie, or if not both of them, at least he did. Twenty years later, he saw that now.

Nor did she show him her poetry. The highest poetry, she told him, and the highest politics, couldn't be reconciled. She crossed that line only once, after the throes of lovemaking. She said:

> We carve out war shadows
> and stack them around us
> that is our intimacy
> you with the darkness slingshot
> you with the stone

"And you?" he said.

She said:

> The darkblood
> on the dark hoof's claw

When he launched a flotilla to prowl the Volga, she'd begged him to let her go, alone, without him. She'd return, she said. At that point there was little he could refuse her. She was shot by a sniper on the Kama River. They buried her in the water. When the telegram arrived, notifying him of her death, it was the only time he wept during the Civil War. That was the end of that future. Maybe she'd escaped the no future they were living in. That glorious walk in a dark place with no way out. She'd found her way out. And since then, he'd not gone back. Twenty years later he stood in that doorway again.

He tethered the gray to a tree next to the river. Stripped and put his clothes over the saddle. Swam. Burial at sea.

Then he mounted for his return to the cottage. He thought of the deaths of his children: Nina and Zina, Sergei, and now Lyova. The massacre of his old allies and friends. The execution of his brother, his sister, their children. His isolation with Sedova weighed on him. After thirty years, the stone of no future returned with the irony of aging. He struggled with the claustrophobia of her submission to their doomful concatenation, stalked by execution, passive hiding, and fear. Maybe a risk was at hand. A few moments of dark glory with no way out.

He didn't race back. He walked and trotted. And as he did, he filled with anticipation.

A second car was parked outside. He asked his guard to undress and cool the stallion, then went inside where Kahlo was waiting just inside the door. Her hair was down. Wordlessly she removed his glasses and tore off his cap, took down his pants, raised her skirts and was upon him, her strong arms around his neck, her lips smothering his; he held her pumping buttocks, absorbed her passionate groans that peeked to shrill, joyous, yelps. He was mad for her, mad with joy. She smelled the sweet musk of the horse mixed with his sweat, she smelled the river. She clutched at him, his shoulders, his hair; he felt her wild beyond ecstasy, his own pleasure coursing through him, there had been nothing like this ever. When he brought her down to the floor, gathering nearby pillows, she was on top of him, falling over him, he held her heaving breasts. The sounds she made, bursting from her labored breath, cries on the edge of pain. "This is the end of the world!" she screamed. She leaned back, pushing him up against the roof of her sex, and then he felt every cell of her quiver, release, contract, enfold him in her soft fist.

When they were done she rumbled like a huge cat. "I fucked the whole Red Army!" she said, her voice a rasp, not a voice. "I am almost dead."

Now she undressed, kicking away her shoes, slipping from her blouse, though letting her skirt fall over her polio withered leg. Then she undressed him. She spoke as she did. "I felt war," she said. "I felt steel. The dance of darkblood." Darkblood. The same word he'd heard twenty years ago, bringing back to him the gods of war and death and love. Her chest still heaved while she ran her hand from his chest to his groin. "The eternal, non-existent moment. The gods give. The gods take. Dare we say love, comrade?"

He couldn't think. "I feel infinity," he said, "and abyss."

"A dialectic?" she said. "Now we're free from idiotic destiny." She ran her hand down to his flaccid penis. "Rise up, Comandante. Comandito."

He said, "I'm fifty-eight, not eighteen."

"It's too long of a drive for one fuck," she said to him. She massaged him. "You are with Frida Kahlo," she said. "You are with Frida Kahlo!"

Quickly the smell and texture of her skin raged through him again. He ran his hands from her ears to her cheeks, down the sides of her neck, over her slim shoulders, held her breasts, firm and soft, her youth poured into him, her nipples hardening to his touch. He turned her as he hardened again. With his penis he traced her scar down her back and over her hip to her sex, but she pulled him into a sitting position, straddling his lap. He tried to separate and go down on her, but she pulled herself back onto his lap.

"I just came to fuck you!" she said. "To fuck you. Nothing else!"

She sank her nails into his chest. She clutched his shoulders, his hair, rocked and folded around him. Nothing else mattered. Nothing else would ever matter again until the next time.

Afterward even the air was visceral. He got up and brought whiskey and cigarettes. He sat with her again on the floor. Brushed her hair behind her shoulders.

"Only a mountain can know the core of another mountain," said Kahlo. "Greatness has fucked. In a hundred years, in places throughout the world, people will know this happened."

He lit a cigarette for her. "You were making history?" he said.

"Not *we*? History is made for us, or against us, if I've read you correctly." She let her smoke linger under her nostrils. Inhaled it again as she drank the whiskey. Her reckless sense of destiny charged through him. "I just came to fuck you," she said. "I didn't think, what else? What next?"

Greater than pleasure, greater than necessity, reckless intimacy rolled in his chest.

"Have you ever been happier in your life? Than now?" Frida Kahlo said. She ran the back of her hand on his cheek. "Nothing lasts, Comanadante," she whispered. "That's the beauty of it. Nothing lasts."

After more whiskey and another cigarette, she dressed. He did, too. As she put up her hair and eyed him coyly from underneath her arm, he noticed the firmness of her triceps. She arched an eyebrow and pirouetted to him. She took his hands. Rubbed her forehead softly on his nose. "I want you to tell me about war," said Frida Kahlo.

"War isn't a story," said Trotsky.

"I'll coax it out of you."

"You don't have much coax in you," he said.

She laughed and went to the door. "I'll find you," she said before she left. "You won't have to wait long."

When Sedova noticed that Frida was gone she was afraid that she knew where she went. She asked Van, the head of the guards, but he was mute. What could she expect? And what could come of any of it? She asked him to get her a car and had him drive to the city, getting out at Sanborn's.

"Alone?" the guard said.

"I imagine Stalin's eyes are somewhere else right now," she said. "I'll be safe. Wait for me."

She went in and took a booth. The interior expanded under giant, ornately painted arches, the walls tiled with remarkable blue squares, that deep, cobalt blue that you could only find in Mexico. A huge marble fountain stood at the end of the hall. She ordered tequila and beer. Artists met here. She wanted to feel that, feel it somewhere else than Casa Azul. She sipped the tequila. Watched the men in fedoras drinking and smoking at the bar. Some of them smoked cigars. She'd smoked a cigar or two in Paris. Back then, if she was alone, she wouldn't be alone for long. But now she was too old to turn a man's head. Or so she thought. Yet a man approached the booth. He wasn't a young man, late middle age at best. He wore a gray suit and trousers, a black tie with white angled stripes. He took off his hat. His hair was thick, graying a little, eyes light brown, almost amber.

"Are you meeting someone?" he asked.

"Ne pas," she said.

He switched to French. "Do you wish to be alone?"

She nodded to the seat across from her.

He sat. When the waiter approached he ordered brandy and soda, no ice.

"I am Leonid," he said to her. "Leonov."

"Russian then," she said to him in Russian. "Natalia." She immediately wondered if it was a mistake to give her real name, though given the situation, how much could it matter? Everyone was someone's agent.

The waiter brought Leonid his drink. He sipped it. "I learned this in Spain, from an American writer. Hemingway." He waited for her to recognize the name, but she didn't.

She knew the leftists. "Dos Passos," she said. "Modotti."

"But their government was no help." Unselfconsciously he offered her a taste of his drink.

She took a sip and liked it, liked the way the soda tempered the heaviness of the brandy.

He waved his hand toward the arched ceiling. "It's difficult to find a place here that serves it. You'd think that something so common in Spain . . ."

"One speaks Mexican here, not Spanish," she said. "You fought?"

"I'm a little old for battle," he said. "Volunteer medical corps." He called the waiter and ordered a brandy and soda for her. "Natalia," he said. "Not Sedova, I hope."

"You hope not?"

"I'm Trotskyist," he said. "I met Victor Serge in Paris."

"Serge is often ambivalent," she said. "Lyova?"

"No," he said. He paused. "I'm sorry."

She held herself on the verge of tears. Sipped the drink.

"Are you a member?" she said.

"No," he said. "Too visible."

"There aren't many Mexican Trotskyists and the few there are fight with each other," Sedova said.

"You're unguarded?" said Leonov.

"There's a car outside."

He took out a pack cigarettes and offered her one. She declined, but nodded to him. He lit. Smoked. Exhaled. "I was hoping you'd be someone less renowned," he said to her. He offered an ironic smile.

"Lev is hunting and fishing in the north," she said.

A violinist approached. Leonid looked at her and she shook her head. He waved the man off. "The Alameda is nearby. Would you like to take a walk?"

He put down some pesos and they finished their drinks. He accompanied her outside where she signaled Van to follow them.

They crossed an avenue to the eastern spur of the Alameda. He pointed to the Palacio del Belles Artes across the way. "Trotsky is in Rivera's mural there," he said, "standing with Marx and Lenin."

She barely turned. "I see plenty of Trotsky," she said. "And Rivera."

"I imagine it's difficult to find time alone now," he said.

They walked to the center of the park that stretched along La Avenida Hidalgo. She bought some seeds to feed the pigeons. Overhead the sky began to cloud with the approaching afternoon showers. Anyway, they sat on a bench and fed the birds.

"It was hard to follow the war from here," she said.

"It was hard to follow it there," he said. "We had no leaders, really. The GPU divided the workers from the intellectuals, the peasants from the industrial workers. We fought among ourselves before we ever faced Franco."

"You could be GPU," she said.

"You could be GPU," said Leonid and they both laughed. "I couldn't get into the States. I have an apartment on Orizaba. There's a law office nearby. It's not hard work." He brought out his cigarettes again. This time she smoked with him.

"Mexican cigarettes aren't bad," she said. "And they're cheaper than American."

"A metaphor for Mexico."

A pigeon fluttered in front of her and she blew smoke at it. It circled to her feet. "Another metaphor," she said. "Are you underground?"

"Everyone is underground. And no one. Everyone knows everything, whether it's true or not."

"Everything," she said. She wondered how much.

"Cardenas is giving asylum to Republican volunteers from Poland,

Finland, Germany, Austria," said Leonov. "There's bound to be GPU assassins among them."

"Cardenas is in trouble," she said. "Inevitably. Even Leon is split in two. How can you support the Soviet Union yet oppose Stalin?"

"I know. I've read your work in *The Social Appeal*. And your essays advocating more party participation for women," he said to her. "You're powerful and articulate. The role of women hasn't really been taken on by the Bolsheviks."

"They're too busy killing each other," she said.

They put out their cigarettes on the bench and then threw them on the ground. He had a flask in the inner pocket of his jacket. "Just more brandy," he said.

She took a sip. "There should be no roles. Jobs, not roles."

"Roles are bourgeois." He laughed. Like his voice, it was sonorous.

"If only that," she said. "But if no bourgeoisie, then no proletariat to replace them. You know all that." She took another sip and then gave him the flask. "But it would seem we're on the verge of world war, not world liberation."

He put the flask in his jacket. Briefly, he leaned on his knees with his elbows, she sat up and turned to her. "You're very beautiful," he said.

She wanted to be offended by that, but how long had it been since Lev had said that to her? If love had welded them through exile, turmoil, death, where was it now? Silently, they had another cigarette and a sip of brandy.

"You know we're at Casa Azul," she said.

"Everyone knows. Rivera and Kahlo are in San Angel."

"Mostly," she said.

"When he's not fucking models. And she . . ." he paused.

"When she's not chasing my husband."

"Not much of a chase?" he said to her. He looked her in the eyes again. "I've gone beyond propriety," he said.

"Here," she said "at the end of time, at the end of the world, at the edge of total defeat."

She asked him for more brandy, then stood. "Will you help me buy a gun?" she said to him.

"Is there someone you want to shoot?"

She laughed. She said, "Frida Kahlo?"

They walked the crowded streets to the Zócalo, the inner square lined with merchants selling jewelry, sunglasses, socks, shirts, sundries on spread blankets, tables piled with fruits and vegetables. Van parked the car and now followed them on foot. She felt as if she was walking with a spy followed by a spy. Leonov had been wearing sunglasses, but he took them off and put them deep in his pants pocket.

"They'll steal them off your face and sell them from a blanket," he said.

"It's a living, comrade Leonov," she said.

He simply nodded. He raised his hand toward the Cathedral.

"No religion, thank you," said Sedova.

"One religion replaces another," said Leonov. "I hope it isn't that simple in politics."

"Heresy, comrade?" she laughed. Did he get the pun?

"Opposition?" he said. He laughed too.

"That, one hopes, is the difference," she said.

On a side street ran a row of gun shops. He led her to one.

"I was sure you'd know," Sedova said.

"One must know," he said.

The proprietor, dark and mustached, nodded at Leonid Leonov who explained that Sedova was looking for a pistol, light enough to handle but powerful enough to stop a man at ten feet. She understood enough of it and when he began to reiterate to her in Russian, she lifted her hand and said, "I approve." The man showed her a .38 Browning. She turned away from the counter and lifted it, her left hand steadying her right. Then she released the safety and clicked the trigger with a steady squeeze.

"Not the first time, I see," said Leonov.

"Unfortunately," she said. "Unfortunately."

Sedova purchased the gun and some ammunition and put it in her bag. She took Leonov's arm and they left the store. Van spotted them immediately and stepped toward them. She put up her hand to stop him.

When she faced Leonov he said, "May I see you again?"

She agreed to meet him in a week at Sanborn's. He kissed her hand.

Then she walked to Van and let him lead her to the car.

Van, the head of their security now, said to her, "Am I permitted an opinion?"

"If you keep it to yourself," she said. It was too early for opinions. As of yet there were no facts, only innuendo. In the case of Leonov, double agent or not, it felt good to be the center of attention, to have someone understand that she was powerful, and if jealous, neither meek nor resentful. After that, who knew?

When she returned to Casa Azul there was a note. Lev Davidovich had called. There was a short message in simple Spanish. A surprise visit from Frida and her brother-in-law. They stayed only briefly, shared some tea. But he thought it best to let her know. This told her more than she wanted to know. She thought of Leonid Leonov. She had no doubt that he might be GPU, or was once GPU, now the NKVD. If you were outside the inner circle of power, there was no other way to advance, as long as you didn't advance too far. Not even the military was safe. The top generals had been executed, too. You couldn't leave the agency without leaving Russia. Even so, you could be recruited again and anyone close enough to recruit you was close enough to kill you. Everyone was suspect. That brought her new fear, though she feared Kahlo more, however foolish that might be. Yet however jealous she felt, Kahlo's game could not last, though as long as it did, it would be humiliating. She couldn't predict more than that.

Now she thought of the boy in Petrograd, Mikail, though to think of him as a boy was the thinking of a middle-aged woman. Then she was a young woman and he was a younger man. When she gave into him, finally—how long had she resisted? it seemed like a very long time—when she kissed him, as they knelt together beside his bike, balanced upside down on its handle bars and seat so they could re-engage the chain that had come loose from its sprocket; he seemed to be struggling with it and she got down next to him to hold the pedal while he nudged the chain into place; she pushed the pedal and the chain slipped onto the gear. "Ah," he said, "success!" He kissed her cheek. Then she turned to him and they touched lips. It was mutual. Things fall away when that happens. Consequences, the future, fall away. They lay on the grass, behind some shrubs. He'd brought a blanket in a basket behind his seat.

"You planned?" she said.

"I had no plans, just preparations," he said to her.

"I'm certainly not your first," she said.

"My first in some ways," he said.

"Your first with someone older?"

"You're hardly older," he said. "My first with a woman of authority. My first with someone smarter than me." He thought for a moment. "My first with someone dangerous."

"Dangerous," she said. "This is dangerous, but I'm not dangerous."

"You're dangerous in every way." He leaned to her and kissed her. He was ready again.

And now, thinking back, he was right. It added to it. The danger. As well as the helpless impossibility of it ever working out. So when she stayed late at work, he stayed late too, and when the building was abandoned they found an unused office and met there. Into the chill of fall, the darkening afternoons and the first snow, they watched the white blanket quiet the city.

"I'm not such a good communist," he said to her once. "I believe in God."

"Which one?" she said.

"The one who touches me at night when I wake up in fear. The one who speaks to me when I wake up alone without you."

"People get fatal diseases, then pray to God to cure them," she said to him. "Who do they think gave them the disease?"

"That's the test," he said. "Will you turn to God who gave you the disease, thank Him for your life and ask for forgiveness and cure?"

"*Him* is it?"

"Merely a pronoun. You prefer *Her*?"

"I prefer nothing at all," she said. "You would make love to me even if you didn't believe in God. Are you making love to me because you do? Are you asking God to forgive you for fucking another man's wife?"

"Not yet," he said. "Besides, you're not married."

That he knew surprised her. "Marriage, like God, changes nothing," she said, kissing him.

He was handsome, his body and hair golden, his skin almost hairless. He was an attentive lover. And her husband, though it was true they never really married, was thousands of miles away, parlaying his own transgressions. Did one give up everything to revolution? Briefly, in France, before Lev Davidovich, she was very young and very free. What did that change? Fidelity, like marriage, was not a law, not a thing, but a habit, an ideological cloak for vanity and jealousy and the deeper you fell into it, the deeper the risks for pain. It wasn't something you plotted to abandon, but it could happen, with loneliness, with distance.

"Do you love me?" he asked.

And with that, he crossed the line. Now he'd entered into the same labyrinth as God and marriage and fidelity.

"Do you really want that?" she asked him. "We are doomed by brevity. We are all doomed by it. This love making even more so. I have a revolution to attend to. And sons. But whether or not Leon Trotsky leads the Red army to victory or returns home in a coffin, you and I, this crack in time, must end."

"But do you love me?" he said.

And she turned away from him.

So the day he stood in front of her with his transfer papers to Tsaritsin in hand, he wept.

"Be a man," she said to him. "Be the man who was brave enough to love me."

"I'll be shot in the back."

"Only if you turn your back," she whispered. She touched his cheek. "We were foolish," she said. "Now let's not be fools." In this, women were stronger than men, their lives both more complex and more tenuous. That day it was a lover. One day it would be her sons. And even Lev Davidovich himself. She kissed Mikail. He stepped back and saluted her. "That's better, dear one," she said.

HORROR OF LOVE

HE WAS OBSESSED with Frida Kahlo: the delicacy of her fingers and wrists, the dance of her mind, the way the collar of her blouse fell from her collar bone to reveal her throat which he envisioned as something pure. He remembered her lips accepting his, her tongue searching for his throat, the two of them muffling each other's screams. In the fanaticism of desire he dreamed of escaping with her to Acapulco and piloting a boat to Cabo San Lucas, exiling themselves in some obscure town on the western Baja. He'd sell his Stalin biography, and then one on Lenin, turning the heads of New York publishing. Afternoons, when the light poured perfectly through their cottage windows, he'd watch her back as she painted, the ballet of her shoulders and arms guiding her brush strokes. After arguing about Bolshevism and art, they would make love passionately on the shore, in the waves. There would be photographs of the two of them on the beach, grinning with visages of hope and doom like Cleopatra and Anthony waiting for Octavius. For a man in this state of infatuation, only the impossible could be imagined. He took long walks and began collecting cacti, which he imagined as metaphors of himself, bristling and dangerous, delicate yet full. He couldn't write anything.

Sedova almost didn't come to Tlaxco. She waited a day, another day.

She thought of approaching Rivera, but couldn't imagine broaching the subject, even if, like the last time she spoke to him, she could likely just stand in front of him and wait for him to speak, she yet didn't want to be a harbinger. It was too early. To early for anyone to really know anything. She watched when Kahlo returned from Tlaxco and gathered some of her things before heading for San Angel. Now, for certain, it was both too early and too late. She swam in unappetizing choices. So many that she couldn't eat. She made up her mind that she could leave Leon. But it was all preemptive. She could be imagining it all. Maybe they just had tea. But then she thought of the way that Kahlo followed Lev with her shadowed, down turned eyes, the way she lifted her hand to say good night, in English, "Good night, my dear," or "Good night, love." Sedova's English was at least that good. This is how they found each other when Van drove her to Tlaxco on Trotsky's second to last day there.

At the door of the cottage he greeted her and held her, each looking at the other too hard because it was too hard to know what to feel. They made love. For him it was a distraction from his obsession, but he told himself as well that it was an outpouring of his true love, his lasting love, a real love in this real world, not the impossible imagination where he now spent his time. For her his passion was almost too desperate, as if he was acting the part of her lover, and so in every gesture she felt the opposite confirmed. Yet she did love him, didn't she?

Afterwards, he showed her his first collected cactuses. "Do you think I should learn their names?" he asked.

"Latin, botanical names?" she said. "Mexican names?"

He pointed to the thorny tip of a bulbous, furry plant. "This one is about to flower," he said.

"Are they soldiers?" she said. "Lovers?"

"Can't they just be cactuses?"

Could anything just be what was in front of their faces anymore? What had Breton said? That all of Mexico was surreal, a land of the unconscious pouring itself out around every corner; that all you had to do was look straight ahead and you'd be turning the corner again and again, or as if the world existed in your peripheral vision and what stood in front of you, or lay in front of you or burned or bled in front of you exploded to those edges, so psychologically, emotionally, you lived on the edge of panic. She stood with Leon Trotsky, thirty years her lover, in Mexico, in front of cactuses.

Love these cactuses, he thought, stroking her hair. That's all you have to do. But in that he was already infected with Mexico, seduced without even realizing it. He wondered, now, what was he willing to give up? What did he have? What could he walk away from? If ten years ago he'd written his autobiography, what life was he writing now? Would he remember this moment, the moment he met with his wife after he'd made love to Frida Kahlo? Would he write it down? Would anyone?

"This is how we live, where we live," he said softly.

"Lev Davidovich, we die alone," she said. "We do not meet again anywhere but under a gravestone."

Though they met in front of one in Paris. She was thinking of that.

On the ride back to Coyoacán she let him take her hand, his fingers moving over it as if it were an act of meditation. But that night in bed, she waited for him to fall asleep and then moved away from his spooning and lay on her back. She watched his eyes quiver and his lips move. He was dreaming. In his dream he lay on his back in the great iron train, the train rumbling under him, his leather pants open, his genitals exposed, the ghost of Maria Siszkaya sits upon him, takes out her heart and offers it to an army of men, their rifles raised, but they aren't an army of living men, they are an army of the dead.

The next day he returned with his papers and books to his office near Chapultepec. He needed some space away from Casa Azul to get back to work. But on his work desk he found a paper Mexican flag folded around a fountain pen with his name engraved on the barrel. On the white side of the unfolded flag a note that read, "I am having comida corrida at Tina's." It was unsigned, but he knew that during Frida and Diego's courtship, she often brought a lunch to him that they shared on his scaffolding. How many of Diego's models, lovers, brought him lunch, or was that the one ritual left for Frida alone? Yet not today. He put the pen in his coat pocket, left the office and signaled to Hansen, his American guard. As always, he sat slumped in the back seat of the Dodge. He had his body guard drive north through the park, then circle back to the west and then south for Coyoacán where they stopped a half block from Tina's apartment. "I have a meeting. Wait here," he said. He went up the interior steps where Frida Kahlo waited bare breasted at the open apartment door, a black target drawn around her right breast.

"I know the sound of your footsteps," she said. "I heard them before I was born. In my sleep, I know where you are. I feel your breath in my ear. I'm full of the world. I wait for you and nothing else." She held her targeted breast to his lips. It tasted like anise.

They made love. She didn't want him to go down on her. Didn't want to lie on the bed, remove her skirts. She didn't want him to do anything that he did with Sedova.

She rolled on her side, onto her good leg, pushing him inside her, her elbows into his chest, her eyes deepening, black and far away like space. She moaned to him. The sounds floated on her breath, felt as much as heard. She put his hand on her clitoris and guided his fingers against her lunging until she came. Then he came.

Afterward, he lay there, trying to find a thought, but he couldn't find one. For the first time in his life his mind was blank, while she came from the kitchen with a platter of sliced watermelon that she'd dipped in vodka.

"You'll never eat watermelon the same again," she said to him. "You'll never see it the same again. In my paintings, watermelon, as red as blood."

They fed each other pieces.

"How must this end?" he said now.

"When?" she said. "And where? Do you think Diego will shoot you?"

"Diego will never shoot anyone," he said.

"I think of that man in Xochimilco. I think of that look on his face when he saw eternity. That's when I wanted you. That's what I wanted to feel when you fucked me."

"And I'm not supposed to ask you if you did," said Trotsky.

"No man would dare."

"So did you?"

"Only just then, when you asked." She smiled demurely. "Do you think I mean anything that I say? Words are just sounds."

"Gunfire is just sounds."

"And 'bullet' is just a word? 'Death' just a word? 'Wound' does not mean wound?"

He put his hand on her sex. "Cunt?" he said in Russian.

"You see?" she said. 'Who needs to know the word?" She aroused him and placed him inside her. "A word," she said. "A sound. This is real. This is all that's real."

And wrapped inside her, again he was thoughtless. When they finished, they bathed each other, though quickly. They couldn't take much more time. As he dried her back, he said to her, "Have you read the American, Whitman?"

"An imperialist?" she said.

"Quite the opposite," he said. "All is sex, even death."

"Is that how you explained shooting deserters?"

"I never shot them. I rallied them. I shot the generals who led their men in retreat."

She turned to him. "No retreat then," she said softly.

Dressing, he put on his jacket and retrieved her gift, the engraved pen. "Thank you," he said.

"A birthday present," said Kahlo.

"But I would have preferred your signature."

"Tu pistola?" said Kahlo.

He touched the other side of his coat.

"Would you give me a pistol with my name on it?" she said.

When he put the pen back and said nothing she said, "I love it. You don't trust me."

"A gun changes everything," said Leon Trotsky.

The phone rang once, twice, then stopped. Then it rang again, once.

"Tina has signaled it's clear for you to leave unseen," Frida Kahlo said.

He touched her cheek, left the apartment, found Hansen waiting and returned to Hidalgo's cottage and his book on Stalin, his thoughts obsessed with sex, treachery, retreat.

Sedova didn't need to find Rivera. He was waiting in the garden below her room as she readied to leave for Sanborn's.

"You look exceptionally beautiful today, Natalia Sedova," he said to her.

She might have objected if she hadn't, in fact, tried a little: fresh make up; she'd curled her hair, wore a beret and a rose colored blouse with her black skirt. He wasn't wearing his painter overalls, but a brown suit and one of his characteristic wide neck ties, a fedora, not a sombrero.

"Leon gave me the most honorific praise in the *Partisan Review*."

"'The hidden springs of social revolution,'" Sedova quoted. "But he's not here right now."

"Hidalgo's?" said Rivera. "I think my appearance there might scare him to death."

"There's no one left to die," said Sedova.

"Seva?" said Diego.

"I suppose there's always someone."

"You are always so perilously direct," Diego said. "There is no phone there. Are you going to see him?"

"No," she said. "I don't want to find him."

"I see," he said. "I have things I needn't have confirmed, as well." He removed his hat and wiped his brow with is handkerchief. "Soon," he said, "Breton will arrive again. Frida will be in New York, then Paris. She'll have other admirers there. Kandinsky, Duchamp. Picasso will go mad for her."

"By reputation you're a more jealous man than that," said Sedova. She glanced at her watch.

"You have a meeting," he said. "Be careful. Leonov is not his real name."

She didn't want to ask how he knew about Leonid. "A deadly friendship?" she said. "Like Siqueiros?"

"He fought in Spain. He hates Trotsky. He thinks Leon is working for the Nazis and the FBI." He put his hat on again. "I met Mussolini. Stalin too. They liked me."

"Rockefeller?" she said. She offered a short laugh.

"At first. Really. At first. I'm a famous artist. I must meet people."

"You've been very kind to us here," said Natalia Sedova.

"I have a new model now," said Rivera. "A Hungarian painter. I might marry her."

"Divorce Frida?" said Natalia Sedova.

"Not that marriage matters, as you know."

"I see," she said. "I have to wonder what regard, or disregard, earns me your confessions."

"My Catholicism is upside down," he said, then grinned almost sheepishly. He held the brim of his hat, then released it.

"I'm too old to model," she said.

"You're not. You are a beautiful and articulate woman."

She let him kiss her hand. Even in such a casual gesture, his manner was sensual, his lips soft and seductive.

"I've arranged a trip to Guadalajara when Breton and Lamba arrive," he said. "Let's do that and see what happens after."

In the car with Van she wondered what to make of it, this piling up of implicit loyalties and disloyalties, as if living an impassioned life, driven by art, by politics, fed his passionate transgressions. What had he come to tell her, really? She should have pressed him more directly about Leonov, though it would likely have resulted in yet another diversion. Were they at the center of the world? The edge? Mexico City. The higher up you went, the harder it was to breathe.

Leonid was waiting in the same booth at Sanborn's, her brandy and soda waiting for her as well. He kissed her hand. It was a day for hand kissing.

"You look beautiful," he said.

"I'm having a beautiful day."

"You've added beauty to my day, Natalia Sedova. I'm glad you came."

She sat across from him. "I told you I would. A lot has happened."

Leonid removed his hat and placed it next to him. "You sound upset," he said. "Can we talk about it?"

She sipped the drink. Looked him in the eyes. "Let's find out," she said.

He returned the directness of her stare. "That's a frightening tone, Natalia Sedova. Really. Like that, we'll never get to the bottom of anything."

"What did you know about the POUM in Spain?"

"The workers' party?" he said.

"The Workers Party for Marxist Unification," she said.

El Partido Obrere de Unificación Marxista," said Leonov. "I was there, Natalia.

Spain was upside down. I don't think anyone knew what they were fighting for."

"Franco seemed to," she said.

"Basic Catholic values?"

"You need an army to do that?"

"I was joking. Power, pure and simple. We were confused. Many of us went there to fight for the Republic. We ended up just fighting," he said.

"You didn't join?"

"The POUM? They were Spanish. I am Russian."

"They were Trotskyists," said Sedova.

Leonid took a deep swallow and sat back. "Do you think any of them ever heard of Dialectal Materialism, let alone believed in it?"

"They were for permanent revolution," said Sedova. "And collectivization. From each according to their ability, to each according to their need."

"There were dozens of parties among the Republicans," he said. "One of the reasons for their demise. Franco understands this, as did Lenin, and Trotsky too. And so, now, does Stalin."

"And Hitler."

"Was elected," said Leonid Leonov. "And the Communists were divided and crushed. People want stability, not permanent revolution."

"The rich do," she said. "The bourgeoisie."

"The POUM was infiltrated by the Fascists," said Leonid.

"And the GPU," she said.

"Now the NKVD," he said. "But they were everywhere. I think Stalin's plan was for everyone to infiltrate everybody, no one wins, Hitler is thwarted."

"Which are you?" she said.

"The POUM leaders will be tried for spying for Franco."

"By the Soviets," she said. "The same rhetoric Stalin used on the old Bolsheviks and is yet used on Leon Trotsky."

"That's why I'm on the run," said Leonid Leonov. "Are you aware of Orlov?"

Orlov had been one on Stalin's GPU ringleaders who defected to Mexico.

"Yes," she said.

"I was sent here to kill him. And to help turn the Communist press here against Trotsky. The first I've refused to do. The second I didn't need to do."

She finished her drink.

"Unlike your dear husband," said Leonov, "my idealism is dead." He finished his drink, too. "Can we walk?

She brought him to the car where Van waited outside the driver's door.

"This is comrade Leonov," she said to Van.

The men didn't shake hands.

"Is this wise, comrade Sedova?" said Van.

"In fact, I think it is quite wise," said Natalia Sedova.

Van parked and followed them as they walked. The peculiar crows with a white stripe under their wings hopped around them, expecting food. An iguana lay on a tree branch. They stopped at the Emperor's fountain and listened to the water.

"Do you have family?" Sedova asked Leonid.

"A wife. Two daughters. Gladly, no sons. Daughters are safer."

"They aren't."

"Regardless, I left them early on. I spoke of losing my ideals, but in fact I understood, going in, that I would be murdered by ideals. The difference, after Lenin's death, is that the terms changed from loyalty to survival."

"Can you contact them?" she said.

"I don't contact anyone," he said. "In Paris, everything Trotsky sent to Lyova was intercepted by Zborowski and sent to Orlov, then from Orlov to Stalin. Everything is that way."

"We'd come to suspect it," she said. "Then you knew, too."

"Our very thoughts are recorded in the Kremlin. I live like a Dostoyevsky character."

"There are many."

"The loneliest," he said. "There are no good choices."

"Survival is a choice. Suicide," she said.

"Those are good choices?" He laughed. "But right now," he said, "right now, in this moment, it has never been better." He took her by the hand and led her behind the fountain. She knew that in that moment alone he could end her life. But she didn't fear it. Survival. Take it out of her hands. He turned to her, lifted her head, and kissed her lips. She returned the kiss.

"That felt good," he said.

It felt good to her, too, her own self-willed playing with fire.

When they stepped out Van had already come a good way toward the fountain, but he stopped when he saw them.

"I can find my way home from here," Leonid said. He doffed his hat. "Do you think I'm a threat to you?"

"No," she said, "I think you're a threat to Leon Trotsky."

EVERYTHING IS RED

IT WAS THE DAY OF THE DEAD. And Trotsky's birthday, too. Diego gave him a candied skull with "Stalin" printed on its forehead.

"Diego has bad taste," said Frida.

"On the contrary," said Leon.

"Good taste is spineless," said Jacqueline Lamba.

The room filled with Kahlo's animal magic, the screech of Fulang Chang and the parrots; the monkey chased the dogs; Lorca, who Leon had brought for the occasion, hissed at the scurrying canines. Diego toasted the coming trip to "the land of Orozco's fire!" He left for Guadalajara alone that night.

The group followed the next day, with Hansen driving Trotsky's Dodge, Breton up front and Natalia and Leon in the back. In the second car, Rivera's Ford, one of Diego's men, Sixto, drove with Van at shot gun, Jacqueline and Frida in the back seat.

Breton had worked on the draft of *Revolution and Art* in Paris but struggled with reconciling the spontaneity of his surrealism with the apparent determinism of Marx. He was to have brought his final draft for Trotsky to edit before they put together the final manuscript and sent it off to the *Partisan Review*. He was nervous about showing it to Trotsky.

Leon wanted to see it. Natalia sensed a tension between them, but there was tension everywhere.

Breton turned toward the back seat. "You seem to be very fond of your little cat," he said. He spoke in French. The three of them all spoke French.

Trotsky grunted. He was always irritated by the small talk that avoided big talk.

"He's always been fond of animals," Natalia said. "But it's been hard to find time or space, especially during the exiles."

"The dogs at the house are small and yappy," said Trotsky. "The parrots squawk too much nonsense. I like the rabbits. They're honest and quiet."

"Honest?" said André.

"With their emotions."

"So you think they have feelings?" said Breton.

"Thoughts and feelings. I watch them everyday."

"But that is absurd, my friend," Breton said.

Natalia laughed. "André Breton has called thinking rabbits absurd."

Breton tightened his cheeks and narrowed his eyes at her. "I doubt they possess an unconscious," he said.

"They taste, they hear, smell, feel, see," said Trotsky. "And thus think."

"They contemplate their carrots?"

"They know a good one from a bad one."

"But they don't know that they know it," Breton said.

"He's French, my love," Sedova said to Leon. "He's up to his ears in Descartes."

"Maybe we should invite them to join the Fourth International," said André Breton. "Do you ask them, 'Who would like to be eaten for dinner?'"

"I don't eat them," said Trotsky.

"Chickens, sheep, cows?"

"Ducks and geese?" laughed Natalia.

"We don't eat horses and dogs," said Trotsky. "We reward their loyalty."

"Cats?" Sedova said.

"Maybe we should eat them," said Breton. He was irritated now. "Maybe we should eat all of them!"

"They're sentient," Leon Trotsky said. "But first the workers utopia, then the utopia of sentience."

"Stop the car!" yelled André Breton.

Hansen slowed to a stop. They were well outside the city, surrounded by jungle covered hills. Breton leapt from his seat and stood on the road, staring hard at the Ford as it slowed to a stop behind them. Though Trotsky sat, unmoving, Natalia jumped out of her seat, too, as Breton stepped toward the Ford. She stepped in front of him.

"He's a rigid madman," he said.

When Breton tried to walk around her, she put a hand in his chest. "He's just speaking his unconscious mind," she said. She smirked at him, and though he was slightly taller, she managed to give the impression she was looking down at him. "Do you think you'll find Frida Kahlo's insouciance more compatible?" She knew Lev Davidovich only too well. He'd baited Breton. And Breton him. She'd wondered from the start whether it was her presence that agitated the men, that in this upside-down pressure cooker she'd become, for lack of a better phrase, the unconscious fulcrum. "Get back in the car, André," she said. "You two have work to do, now and when we get back. I'm getting in the other car." And she spun from him and walked to the Ford, quickly contemplating whether it would be better to sit next to Frida Kahlo or put Lamba between them.

Well at this point she had nothing to lose or prove, nothing she could lose or prove. She opened the car door and sat next to Frida.

"The men are fighting about whether or not rabbits think," she said.

These three could converse in French, too, though Frida slipped into Spanish as well.

"André doesn't think about animals, let alone what they think," said Jacqueline Lamba. "Doesn't Alice follow a rabbit into Wonderland?"

"Is that Surrealism?" Natalia asked Kahlo.

"I don't know anything about Surrealism," said Frida Kahlo.

"Lewis Carrol is far too rational to be surreal," Lamba said.

"He liked children," said Frida.

"Maybe too much," said Lamba.

"And Lev," said Frida, she paused, "Leon likes rabbits."

"But not too much," said Sedova.

The three of them laughed.

"If they want to talk about bunnies then let's not," said Frida Kahlo.

"Not bunnies nor men," said Natalia Sedova.

Kahlo said, "Let's sing instead. I'll sing a line and you both repeat it, then I'll sing another and you'll repeat, and when that's done, we'll all sing it together, and when we know it well enough I'll start another." She brought out a flask of tequila and they passed it back and forth and Frida began a song by Agustin Lara, "Se me hizo facil."

"Voy a buscar, un amor que me comprenda," sang Frida.

She motioned with her hands as the two women repeated the tune and lyrics.

"La otra la olvido cada día mas y mas," Kahlo sang.

When they could sing the whole song together Frida taught them "Amor de mis amores" and "Aventureara."

They sang and drank tequila.

Ahead in the Dodge Trotsky asked Breton, "What are you so edgy about?"

"I'm not edgy," said Breton. "What are you angry about?"

"Frankly," said Leon, "I'm angry about the *retablos* you stole from that church in Puebla."

"Now? That was some time ago. You're angry about that?"

"I was angry then. I should have stopped you. They were the prayers of poor people."

"Prayers?" said Breton. "You don't believe in prayer."

"But they did," said Trotsky. "Besides, I don't have to believe in it to admire it."

"Kahlo has a wall of them!" said Breton.

"And since I have you alone, I think you underestimate Zola and overestimate Freud."

"That makes you angry?"

"Is Freud in your draft of *Revolution and Art*?" Trotsky said.

"Yes. That's what you're upset about?" Breton said.

"And you are upset that I talk to rabbits."

"You talk at rabbits," said André Breton. "One can't talk to them."

"You can't reconcile Surrealism or Freud with Marx because neither of them is sociological. Is that why you can't finish your draft of the essay?"

"I have a draft. But you're questioning my commitment to our cause," said Breton.

"Your intellectual commitment to dialectical materialism," said Leon Trotsky.

"Many good communists and socialists question dialectical materialism."

"Not intellectual communists."

"In America they do," Breton said. "Even your biographer, Monsieur Eastman."

"An anti-intellectual," said Trotsky.

"Bertram Wolfe?"

"A Rivera sycophant. Name one American idea, one theory that has had any real influence in Europe," said Trotsky.

"Your friend Dewey's Pragmatism?"

"Pragmatism is a method," said Leon Trotsky, "not a theory."

"Victor Serge? Boris Souvarine?"

"Political corpses," said Leon Trotsky.

"Your allies and friends," said Breton.

"Their loyalty is irrelevant to the argument," Trotsky said. "You should spend more time with animals."

"You'll have my draft when we return to Coyoacán," Breton said to him.

"When the workers are sheltered and well fed, with the leisure and freedom to think, they will make their own art."

"There will always be artists," said André Breton. "Even in utopia. But are you sleeping with Frida yet?"

Trotsky hesitated and that was enough. If he denied it now, it would be no different than admitting it.

Behind them, in the Ford, the women sang. An hour later, when they pulled into a café outside Zitacuaro, Breton and Trotsky were not talking to each other and the women were still singing. Breton complained that he was suffering from an attack of aphasia and needed to be near Jacqueline, so Sedova joined Trotsky again in the Dodge.

"He's very sensitive, Lev," Natalia said to Trotsky when they were off again.

"Not about animals," Trotsky said.

"You can't quarrel with Breton," she said. She took his hand and put it on her lap. "You need to work together."

"This trip is a mistake," he said.

"Of course it is," said Natalia Sedova. "But now what?"

"Yes," he said. "Now what?" Because he wasn't thinking of André Breton or art and politics. He was thinking of Frida Kahlo in the car behind him.

So when they arrived at their hotel in Guadalajara Trotsky was preoccupied and irascible. Sedova had to arrange for their room while Trotsky ignored everyone, finally following her to the room and throwing his bags in.

"I'm going to find Orozco," he said.

"Alone?" said Natalia Sedova.

That startled him a little because it intimated the truth, that he might have permitted himself to find Frida Kahlo before Diego showed up. For her part, it was exactly what she meant. "I introduced you to art, many years ago, in Paris, my love," she said.

He softened. He yet loved Natalia Sedova. He must quell his obsession. And yet his mind leapt to the end of this purported vacation and to their return to Coyoacán, and then, soon after, Frida would be in New York, then Paris, and their interlude would be punctuated. He was gulping time. What did Natalia know? What did she suspect?

"Let's find Van and Olsen," he said. "And go, alone together."

They stopped first at the Governor's Palace where Orozco had covered the archways and domed ceilings with myriad shades of red, gigantically depicting the suffering of Indian workers chained to their hammers and axes, half-monster soldiers prodding them with medieval weaponry. The paintings rolled and flowed from one archway, one scene to the next. Trotsky was astounded and moved. Rivera's murals tended to explode with determination and brightness, depicting a humanity growing liberated by technology. Orozco painted machines as oppressors, the workers' earth as a workers' hell.

They drove to the Hospicio Cabañas, an abandoned church where they found José Clemente Orozco at work on his mural *The Spanish Conquest of Mexico*, an equally dark portrayal of Indians, workers, conquerors, false inventors and false prophets of politics, technology, and religion.

Though Van had arranged the meeting, Orozco seemed surprised to be interrupted. He turned, a stocky man both pale and dark, thick glasses and thick mustache, his left arm ending in a stump.

"This is genius," said Trotsky.

"No," said Orozco. "I don't believe in genius."

"Like Dostoevsky," said Trotsky.

"You're Spanish," Natalia said to Orozco.

"Only by birth. I studied painting in El Norte, not in Europe. I am Mexican."

Trotsky pointed to the figures of three dubious looking men, presented in the guise of false prophets. Did one of them resemble him?

"That's me," Trotsky said.

"No one here is real," said Orozco.

"I've heard you called a nihilist," said Sedova. "But this work is political, not nihilistic."

"I don't care," said José Clemente Orozco.

"I don't care either," said Leon Trotsky.

They sat at a small table then, sharing a pot of tea as Trotsky's eyes roved over the mural again and again.

"I'm very moved," Trotsky said.

"It doesn't matter," said Orozco.

But Trotsky, who once saw Rivera as the personification of revolutionary art, now, suddenly, felt that vision falling apart and coming together again in a sequence of epiphanies, feeling in that moment the vision of Breton, a synthesis of abstraction, surrealism, and socialism, a vision melding communism and freedom. When they left he said to Natalia, "I must see Siqueiros, too."

"He's Stalinist," said Natalia. "He wants to kill you."

"Kahlo is Stalinist, too, don't you think?" he said to her.

"Then you know more than me," she said. She saw Van's eyes in the rearview mirror, searching her and scolding her. How much did he know? Had he told Lev about Leonid? Did he know, or suspect as she did, about Leon and Kahlo? She felt herself in a vortex where no one knew anything and everyone knew too much. And for Lev to bring up Kahlo now, to her, Sedova, was a self-conscious attempt to appear as if he were distancing himself when in fact he meant the opposite.

"I will see Siqueiros," said Trotsky. "Can we do that, Van?" he said.

"Maybe," said Van, "but it will have to be carefully arranged."

"When we get back to Coyoacán," Trotsky said.

When they got back to the hotel in Guadalajara Trotsky told Natalia that he had to see Breton immediately. In fact, he told himself he meant to, and would, if he were not interrupted, but after he consulted the reception desk for the location of Breton's room, he crossed the plaza at the center of the hotel and Frida Kahlo spoke to him from the shadows beneath a corner balcony.

"Come, Lev," she said. "Diego arrives in the morning."

He followed her to a room near the kitchen on the bottom floor, sometimes used by the kitchen help.

"This way you'll smell like food and not of me," she said.

They made love feverishly on blankets she'd laid on the floor. Then, inside her, clutching her, was the only time his mind quieted away from his obsession, and when he was done, when he was no longer inside her, his thoughts raged with when he would possess her again. She had tequila and they drank from the bottle, a pint.

"I saw Orozco," he said to her.

"I don't like him," she said. "He has passion and nothing else."

"Paint," said Trotsky. "Vision. Surreality."

"I am not a surrealist," Kahlo said.

"Breton thinks you are."

"Breton is a silly man," Frida said. "I simply paint myself, from the insides out."

"Not so simply," Trotsky said. "No one else has done it."

"Hieronymus Bosch? Maybe now, Dali."

"They paint the hellish world," he said. "You paint the hell inside. Freud, maybe, if he could paint. But he would paint others, not himself."

She put her hand in his thick hair. "Life is meaningless or futile, my darling," she said. "Blood, guts, dreams, wombs full or empty. Graves."

"All of that," said Leon Trotsky. He took her in his arms and let her take him away again.

Then they heard shuffling in the hallway. Diego's voice. "Frida! Frida!"

"He's early," she said. "Leave through the kitchen."

She gathered the blankets and threw them in a corner. Trotsky spied her as he quickly dressed. The doorknob rattled. He could hear keys being fumbled. Why would Rivera come to this room? Why would he have keys? It was almost as if she'd planned to be caught. He should face Rivera now. But he couldn't think what would happen next. When she went to the door, half dressed and disheveled, she turned to offer him a final glance. He left through the darkened kitchen.

What would Diego think? What would anyone think? They'd both been unfaithful to each other many times before. If he was suspicious, there could be any number of suspects, female as well as male, even Lamba or Breton. In the unlit dining room now, he heard Rivera rush into the kitchen, but Leon had already ducked behind the bar. Rivera glanced around, then went back. There was shouting. A gunshot. But Diego wouldn't shoot Frida. Leon stood and headed back to his room. He'd now done the most cowardly thing he'd ever done. He'd stooped that low for passion. But he couldn't say he wouldn't do it again.

In his chamber, Sedova sat in bed, reading. He didn't look at her and quickly undressed and showered. He dried and threw on a night shirt.

"There was commotion?" she said to him.

"I heard it," he said.

"Did you find André?"

"No."

"You smelled of food when you came in. Did you eat something?" she asked.

"The cook had me taste some tomatillo that he was making for tomorrow," Trotsky said. "We shared a beer."

She didn't believe him. She couldn't remember the last time she didn't believe him. She felt a swell of jealousy. Quieted it. This would end, she told herself, but she didn't know how it would end.

"Let's leave tomorrow morning," he said to her.

"Yes," she said. "I think that would be fine." She got up. Met his gaze. "I'm going to read in a chair," she said. She went to the adjacent room that had a desk, a couch, a reading chair in which she sat down after lighting a nearby lamp. When he fell asleep quickly, uncommon because he was often plagued at night by headaches and sleeplessness, she returned to the bed, though she didn't move next to him or touch him but lay on her back, dismissing one thought after another until the dawn when she couldn't really say she'd slept at all.

In the morning he corralled Van and Hansen and they left without saying goodbye to anyone. She stared out the window. He stared straight ahead. They couldn't talk openly in the presence of their guards, maybe for the better. In a very low tone Trotsky began to speak.

"We never reached Obdorsk," he said. It was the destination of his Siberian exile, after fifteen months in prison for the failed revolution of 1905. He recalled it now to avoid talking to Natalia Sedova and avoid thinking of Frida Kahlo. "I always preferred prison, very often I preferred it to being free. My cells were always filled with books. My thoughts free. On the eastern edge of the Urals we'd abandoned the train and were tugged along by reindeer pulling sleds. There were fewer and fewer guards because there was nothing anywhere but woods, snow, and reindeer, though the guards called them deer. It took a month, trudging through snow as deep as the deers' chests. When we stopped in Berezev I walked away. Hired a sled driver with money I'd hidden in my boots, and headed back, hiding under a wagon load of hay. For days we lived on liquor and snow. But we found a train depot and I boarded, heading for St. Petersburg. I arrived there after only eleven days of leaving Berezev. You were all I could think of. When I got off the train I saw you running through the train cars. You'd found my overcoat and carried it against your chest as you ran. I jumped back on the train and ran toward you."

"I'd been in prison, too," she said.

"We fled to Finland to join Lenin and Martov."

"We clung to each other. Through ten years of exile," she said.

"And hope," said Leon Trotsky.

"Now ten years more," she said. "And less hope." Because they were older now, now their children were dead, and now the enemy was not the czar, but Stalin. And then they'd been deeply in love and she had him to cling to. And he to her. Was he abandoning that? Now, to what could she cling?

Despair. Could she cling to despair? Clutch it to her heart? Nothing more to hope for. Was there freedom there? She could leave Casa Azul. She could leave Lev Davidovich. Leave Leon Trotsky.

"André and Lamba have already planned another vacation," said Leon.

"The essay," said Natalia.

"Precisely," said Trotsky.

"First he will have his holiday," said Sedova. "Maybe he's thinking."

"If he will just give me what he has I can finish it."

"Orozco," said Sedova. "He solved something for you."

"I must see Siqueiros," said Leon.

Even now he lined up what he must do next, who he must see. How he might yet change the unlistening world. Once she was a part of those plans. Maybe it was a subtle shift. But in that world she felt she'd disappeared. What must she do now? What could she do?

Back in Coyoacán he awoke in the middle of the night and listened to the car return with the other four vacationers. In the adjacent room he made a pencil sketch, if a poor one, of himself with a monkey around his neck. He stepped out and found Hansen dozing in the garden. He woke the embarrassed guard and gave him the drawing. "Take it to Frida," he said. "Don't tell Van." He knew that Hansen suspected. The guard had tailed him to Tina's, part of his job. In the morning Trotsky left early and met with Breton who gave him a copy of their essay.

"Comrade," said Breton. "Fix it."

But without glancing at the papers he left for Tina's apartment where he knew Frida Kahlo would be waiting. And she was. At the door. Though she wore her full skirt, her torso was naked; her back brace and bra lay on the floor. She held a hand on each breast, lifting them slightly with her palms, her red, red nails blazing. When she took his face in her hands, she exposed her nipples, both of them encircled twice in red rouge. When he bent to lick them they tasted sweet and her nipples rose to his lips, hard and erect. He lowered his pants, lifted her by her butt and she placed herself on his hard penis, her tresses falling over his shoulders, her skirts enveloping their bodies. For a moment, for a moment, they were one.

"I haven't much time today," she said as he helped her dress. "We can't do it twice. But I've been thinking about you. Do your countrymen even know that you invented the Soviet Union? And then that you saved it?"

"Marx and Lenin invented it. Battle saved it."

She turned on him angrily. "Don't make light of my sympathy," she said. "Damn your historical inevitabilities! Am I some mere inevitability? My passion, my madness, my pain? I'm not some soldier you can just shoot in the back."

"You are the world's greatest living artist," Trotsky said.

"Does yours and Breton's little essay explain that?"

"What will happen to us when you leave for New York?" he said.

"I don't know!" she said. "I don't know. From moment to moment I don't know!"

He took her hand. "I want to see Siqueiros," he said.

"David Alfaro," said Kahlo. "He was Diego's best friend until Diego convinced Cardenas to give you exile."

"Then he threw Rivera out of the party."

"For being an anarchist, Fascist, Trotskyist!"

"And you know better now?" he said.

"I know nothing, but that the people are oppressed," said Kahlo.

"I am a Bolshevik."

"You created Bolshevism!"

She'd pulled her hand away but he took it again. "Is this a lovers' quarrel?" he said. "I'd almost forgotten." It had been a long time since he'd engaged a woman this fiercely. Over decades he and Sedova had found ways to almost immediately calculate the level of a disagreement, and alleviate it. He supposed, as well, that their passion was alleviated too.

She tore her hand from him again. "This is no lovers' quarrel! I haven't struck you. I haven't thrown anything at you!"

"Will you help me meet Siqueiros?"

She glared at him. He saw fear, sympathy, anger, and admiration sweep across her face. Her lips trembled. "He wants you dead."

"He won't kill me like that." He instinctively raised his right hand to the inner breast pocket of his jacket.

"And you will not kill him."

"I will not."

"Then what will you do?"

"I'll see him. That might be enough."

She relaxed. Her shoulders sagged for a moment, then she straightened them. "We've wasted time that we could have spent making love," she said. Her features hardened again. "I've slept with him."

He stepped toward her and took her wrists. "It's the past."

And she came to him and kissed him passionately. "Everything is eventual," she whispered. "Everything is so deeply transient it barely exists."

"We'll go before you vacation again. Van will drive us," he said.

"You're not coming to Pátzcuaro?"

"I have to finish the essay."

"All the men I've loved have placed their work ahead of me. But if they don't, I can't love them."

"You do the same," he said. "Work first."

She took out his drawing of himself with the monkey. "A poor rendering, Lev Davidovich," she said.

"Rendered nonetheless."

"That is you, always. Nonetheless," Frida said. "The day after tomorrow. I'll take you."

In the apartment Sedova was waiting for him.

"You've worked it out with Breton?" she said.

"Yes, I can finish it now, after I see Siqueiros."

"You're determined."

"Frida will take me to him," Trotsky said.

"Frida," she said.

"He hates Rivera."

"I know this," she said. "And Lake Pátzcuaro?"

"I need to stay and work," said Trotsky. "You can go. You enjoy them all."

"Is Frida going?"

"I assume she is," he said.

"You can bear being without her that long?"

He paused, hesitated, then said, "She'll be in New York and Paris soon enough."

"You see that as some sort of resolution," said Sedova.

He stepped toward her but she stepped back. "I have always loved you," he said, "from the first."

She supposed that if she was going to blow up at him, now was the time, but decided not to display her jealousy, her pain. If she couldn't match his passion for Frida with her own passion, neither could she win a war of passion with her. Kahlo would always be the guerrilla lover. "You have been my sole passion. I gave my life to a cause and gave my life to you. I am bitter, Lev Davidovich. I can't share our bed."

He wanted to say he was sorry, but he wasn't sorry yet. She left him there, not knowing what to do. When she was gone, he turned his attention to Breton's draft of "Revolution and Art." She went to the kitchen where she knew she'd find Rivera.

He was there and Frida was with him.

"May I speak with Diego," Sedova said.

Frida lowered her head and clutched Diego Rivera's arm. Then she released it and walked out to the garden.

"You want to tell me something," said Diego.

"I don't need to tell you," she said.

"Then I don't need to know. But neither will you solve this with

140

Leonov."

"It's just solace," she said. "He's Russian. He's someone who doesn't live in this house."

"Precisely the problem. He likely knows more about what's going on here than any one of us. He was in Spain?"

"As a nurse," she said.

"Natalia Sedova," said Diego, "he didn't fight for the Republic. Leonov is not his real name."

"Who can use their real name?" she said.

"Natalia," he said, "your personal life isn't my business. But protect yourself and your husband. Find out who Leonov really is."

"You can't tell me?"

"I don't know details." Rivera retrieved a pack of cigarettes from his jacket. Extracted a cigarette. He offered one to Natalia who refused. "Frida is taking Leon to see David Alfaro," he said.

"I know this," she said.

"Siqueiros might know."

"How would that come up?" said Sedova.

"But you can find out." He smoked. "The way any woman can find things out."

Sedova pointed to the bottles on the counter. "Might I have a drink?"

Diego extinguished his cigarette and poured two shots, but Frida came back into the house, looked at Diego and then Sedova, then back at Diego. "Drinking without me?" she said. Rivera poured a third. They raised their cups.

"He's finishing the essay?" said Rivera.

"But he won't sign it," Natalia said.

"I'll sign it," said Rivera. "Everyone will know anyways."

"Pátzcuaro?" said Frida.

"He's going to stay and work."

"And you, comrade?" said Frida.

141

"I'll stay here with him."

"He can spend some time with his little cat," Frida said.

Sedova noted a hint of jealousy in Kahlo's tone, though she couldn't quite speculate as to its cause. Maybe a woman like Frida Kahlo, who was open to all possibilities, could be jealous of everything.

"I'm loyal to Leon Trotsky," said Rivera. "Perhaps too loyal." He looked at Frida, finished his drink and poured another. Stoically, Kahlo held out her glass and then Sedova did, too. He poured, then put the bottle down and retrieved his cigarettes again. Frida took one and this time Natalia did, too. He lit Sedova's, then Frida's, then his own. "This occasion is far too serious." He raised his cup. "Salud."

Smoke curled around the three of them, for Sedova, some metaphor for Trotsky, the man who wasn't there. When they touched glasses, she sought out Frida's eyes. They were dark and clear.

OBSCURO

THEY DROVE TO A WAREHOUSE southeast of Xochimilco. Siqueiros was inside, alone, working under the light that poured from a bank of windows above him. The canvas was part of a mock up for his planned history of Mexico; a bald eagle clutched an American flag and a crucifix, casting a shadow over a muscled and chained Mexican worker. The figures were dramatic and expressive in sweeping strokes of yellow and brown. Spent .22 cartridges and cigarette butts were strewn on the floor, but Trotsky didn't see a gun. What was prominent, on the wall behind the canvas, was a large metal horse shoe, obviously from a draft horse. One of Siqueiros' notorious nicknames was "Wild Horse." David Alfaro looked up, a large, big-faced man with thick, wavy hair. He turned to face Trotsky and Kahlo. He blinked.

"How many times must you betray me," he said to Frida. He put down his brush and spoke to Trotsky. "I am a Stalinist and you are a traitor. I've vowed to kill you."

Trotsky didn't raise his hand to his gun pocket. He looked at Siqueiros. He scanned the easels around the room, some propped against the walls, others flat on the floor amidst the spent cartridges, the color and figures all around exploding with passion.

"I simply wanted to see you," Leon Trotsky said. "I admire your work."

"I am not so optimistic as your friend, Rivera."

He went to an icebox and returned with three beers. Opened them.

Frida took one and said, "I'll drink this in the car."

Wordlessly, they watched her leave. Siqueiros sat down at a small wooden table. Drank. He said, "Why weren't you in Spain?"

"Who would I lead?" said Trotsky.

"You must always lead? Besides, there were Trotskyists."

"The POUM," said Trotsky. "But they were far from a majority. Anyway, the Stalinists rubbed them out."

"There were Russians," said Siqueiros.

"Not volunteers?" said Trotsky.

"I fought in an international brigade," Siqueiros said.

"The other Russians were Stalinists," Trotsky said. "Many were double agents, no? More so, in our civil war, the Whites, the Monarchists, the Cossacks, the warlords were all divided into factions. We Reds were united. In Spain it was the opposite. Franco had the unity of purpose. And trained armies, the Moroccans and Italians. The Republic was divided. But even if I could unite them, would Stalin permit a Bolshevik Spain under my principles?"

"You have no principles," said David Alfaro.

"What principles will guide Stalin's pact with Hitler?"

Siqueiros winced. Drank.

Trotsky paused, too. Drank some beer. He again scanned the warehouse. "Besides, I am an old man now," Trotsky said.

"The Fascists chanted, 'Down with intelligence! Long live death!'" Siqueiros said to him.

"The defenders of Catholicism?" said Leon Trotsky.

"Stalin is our only hope now," Siqueiros said. "The hope of the world."

"While he allows the Germans to annex Austria and Czechoslovakia. To firebomb London."

"He's buying time," said David Alfaro Siqueiros.

"Understand me," said Leon Trotsky. "I would prefer the survival of Russia and the Soviet Union, even if it takes Stalin to do it. But Hitler will turn on him and Blitzkrieg to Moscow."

Siqueiros drank again. Lit a cigarette. An American Lucky Strike. An odd preference for a Bolshevik.

Siqueiros shook the pack and shifted one forward. Trotsky took it and let his enemy light it.

David Alfaro breathed in deeply and exhaled a great cloud of smoke. "They're good, aren't they?" he said. He drew in smoke again and let the smoke escape from his mouth as he spoke. "You are very beguiling. And fearless. But not enough so."

"You prefer *Pravda* to what you see and hear with your own eyes and ears," said Trotsky.

Siqueiros offered him a weighted and emphatic shrug. "I've seen and heard plenty, enough to make my own political judgments."

For a while, the two men drank and smoked in silence. Trotsky finished his cigarette and seeing no ash tray, put it out on the floor.

"I didn't come to talk things out," he said. "Or persuade."

"Why did you bring Kahlo?"

"Who else could bring me?" He was no expert on the intricacies of passion and infidelity, but if Siqueiros had slept with Frida then another triangle of conflict could be drawn. Her presence, now, could be read as an insult. He wondered how much that emotional labyrinth lay between Siqueiros and Rivera. And how close to the surface it lay beneath Rivera and himself. "This is not about Frida Kahlo," Leon Trotsky said.

"Politics. Art. Death. Love too?" Siqueiros said.

"You are a revolutionary. I am too. I came to see in person the man who made this revolutionary art." Trotsky stood and offered his hand. "Comrade Siqueiros," he said.

Siqueiros looked at the hand. He raised his own, but only touched

Trotsky's fingertips. "Señor Trotsky," he said.

Trotsky turned, and lending his back to whatever weapon could be raised against it, walked out of the studio.

Van had the engine running and drove off immediately.

"He didn't shoot you," Frida said.

"Nor I, him," said Trotsky.

"I want to talk," she said.

"I'm sure Van has perceived the obvious," said Leon.

Van made eye contact with him in the rearview mirror. Everyone knew now, it seemed. He wondered about Rivera.

Frida directed Van into the city, onto the Paseo de la Reforma, east of Chapultepec to a gallery of shops, booths of mostly clothes and jewelry. Trotsky followed her down several aisles to a flight of stairs where Frida told Van to wait, then led Leon to the second floor. There was a pale blue door that Frida unlocked. There was a bed, but she never made love to him in bed.

"Have others used the bed?" he said.

"With me?" she said. "Yes." She pulled him to her. "But they aren't here now. We're here now. I'm leaving soon and this will end. Maybe it is ending."

They made love quickly. He couldn't help but feel that this was one of their least passionate encounters.

"You're not coming to Pátzcuaro," she said. "A show of strength?"

"I'm never strong around you," he said.

"I'm never strong at all," she said, "let alone around you." She put herself back together, straightened the hair atop her head. "Once more then, before I leave for New York. I have a gift for you."

"A parting gift."

She put her hands in his hair. He cupped the back of her head in his hand.

"I won't forget the authority of these hands of yours. But all things end—power, passion."

"Love?"

"You don't love me, Lev Davidovich. You only changed my life forever."

With his other hand he ran his fingers over her brace where he knew he was massaging the scars on her back. She quivered and it raced through him.

"Soon I won't be able to walk, let alone make love," she said.

"Not so soon," he said.

"Very soon. I'm divorcing Diego. When we get back together, as inevitably we will, I will be through with love making. Incapable." She took his hand and led him out of the room. "I'll meet you one more time."

Sedova went to her doctor and procured some laudanum to help her sleep, though she didn't plan to use it on herself. She put it in her purse along with her pistol. She brushed her hair and put on some makeup, then found Hansen and had him drive her to the blue tiled Casa de los Azulejos across from the Palacio. Inside the Sanborn's she walked up the stairway at the back of the restaurant and stood in front of the Orozco mural at the top of the stairs, its figures giant and red, angry with power. Leonid Leonov followed her and stood behind her.

"Talent and vision too powerful to believe," he said.

"Have you met him?" she said without turning.

"I have not."

"We just did in Guadalajara." She turned around, meeting his eyes that peered from under his hat brim. "Leon is seeing Siqueiros now."

"His sworn enemy," said Leonov. "Is Kahlo with him?" He took her hand.

"I'm afraid so," she said. "I might have to leave him."

"A big step," he said. "Who do you know here?"

Keeping hold of his hand she led him back down the marble stairs with their clean brass railings, the walls of remarkable blue tile.

"It's said the tiles and brass came from China," he said.

"In the Sixteenth Century?" she said. "More likely Puebla."

When they sat, the waiter brought them brandy and soda without their ordering.

"Everybody knows everything," she said.

"Do you mean that existentially?" he said.

She laughed and toasted in French. "Salut," she said, and he said "Salut, dear one." And she felt herself blush.

"Would you move in with me? Or near me?" said Leonov.

"One ship for another? Too quick," she said. "And too intimate."

"We could start with a little intimacy," he said. "Then see."

It felt good to be charmed, despite everything. She looked into his blue eyes. "I want to go to the Palacio now," she said.

He nodded, finished his drink, and again offered his hand, which she took, though her eyes settled on the silver bracelet that Lev had given her after his first afternoon with Frida. She looked at the name on it, Sergei. She felt hot and felt a chill, as well. She got up. He put down some pesos and as they left the building she nodded to Hansen who followed.

"Do you ever wish to be free of that?" said Leonid.

"Always," she said. "But what of wishes?" She waved her hand. "Worlds? Dreams? War? Betrayal?"

He laughed. "You are too deep and too quick witted for me."

"And for me!" she said, and laughed with him.

They crossed at the corner where Avenida 5 de Mayo met both San Juan de Letran and Lazaro Cardenas Leyva at the corner of the Palace. Amid the fountains and sculptures in the courtyard, young lovers caressed and kissed. The Palace loomed over them, another concrete symbol of Mexico, the cultures of the Spanish and Indians, both committed to the monumental, said Leonid.

"And blood," Sedova said.

"And blood," Leonov said softly.

They entered the grand atrium and took the marble stairway where

Diego's Rockefeller mural, El hombre en cruce caminos, spread across the wall. A blond pilot navigated four cosmically painted propellers, guiding Mexico into her future. Just below his left arm stood Lenin, surrounded by men, women, children, a worker, and a soldier, their hands clasped over his. And behind him to his upper left, in front of Marx and Engels, stood Trotsky holding a red banner that proclaimed in English, then Spanish below it, "Workers of the World Unite."

In many of his murals he usually painted Frida, helping out children or passing out rifles, Frida, who Breton described as a bomb disguised as a butterfly, Frida with children and guns, but Frida wasn't there; right now, Natalia guessed, Kahlo was in the arms of Trotsky, Sedova's lover who once stood on the cusp of liberating the world. She once stood there with him. She imagined herself in the painting, together with him, holding the banner. Now their banner was gone. Natalia Sedova, how long have you been invisible?

"It's impressive," Leonov said.

A crowd of school children rushed up the stairs, a teacher exhorting them in Spanish, in Mexican. "This is our past! This is our future!" she yelled. "Our revolution!"

Sedova turned away.

"Do you want to see the other murals?" he said

She shook her head. "Let's go to your place," she said.

Outside she told Hansen to meet her at home. When he objected she told him that she was protected enough with Leonid. She caught a cab with him. She knew Hansen would follow anyways.

Orizaba Street was tree lined but had a wide boulevard with benches, shrubs, and trees. The benches were full of young lovers. Leonid's apartment, reached by a wooden stairway to the second floor, had a small kitchen and a second room with a made bed, a reading chair and lamp, and a small table on which lay a copy of El Popular, a Stalinist leaning news daily.

"One must keep up with the opposing opinions," Leonov said.

"Indeed," said Sedova.

On the walls hung a few landscapes and still-lifes, more in the style of folk retablos. The place was neat and clean. There was a coat stand and he hung his hat on it.

"Of course, I have cleaning help," said Leonid.

"Are they Stalinists?" said Sedova.

Leonov laughed. "I'm afraid they're Catholic Indio," he said. "I doubt they read at all."

He went to a cupboard and extracted a bottle of amber-brown liquor, poured it into two short glasses.

"Have you ever had Scotch?" he asked her.

"Seldom," she said. "Russia and Britain."

"Have never been friends," he said. "But this is good liquor." He raised his glass to her. "And this is a special occasion."

It was very smooth, and more subtle and complex than the brandy and soda.

"Were you in Madrid?" said Sedova.

"Until the stalemate, then I went north to Santander until we were swept out, by well-armed Italians and Moroccans. There was hard fighting. Lots of bombing."

"Guernica," said Natalia.

"That was the Germans," he said. "The Black Condors. It was an experiment in terror."

"There weren't Russians on the ground?"

"Nobody was there, officially. Hitler, and Stalin too, I think, were just buying time."

"Now they're holding hands."

"Not for long. There are German agents all over Mexico trying to turn the masses against Cardenas. A Nazi Mexico will distract the United States. Hitler will sweep through France, then Britain."

"Then Russia," she said. She sat down at the table and finished her whisky, pushed her glass forward. He finished his and poured two more.

He sat down across from her. "And then it's over," he said.

"If all goes as planned," she said. "When does that ever happen?"

"Certainly, you're right," Leonid said. "Britain has the ocean, Russia has geographic space, and winter."

"When are you going back?" Sedova said. She wondered how well he could hold his liquor. If he was Russian, he was a drinker. But she was Russian, too. If she must, she'd create her own distraction. What she hoped, what she truly hoped, is that when she had her opportunity, she'd find nothing on him, then it would just be a matter of ending things.

"Can you go back?" he said. "No." He drank and put down his glass. "Unless the Old Man is dead."

"Old Man," she said. "Leon Trotsky."

"Then there would be no need to kill you."

"You mean no need for Stalin to kill me," she said. She drank, as well.

"Of course," he said.

He liked knowing things and his desire to impress her was putting him on the brink of showing he knew too much. He must have felt it, too, because he got up and took the whisky to the kitchen, though when he returned he went to his knees in front of her.

"Old Man," she said again. She'd heard it before, yet usually with more affection.

He kissed her lips. "Let's change the subject," he said.

From there it happened pretty quickly. They undressed each other on the bed and made love. He was neither indulgent nor passionate, really, though a man whose love making was more about himself in that he took pride in his attentiveness. Afterwards she lay with him a while, then wrapped a sheet around herself and got up. She said, "I'll make another round." On her way to the kitchen she went to her purse for a handkerchief and slipped the laudanum into her hand. In the kitchen she worked with her back to the doorway, poured two big drinks and poured the laudanum into his.

When she returned she put her handkerchief and the laudanum back in her purse, then she gave him his drink and stood in front of him, throwing back her glass of Scotch in one swallow.

He laughed. "A waste of good liquor," he said, and like a good Russian downed his whole glass too. "It tastes odd," he said. He made a face, his brow wrinkling, so she quickly took his empty glass and fetched them both another round.

"You just need another," she said. She drank hers in two gulps. He smiled wryly and drank his in one. If he suspected anything it was too late. He reached for her and she came to him. He yawned, but proceeded, running his hand from her shoulder to her wrist. She kissed his forehead. He yawned again and closed his eyes, and then fell asleep.

She dressed quickly, then went to the drawer at the front of the table. She found what she was looking for buried under a pile of envelopes and folders. His name was Eitingon, not Leonov. Old Man was a code name for Trotsky. Eitingon's code name was Dragon. His job was to infiltrate Casa Azul.

She told herself that now was not the time to think, but she couldn't help but wonder why he'd made it so easy, why he hadn't thought beyond seducing her. Overconfident? Did he have a plan? Did he think, like Frida, that next she would introduce him to Trotsky, making the blatant incomprehensible? Now it didn't matter. She retrieved her revolver and opened the chamber, making sure each cartridge was loaded. She again found her handkerchief, then watched him, counting his slow steady breaths. She calculated how, if he'd shot himself, where his hand would fall, where the gun would land.

She'd have to be quick and accurate. She would rather have his fingerprints on the handle, but calculated that it would be difficult and time consuming. She watched him again and moved to the bed where he lay on his side, facing where only moments ago she lay in his arms. She put the muzzle near his temple. Her thoughts flew now. Time stopped. Stalin never had to hold a gun to anyone's head. He had his fearful minions, layers of bureaucracy, obedient, mindless automatons between him and his victims. Where was she on this dialectic of executions? She exhaled. Released the safety on the gun. Put pressure on the trigger. She'd have to put the muzzle on his head and discharge the weapon immediately in case the contact woke him. She counted, one, two, then stepped back. She went to her purse and found a writing tablet and pen. She wrote, "Never try to see me again," and tore out the page. Then she opened the gun's chamber and retrieved a single bullet, closed the chamber, walked to the bed and put the note near his face and put the bullet on the note. As she assumed, Hansen was outside waiting.

SEPARATIONS

TROTSKY WAS WAITING for her in their room. He came to her but she stepped back. Yet he was close enough to smell her breath.

"Whisky?" he said to her.

"You showered," she said.

He said, "I was sweating."

She said, "I can imagine." She went to the closet and brought out her suitcase. She'd already made reservations at the city Ritz, a moderately priced hotel in city center, midway between the Arts Palace and the Zócalo. "I can't live like this. I'm leaving you," she said.

"How can you?"

"I pack my things and I walk out."

"To where?"

"In a week or so I'll try to let you know where I am," she said. "I can't take this anymore."

"I'll end it," he said. In that moment, facing her, seeing the fusillade of the laden past and the shattering future explode in front of him, his heart leapt toward her. She'd been everything. She'd been the only thing.

"It's too late," she said. She put clothes in her suitcase. She looked up. "The revolution is over, Leon. You're a free man." She packed her makeup, but left most of the toiletries. "It's a big city," she said. "I'll find what I need."

He watched in silence as she finished packing. Foolishly he reached for the closed suitcase. She caught his hand by the wrist.

"Please," she said. "I'll do this without your help."

They stared at each other. The end is always hard to imagine, the ending hard to realize. She stood in front of him, powerful and purposeful. She had nothing she had to account for but, possibly, wasting her life. She'd have plenty of time now to deal with that. For his part, looking at her, her makeup and hair slightly disheveled, he knew that he'd not been paying attention. She turned away, then turned to face him again.

"Eitingon is in the city," she said.

He knew how far up Eitingon went in the NKVD. "You saw him?"

"It wasn't hard. He wasn't being careful. Anyone that close to Stalin won't last long. With luck he'll be dead before we are."

"We," he said.

"All right," she said. "You. You won't be safe in this house for very long. The NKVD is everywhere. The Nazis too. The populace is turning on Cardenas."

"You found all this out from who? Eitingon?"

"In fact, yes," she said. She took a grip on herself. She was trying to leave him and trying to save him both. She had loved him for too long.

"So you're leaving?"

"Not to protect myself, not my physical self, I'm protecting my personal self, my self-esteem. So sleep with Frida. Sleep with her wherever and whenever you want."

However foolishly he'd been carrying on, he'd assumed it was a secret. He knew that Van had to suspect, but nothing had ever been said.

"Everyone knows, Lev. I'm humiliated."

"You spoke with Eitingon?"

She would have preferred him to say he was sorry, though it would change nothing now. "There's no time for this. I'm leaving. Protect yourself, Lev Davidovich."

"Do you still love me?" said Leon Trotsky to Natalia Sedova.

She looked at him in silence, then turned and left. She had Hansen drive her to the main bus terminal where she got on a bus, then got off and caught a train to the Zócalo, then walked to the Alameda, circling to the hotel. She checked in, went to her room, then took the stairs down to the bar where she ordered a Scotch, yes, a Scotch, toasted the sad air, and watched.

In his room, Trotsky poured a vodka. He smoked a cigarette, despite his poor blood pressure and the pounding in his temples. He put down his glass and went to Frida's studio. She sat in a wheel chair, painting.

"I hear you," she said without looking up. "I know your sounds, and the sound you don't make between your steps. I smell you, too. And I can feel that you're anxious."

"I have never been anxious," he said.

That's when she turned to him.

"Does Diego know?" said Trotsky.

"We never talk about it," she said.

Which had to mean that Diego knew. If he wasn't anxious, he was ashamed. What price this indulgence?

"What did you expect?" she said. She locked the wheels of the chair and braced her wrists on the arms of the chair. With some difficulty she stood up. "I get a little stiff sometimes," she said. "Come to me."

But he stood, unmoving.

She tilted her head slightly toward her right shoulder and lifted her left eyebrow his way. It was frighteningly seductive. He felt a chill. He took a step toward her and caught himself.

"Something's changed," Frida said.

"Natalia has left me."

"And I'm divorcing Diego before I leave for New York. I suppose now that we're both free to do what we want this is not so exciting."

She turned and walked to a corner of the studio, picked up a canvas covered with a cloth. She came back and gave it to him. "I was going to give this to you after we made love," she said, "but it seems we've entered our after already."

He took off the cloth and revealed a portrait of her. She was standing, fully dressed with a long, rose skirt with embroidered white flowers, a long brown shawl covered her shoulders and fell toward the floor. Her right hand covered her left, which held a sheet of paper and a small bouquet was pinned under her left wrist, a rose in her hair. Unlike a moment ago, she looked to her left, her head didn't tilt, her eyes were not demure but stared into the world. If you didn't know her, you wouldn't read the pain, but he did know her and knew the pain beneath her apparent stoicism and defiance. And though the painting wasn't seductive, the rolled paper she held said, "For Leon Trotsky, from Frida Kahlo."

"It's beautiful," he said.

"You've changed my life," said Frida. She kissed him on the lips, very gently. "Shall we say goodbye now?" she said.

He returned to his office with the portrait and hung it on his wall, then without pausing for thought, got out pen and paper and began a letter.

"Dearest Nata," he wrote. "I have known and loved you for more than half my life. I have made a terrible mistake. I remember staring across the Siberian plain, the snow rolling before me, and behind me, in fact on all sides, spreading out, the wind casting blizzard sweeping away both where I was going and where I had been, equally obliterated, only the vague circle of the sun sending the sled shadow beneath us; that was our only hint of direction, a pale shadow, steering by shadow, sustained by nothing, the beacon of you in my heart my last and only guide. I am there again.

"I have walked away from the petty digression that surrounded me on all sides and blinded me. Ironically, I could never have done it without the confidence that my love for you provided, knowing that I would never leave you, and knowing that permitted me to make a fool of myself. Did I act from self hatred? Would I have done it if I didn't know that even you, in the early days when I was at war, in the depth of your loneliness, even you became distracted by infatuation? You have always said that from beginning to end we live alone and crash into one another out of desperation. I will not relent until I can crash with you again."

He sealed the envelope and found Van. "Can you find her?" he said.

"We can find her," said Van. He located her and began delivering the letters that Trotsky wrote, sometimes as often as twice a day.

She walked in the Alameda. Or taking a cab to Chapultepec, walked there. Once they'd contemplated getting old together and now, were they old? Another letter, then another. He wrote of his fear of growing old, accused Kahlo of exploiting his fear. Finally, she waited for Van to drop off Lev's next letter and had one of her own for him to take to Trotsky.

"My Lion," she wrote. "My Little Lion. How often I have looked in the mirror searching for that woman who was young and vital. Often I felt nothing at all. As in Russia, when the autumn leaves turn their backs to the wind and rattle, the thought of winter was more dreadful than the winter itself. We are never old until we have nothing to do. As for infidelity, I wonder when it begins? In the first moment of the first inkling of desire? The first kiss? If we stepped back then, would we have proven ourselves faithful? Faithful until our two bodies form one beast? My Lion, you are the man who sees the world in terms of a million million inevitabilities, so it was inevitable. Are we to compare them? You have always said the past is the present. Even so, I don't believe that either loves or infidelities can be compared. What are the terms, distance in time? in miles? in intensity? our intentions? In our willingness to throw our past away? Or as you imply, was your faith in me the underbelly of your betrayal? Without your love for me you could not have been unfaithful.

Your reasoning belies the facts. Yet if this personal tragedy foreshadows a reconciliation, then know, as well, that I can live without you."

When he read the letter he knew a dialogue had been opened. She would come back to him. He must continue to push relentlessly, but he'd made a breakthrough. Yet there was much work to be done.

He sought out Kahlo who had returned to living and working at Casa Azul while Diego kept to his studio in San Angel. She could have worked there, in San Angel, across from him in her own studio house connected by a walkway to each other's second stories; she could have worked there and even locked her doors—he didn't have locks—but she'd returned to Coyoacán, working from a wheelchair. The self portrait that she'd given Leon aside, what he'd seen of her work was now painfully disfigured, magnificently so, as if her return home made her both more powerful and more vulnerable, more independent and more available to her tryst with Leon, now abandoned, as well. Something was amiss, and he noticed now that their intimacy had brought him little insight into her psyche, as if his passion blocked it or as if she'd hidden it behind the images of her body torn apart, or if she was, as Breton said, a bomb tied with a ribbon.

Here, outside her studio, the letters he'd been writing to Natalia Sedova seemed more true but, as well, seemed a lie. When he entered and stood behind Kahlo she neither looked up nor spoke.

"I need to destroy our correspondence," he said. "If it fell into the wrong hands it could prove disastrous."

She continued to paint. "Whose hands might that be?" she said. "And disastrous to whom?"

"The GPU?" he said. "Journalists?"

"Husbands?" she said. "Wives? Lovers? My paintings are disasters. My life a disaster."

He stepped closer. "Your paintings are the most unique and amazing artwork in the world."

"Did Natalia tell you that?" she said.

"Diego," he said.

She pushed her chair back and struggled to stand, falling back toward the chair. She subdued a screech or scream of pain and he rushed to her, caught her forearms from behind and lifted her to her feet. She fell into him, his face in her neck, her perfume and perspiration, now so familiar, mixed in his nostrils. He remembered the sweet smell of the bullets that flew by him in Petrograd.

She turned to him, taking his shirt in both her hands. "There now," she said. "Is this what we came for?"

When she kissed him his penis sprung to stiffened life. He thought of Sedova's letter. When did this passion begin? How could it end? It couldn't end. They went to their knees and with all this inner strength, softly, he said, "Frida, I shall reconcile with Natalia."

Her hands on his cheeks, he felt her searching inside him with her eyes. Of course, he knew her thoughts. What did his reconciliation have to do with this? Very slowly she ran her tongue between the inside of her lips. "Help me up," she whispered. "I'll get the letters."

That afternoon, in the garden, he burned the letters he'd sent her, and then the letters she'd sent him. He watched the flames. What would Frida say? All is fire. All is change. Nothing lasts.

Rivera wasn't painting frescoes just then. Between his art and some careless political affiliations, governments in Italy, Germany, and Russia were pulling back on commitments to his work. He'd traveled to all those countries, sat with Hitler in Berlin, Mussolini in Rome, and Stalin in Moscow. He'd been too close to all of them and apparently not close enough. It had been hard to tell, he once told Trotsky, what any of them stood for besides power. He didn't paint power, he painted social movement, political prophesy, the banality of fame, the nobility of the ordinary person. Trotsky believed that. But now Rivera was under the gun from both the right and the left. Even Cardenas, his term expiring and his power diminishing even in his own party, was wary of Diego. The Mexican League, the Mexican Trotskyists, were currently divided on whether or not to expel Rivera from their party due his rampant emotionalism and administrative incompetence. At the meeting Trotsky had praised Rivera as invaluable for his imagination, fame, and force of personality, though admitted that his passion for painting made him unfit for political work.

For all of this and more, even before Sedova left him, Trotsky speculated about leaving Casa Azul. Now, trying to rebuild his personal life and put his politics to the forefront, he thought it best to distance himself from Diego, and Frida too.

He found Rivera working in his studio. Covered in paint. Rivera turned to him. He was supposed to be composing a coordinating resolution for the Fourth International, but there he stood, covered in paint.

"Are you here to scold the errant comrade?" Diego said.

"Are you?" said Leon Trotsky. "Errant?"

"The Mexican League says so," said Rivera.

"I'll move you to head of the Pan-American Committee."

"You insult me," said Diego.

"You're a painter," said Trotsky. "Your work is painting. Revolutionary painting."

"Tell that to Siqueiros," Rivera said. "I've read the Party's position. You signed it. It was your coup détat." Rivera dramatically wiped his hands, but it seemed more a gesture of defiance than willingness to talk. "Don't worry about the Fourth International, I've already resigned."

"Instead of writing a resolution," said Trotsky.

"I'll work on my own with the trade unions."

"The unions are anarchists."

"Anti-authoritarian, yes," said Rivera. "And I'm afraid you are an authoritarian. I won't support one of Cardenas' stooges for the presidency. I'll go right wing and support General Mugica. This country needs stability."

"You sound like Stalin," said Leon Trotsky.

"I hope I do!" said Rivera. "He's the only thing, the only man, standing between Hitler and Europe."

"He's hardly between anything," said Trotsky. "Not politically, not geographically."

"I'm creating my own political party," Rivera said.

"Artists?" said Trotsky.

"Peasants and workers." Rivera turned from Leon and walked to the table that held tubes of oil paint. His revolver was there. He lifted it in two hands, but didn't palm the handle.

It had been some time since the two of them, once mutual admirers, had talked, probably not since Trotsky and Frida had begun their affair. Now he wondered how much Rivera knew. How much of this blustering arose, volcanically, from helpless shame.

Trotsky let his hands rest at his side. Surely Rivera knew he carried a pistol and knew how to use it, but more, that this would be the most senseless of senseless gunfights.

"I'm sorry," Trotsky said.

"In your life you've never been sorry for a moment," said Diego Rivera. "Never sorry for anything."

"Natalia and I will leave Casa Azul."

"After I've mortgaged my life to protect it," said Diego.

"I'll repay you," said Leon Trotsky.

"With promises? With impossible ideas? I'm not a fool, Leon Trotsky."

"At one time or another we've all been fools," Trotsky said. "It's just that now we are both fools at the same time."

"You're reuniting with Sedova? When Frida gets back from Paris, we'll divorce. Nothing will matter," said Diego.

"Until we find another place, I'll pay you rent."

"I don't want your fucking money!" said Rivera. He slammed his pistol on the table, spilling paint tubes onto the floor. "Can you ever stop insulting me? I bought the house for Frida. Pay her the rent."

Trotsky turned. He didn't even know why he'd come. In the car he said to Hansen, "You know where she is. Get me her phone number."

She picked up when the phone rang. Who would call her but Lev?

"Thank you for picking up," he said.

"I suppose I was desperate," she said.

"We've been invited to a luncheon," Trotsky said.

"I'm not hungry."

"Tomorrow."

"I won't be hungry tomorrow," said Sedova.

"I can't live without you," said Leon Trotsky.

"You can," she said.

"I am deeply sorry, Nata. I will never stray again."

"You said that after Reisner," said Natalia Sedova. "And after Sheridan."

In 1920, after he'd returned to Moscow from the front, he publicly frolicked with the sculptor Clare Sheridan in England, then, back in Moscow, the free love advocate, Larisa Reisner, had made an open display of her desire to carry Trotsky's child.

"A very long time ago," said Leon. "And I fucked neither of them."

She didn't believe him. Did he believe himself? "Isn't that moot, Lev? The past is present? You fucked Frida Kahlo."

"I'm mad with desire for you, Natalia. Only you. I've told Diego that we are moving out of Casa Azul."

She stopped to calm herself and think, to step back from accusations. Whatever they knew of each other, or admitted to knowing, she had yet hidden things from him, and likely he'd done the same to her. They were no longer young. It seemed that they were doomed upon each other, if not simply doomed. And not just themselves, but the cause they'd fought so hard for. There was no permanent revolution. He'd already written that the revolution was betrayed.

"I found a house," he said.

"In Coyoacán?"

"It doesn't matter. We'll raise rabbits, grow flowers. It will be only me and you."

"And the body guards," she said.

"Till the end," he said to her.

After a little while she said, "I'll meet you tomorrow at the Vienna Café."

"Noon?" he said.

And she said, "Yes."

He brought a bouquet of Black Eyed Susans. She wore the beret that was his favorite, made of velvet so dark blue it looked black in some light, blue in others. Today, the way the light reflected from the cloth, it looked both.

"How beautiful you look," he said.

And when she smiled, it felt to her as if she hadn't smiled in years. "Thank you," she said, her voice barely a whisper.

DEATH EVERYWHERE

WHILE FRIDA KAHLO was in New York and Paris, Leon and Natalia moved out of the Casa Azul. They found a home only a few blocks away on Avenida Viena. Trotsky left the self portrait of Kahlo on the wall of his office in Casa Azul. While in New York and Paris, as Diego had predicted, Frida became an art star of the world, feted by Breton, Kandinsky, Duchamps and Dali. Picasso gave her a diamond. Her picture appeared on the cover of Paris *Vogue*. In New York she had her last torrid affair, an interlude with the photographer Nicolas Murray. It seemed everyone in the world knew but Diego.

Under Frida's portrait, as he packed up the last of his books, Trotsky felt her eyes on the back of his head, a foreshadowing. He found Lorca in the garden, picked her up and brought her with him to the bedroom and Sedova.

"Maybe we should get a dog," she said. "Something that could make some noise."

"A dog would give his life for me," said Leon. "I don't want anything around that would give its life for me."

"Not Van or Hansen?"

"They won't," he said. "I'm going to take a pair of rabbits, too. And get some chickens."

"Germans eat rabbits," she said.

"And the French, too."

"They eat the rabbits and the French?" she said. "The Jews they only kill."

"You are dark, my love," said Trotsky. "We can raise the rabbits, not eat them. There's a huge yard, plenty of room for hutches. Lorca will be our mouser."

"From each according to her ability," said Sedova, and then they both laughed a little.

By the time Frida returned they'd moved out.

Contrary to what either of them expected, the move was joyous. Sedova began planning for the building's security, creating space for their guards, even inviting them to bring their lovers or families. She drew up plans for two watch towers to sit diagonally across the inner yard, to go with a guard room on the roof of the house; any unwanted guests would be caught in a crossfire. Outside, a block away, the Mexican police set up a cottage, a casitas, which was manned day and night by five armed guards.

Sedova helped Leon set up an office with a shortwave radio, a telephone, a typewriter and Dictaphone atop his large makeshift desk of boards and bricks. She set up a typing table and book case for herself, too. She interviewed typists who were fluent in Spanish, English, and Russian, and found a young American Trotskyist who was very efficient at all three and French, too. Natalia set up the kitchen with a cubby that looked out onto the yard where they could watch and listen to the birds in the trees, view a row of white Calla lilies, and eventually espy the rabbit hutches, which Lev built himself, three cages high, out of chicken wire and wood that he painted dark green. Soon they were filling with rabbits that Leon, besides feeding his rabbits and chickens morning and night, wandered to as he pondered the Fourth International. He fed them snacks and petted them. The rabbits came to the cage doors when he arrived and made a kind of soft, inexplicable squeal. Leon used the chickens for eggs. He set up pens for them to roost and gave them the run of the yard. In the mornings, before he sat down to work, he gathered eggs after feeding the birds. He built a cat door for Lorca so she could wander in and out of his office. Though he worried about his headaches and blood pressure, this was as calm as Natalia had seen him since they arrived in Coyoacán.

Leon got in touch with the Rosmers in Paris and arranged for them to bring Sergei's son, Seva, his grandson, to Mexico. The boy was only thirteen, short and slender. He spoke neither Russian nor Spanish, but Trotsky was so anxious to see him that he stood in the lobby waiting for his arrival from Veracruz and when the car carrying Seva and the Rosmers arrived, he ran from the house into the street and hugged the three of them.

Van had left Coyoacán for his home in Minneapolis and when he did, Hansen, who'd returned home to Salt Lake City, came back to Mexico to take charge of the guards. Though his doctor required that he nap at mid-day, Trotsky usually sat with Seva then instead, working on his Spanish and his Russian. Some days they packed Leon's Dodge and with two of the guards, Hansen and a new one, Harold Robins, they drove into the mountains to picnic. Trotsky hired yet another driver, Charley Cornell, who drove with Hansen and Leon to the highlands to collect cactuses, which had become a slight obsession for Trotsky, the yard now filling with Mexican cactus and various chickens: Leghorns, Plymouths, and Rhode Island Reds. Lorca hid under the leaves of a large agave.

Finally, the son of one of Leon's American benefactors, twenty-five year old Robert Sheldon Harte, flew into Mexico City without his father's permission and begged Leon to let him work at what was now called "The Fortress." Slender, with a crop of fuzzy red hair, he reminded Leon of so many of the young intellectuals who surrounded him in the revolutionary years, passionate and angry, full of indefinable fire. Fascinated by all the intrigue surrounding him, he went by the moniker Bobby Shields. At first he followed Leon throughout the complex, arguing about what he found to be the foibles of revolutionary Bolshevism.

"He's annoying," Sedova said to Trotsky. "And all mixed up."

Trotsky laughed. "Our party respects opposition from within. He'll learn. He just needs a job. We'll put him at the garage entrance, our Bolshevik threshold." And he told Hansen to assign him.

"Too young for that much responsibility?" said Hansen. It was Hansen's job to set up the alarms and lights inside the entrance, using trip wires. "He'll have to know where all the switches are."

"You set those," said Trotsky. "All he has to do is keep the gate shut."Nonetheless, with the guards and domestic help taking Sedova's suggestion of inviting their intimates, the grounds were crowded with guards and cooks and drivers and their lovers or wives and their friends, including yet another new hanger-on from Quebec, Frank Jacson, who took to hanging out and smoking with the guards. The Rosmers, who were temporarily taking a room in the Fortress, and fresh from the subversion and chaos of Europe, noticed that Jacson spoke French with an accent neither Quebecois nor Parisian. When they mentioned it, he said it was because of his time doing business in Belgium.

Already alarmed by how her generosity had created too much tumult, when Hansen mentioned Jacson to Sedova she said to him, "Let's keep it simple. Don't let Jacson inside the house."

Soon the guards and friends began partying at night and that's when Trotsky ordered all unemployed companions out of the house to find apartments nearby. Nonetheless, a filmmaker, Al Young, arrived from Cleveland and began filming Leon whenever he got the chance. Trotsky was ambivalent about it, but Young was also an electrician and Natalia Sedova was quick to point out to Leon that the house needed better outside lighting and a real alarm system.

If there was domestic peace inside the chaos of ordering the Fortress, Mexico and the world were in turmoil as the Nazis ravaged Europe. England, which once watched the continent with cool detachment, was forced to abandon it completely when the Germans rolled through

France. The last of the British fled madly, if systematically, from Dunkirk. England was now enduring German bombing raids from the air. With the Stalin-Hitler pact signed, Russia and Germany proceeded to divide Poland between them. In Mexico, while the Stalinists were screaming for Trotsky's head, Trotsky's own party split in two, between Leon's faction that tried to hold the priorities of Permanent Revolution and a smaller faction that wanted to move away from it.

"Toward what?" Trotsky said. "Socialism in one country?"

But for the moment, Trotsky's biggest problem was supporting himself and his entourage. Though several groups of Trotskyists in American, including Bobby's father, sent him money, Trotsky himself engineered a deal with Harvard to buy his archives. He'd gone back to his biography of Stalin and began looking for someone to represent it in New York for an early advance.

When he could, Trotsky wandered down to the garage to talk with Bobby who seemed inflated and excited by his responsibility.

"You are the battle line," Trotsky said.

"Maybe I should have a gun," said Shields.

"There are already too many guns," Leon said. "What do you know about guns?"

"What did you know when you started?" Bobby said.

"I grew up hunting and fishing," said Trotsky. "And reading."

When Bobby said nothing, Leon said, "Ideas are guns. Don't you think?"

"You can't kill anyone with an idea," said Bobby Shields.

"You're wrong," Leon Trotsky said. "You can only kill with an idea."

Shields harrumphed and turned to the barred window next to the gate, staring out, his right hand gripping at his red hair. "You're playing with me," he said. "Condescending."

"I like you," said Leon. "You're very young. I'm pruning your limbs."

"Feeding your rabbits?"

"Far from it. How can you change the world, Bobby Shields?"

"I'm working on it," Bobby said.

When he told Natalia about his conversations with Bobby Shields she said, "You bait him."

"He's hungry," he said.

"And angry," she said. "Can you tell?"

"He came to the front. He came to fight," Trotsky said.

"But whom?"

"You see threats everywhere, my love."

"Someone must. How did you lead a revolution?" she said to him.

"With trust?" he said.

She kissed him. "I'm too deeply inside you," she said.

He said, "Never enough."

Soon after, two very strange things happened. One evening, just after dusk, after Trotsky had finished feeding his menagerie, Lorca was crossing the garden for her evening meal in the kitchen. An owl swept out of the trees and snatched her and flew away.

This saddened Trotsky more than he would have expected. After seeing so many comrades taken out by Stalin, as well as his sons and daughters, how could he be so affected by the loss of a cat?

"It doesn't get easier, my love," said Natalia. "It gets more difficult."

Then Al Rosmer fell ill and entered a French hospital in Mexico City. Oddly, Frank Jacson put himself at the Rosmer's disposal to help Marguerite look after Alfred, ferrying her back and forth in his car. During this, Marguerite learned that Jacson had a girlfriend in New York City, a social worker and Trotskyist named Sylvia Ageloff, who met Al Rosmer in Paris while preparing for the Fourth International. So they were connected, said Jacson; Al was his friend.

Soon after Al Rosmer got out of the hospital, the Rosmers decided to leave Coyoacán and return to New York. Paris, now occupied by the Germans, was no longer a possibility. They arranged for Al Young to drive them to Veracruz in Leon's Dodge to catch a boat and for Natalia

Sedova to accompany them and say goodbye. Though Leon planned to stay at home and work on his book, his farewell to the Rosmers was emotional. He hugged them both.

"You have remarkable hearts," Trotsky said.

"And determined minds," said Marguerite.

"Yes, you have stayed the course," Leon said.

"When all this is done, we'll see you in New York," said Alfred, "or even Paris."

"Make it Moscow," said Leon, and they laughed.

During the drive, Al and Marguerite explained to Natalia their convoluted connection with Frank Jacson.

"He and Sylvia were in Paris with you?" asked Sedova.

"Some," said Al.

"He participated in the Fourth International?"

"She did. He said he had work in Belgium," Al said. "Business."

"His explanations are always so vague," Marguerite said. "And if he was up to any mischief, he's certainly had plenty of opportunity already."

"Or he's very patient," said Sedova.

"Or taking notes for someone," said Alfred Rosmer.

"I'll keep tabs on him," said Young. "Has he been inside the house?"

"No," said Natalia. "I doubt he's even met Lev."

But half way to Veracruz the engine of the Dodge clanged and sputtered to a stop. They were close to a village and Young walked there and hired a tow. At the repair garage they were told that a piston had blown a gasket. It would take a few days to get the part and get the car moving. When they called back to Coyoacán, Hansen picked up in the guardhouse and Jacson was with him. With no other car available, Frank Jacson volunteered to pick up the group in his Buick and drive the Rosmers and Natalia to Veracruz, then bring Sedova back to Coyoacán while Young minded Trotsky's car until it was fixed.

The group conferred. If the Rosmers missed their boat, the delay would prove long and expensive.

"There doesn't seem to be much choice," said Young.

"I can handle him," said Sedova.

"He seems to admire Leon," said Al Rosmer.

"I'm not the prize," said Natalia. She showed them her pistol, which Young knew she carried. "Let's get you to the boat," she said to Al and Marguerite.

Young called back and agreed to Jacson's offering. They waited at a house across the street where, like many rural Mexican homes, the kitchen had been modified to double as café. They drank Coca Cola, warm, rubbing the rims of their glasses with lime. They talked about Seva. His interest in chess. How excited he was to learn he'd be living among rabbits and chickens.

"Lev will teach him a few things," said Natalia.

"About chess or rabbits?" said Al.

"Leon might be surprised," said Marguerite. "Seva can beat either of us."

"He's Russian," said Al Young. "Does he skate? Play hockey?"

"That might be a little hard to do down here," Natalia said. "There must be a rink somewhere in the city."

"He's never really had a home," Marguerite said. "We tried our best."

"He's with family now," said Natalia.

When Jacson arrived Sedova and the Rosmers got in his Buick, Al in front with Frank Jacson, Natalia and Marguerite in the back. They traded some banalities, then Jacson drove them in silence to the dock, said goodbye to the Rosmers, left them off and waited in the car. Natalia didn't follow the Rosmers onto the boat, but said goodbye to them at the foot of the gangplank.

"Thank you so much for everything," she said to them. "For Seva. Lev is happier already. His eyes have life. He smiles."

When she went back to the Buick, Jacson got out and opened the front passenger door.

"You needn't sit in the back alone," he said.

Natalia accepted the front seat. This was her first chance to really get a look at Frank Jacson. He was good looking, if plain. Thick, short cropped hair, angular, almost square features, dark eyes that gave nothing back. She wouldn't call his muted facial expressions stoic. He seemed more like a man with nothing to hide because he had nothing inside, or that what was there was all consuming and it required all of him to hide it.

They started back.

"The Rosmer's told me about Sylvia," she said. She spoke French.

He simply nodded.

"Are you in love?"

Jacson didn't take his eyes from the road. "It's hard to say," he finally said.

If it was hard for him to say, then somebody in the relationship, likely Sylvia, was under a misimpression. As Marguerite had mentioned, his French accent was indiscernible.

"She's coming to Mexico City?"

"Yes," he said. "I think so."

"Can she leave her job?" said Natalia.

"She's trying for a two week leave," he said, "for her asthma."

"Mexico City won't help her asthma," Sedova said. "It's wet and cool." When he didn't respond she said, "This is a nice car. A real asset."

Jacson frowned. "I made money in Belgium," he said.

"Business?"

"I was a middle man. I bought low, sold a little higher."

He didn't extrapolate.

"But you have interest in Trotsky," she said.

His jaw tightened then. He'd yet to glance at her. "He did great things."

"Now Stalin wants him dead," said Natalia Sedova. "At the Fortress you could be in harm's way. Since you've been there, anywhere else you go, you'll be watched."

"Watched?"

"The GPU, now the NKVD, are everywhere."

"Are those Russians?" he said.

"Secret Police."

He nodded his head slightly. How could he not know?

"I'll watch myself," said Frank Jacson.

He reached to the dashboard and turned on the radio. Found some Ranchero music. She assumed that meant he was done talking.

He left her at the gate to the garage where the new guard, the young Bobby Shields, now handled the iron gate. Jacson and he nodded at each other.

"You know him?" Natalia said to Bobby when she got inside.

"He's been around, hasn't he?" Bobby said.

Later, when she and Lev shared a meal of huevos rancheros and beer, she told Lev the story of the day, including her suspicions about Jacson. She wanted to mention Bobby, too, but hesitated so as not to appear paranoid. "I feel Jacson's hiding something," she said.

"I knew of the girlfriend," said Leon. "She was a friend of the Rosmers. She tries to help."

"Doing what?"

"Just errands," Leon said.

"Why is he having her come here?" said Natalia.

"Love?"

"That's not the feeling he gave me," Sedova said. "What should we do?"

"Take them on a picnic?" said Leon Trotsky.

"Leisure, Leon?"

"What better way to keep an eye on him. We'll bring tequila, wine. Maybe find out something when he loosens up."

So two weeks later, driving Leon's Dodge, Al Young took Leon, Natalia, Seva, Sylvia and Jacson to Mount Toluca, some fifty miles west of Mexico City.

They spread some blankets under a shade tree. They shared sandwiches made of well-pounded flank steak, breaded and deep fried. Milanesa. Natalia had learned it from Frida and Eulalia. Al had managed to find some bottles of Italian white wine. He took photos of everyone, even Seva, drank.

They toasted. "To the Majority," laughed Trotsky, "for a change."

Sylvia pressed him a little about the split in the party, now cast as two groups, the Majority and the Minority. He explained, that in Russian Bolshevik simply meant majority and Menshevik meant minority. A lot had happened in twenty years, but he was tempted to call the Minority opposition Mensheviks even now. Like the Mensheviks, their socialism was soft and they weren't committed to Dialectical Materialism. Natalia knew he was about to take off on a lecture, something she once believed was just a bad habit, but as time went on, she saw it as rhetorical and a way of not having to engage an ignorant audience in conversation. He looked at Sylvia and Jacson and went on to explain how Feuerbach turned Hegel on his head, and how Marx and Engel took it from there. It took some time.

"I don't quite get it," said Frank Jacson.

"Read something," said Trotsky.

Al Young laughed and Sylvia blushed. Sedova took hold of Trotsky's forearm and squeezed. When he hesitated, she took a rubber ball from her purse and flipped it to Seva who flipped it to Leon. Young stepped in and showed everyone how to play Pickle, a kind of base running game where a runner tries to time a run between two bases, back and forth from one base to another, without being tagged by the people guarding the bases.

"Like cricket," said Trotsky.

"Baseball," Young said. "Without the bat."

It looked like it might be impossible for the runner to succeed, but the base players had to catch and throw with some agility and accuracy and nobody but Young was good at it, so it continued with some hilarious miscues as Seva successfully ran the bases. After that they had a little more wine and the picnic ended jovially as it began to rain.

That night, after Natalia said good night to Seva and then prepared for bed, Leon said he would be up a little longer to work on the Stalin biography.

"Were you condescending to him?" she said.

"To Jacson? Just trying to find out what our young communists knew, and how smart and how curious?"

"They don't know much," she said.

"And they're neither smart nor very curious," he said.

"So why is he here?"

"Hanging around?" he said. "I don't know. But I'm armed and he's no match for me."

He was willing to take risks for the adulation of the young. He was too trusting, relying on some perceived ability to know a friend or foe by instinct. She was afraid that circumstances had changed too much and become too slippery. "I don't want you to be alone with Jacson," she said. "Never to let your guard down."

And he nodded. "It's why I have guards."

He worked till after eleven as the rainstorm returned. By the time he retired it was raining hard. Then at 4 a.m. the house shook from an explosion. Gunfire poured into the room and smashed the window that looked out to the garage, shattering glass. Natalia grabbed Leon and pulled him off the bed into the tight space between the bed and the wall. They heard Hansen yelling to the guards, "Stay down! Stay down!" so they must have been outgunned and outnumbered . From Seva's room came the smell of burning wood and Seva's scream, "Grandpa! Grandpa!" Machine gun fire rattled against the house and the far bedroom wall was splattered with bullets. Then a bomb exploded at their door, blowing it open. A man entered the room and emptied the chamber of his pistol into the bed, turned and walked out.

A few minutes later it was over. Natalia sprang to her feet and rushed to Seva's room. She grabbed him and took him outside the smoking room. His wardrobe was on fire and she went back and put it out with his blankets. A bullet had grazed his foot and she wrapped it in a shirt before bringing him to their bedroom. Trotsky's face was bleeding from shards of glass embedded in his cheeks and forehead. They both had grazed bullet wounds on their arms.

Trotsky was yet dazed. He touched Seva's cheek, then Sedova's. "They missed," he said.

"I should have rolled on top of you," Sedova said to him.

"And have you save my life? I wouldn't permit it."

By now, Hansen, Young, Cornell, and a fourth guard, Robins, were in the room.

"We were pinned down by the machine gun," said Young. "There were seven or eight of them."

"How did they get into the garage?" said Hansen.

"They must have taken out Bobby," Leon said.

"I saw him in your Dodge as they left," said Cornell.

"Kidnapped. A witness. He'd recognize them," said Trotsky.

"That poor boy," Natalia said.

"He didn't look confined," Cornell said.

"A gun on his ribs would do it," said Leon. He knew Cornell was implying that Shields was complicitous, but he knew as well there'd been some tension between the older guards and Bobby Shields, though he'd attributed it to jealousy and their age difference.

Trotsky walked onto the patio. Fires burned in the garden where bombs and grenades had been thrown. He walked back to his blown-out doorway and noted the .22 caliber shell casings on the floor, and another object lying among them. A horseshoe.

But now the Mexican police arrived on the scene, under a man named Colonel Fernando Salazar. They began gathering up the evidence.

"This is too miraculous that you lived," Salazar said.

"They were bad shots," said Leon Trotsky, "and maybe frightened amateurs."

"But how did they get in?" said Salazar. He was convinced that Bobby Shields was the lynchpin, if not Trotsky himself. Salazar was direct. "A week ago twenty thousand uniformed communists rallied to have you thrown out of Mexico. You could have staged this."

"That would gain their sympathy?" said Natalia.

"Desperation?" said Salazar. "Desperation spawns madness."

"And I'm a madman," said Leon Trotsky.

"I don't know you," Salazar said. "There are a dozen bombs and three hundred cartridges here."

Trotsky pointed to the horseshoe.

"Anyone could have planted that," said Salazar."

"Not the Horse? Siqueiros?"

"We'll look for him," Colonel Salazar said.

"You think I hired some pretty good shots to fire at us in the dark and only graze us," said Leon Trotsky.

"You're remarkably cool," said Salazar.

"Do you know how many times he's been shot at?" said Natalia.

"What about Shields?"

"Impossible," Leon said.

"Who else knew the layout of your house? Where the guards were stationed. Where you slept. Who disarmed the trip wires that were supposed to set off the floodlights and sirens?"

"That isn't your job?" said Trotsky. "Investigation?"

"That's what I'm doing," said Salazar.

"Get your evidence," said Leon. He turned to the four guards. "As soon as they leave we'll spend the night cleaning up," he said to them.

Outside the Fortress, in the casita, they'd found two of the Mexican police guards tied up. Three were missing, though they eventually found them with prostitutes, paid for by someone else. When the police finally left, Hansen turned to Trotsky. "There's some logic about Bobby," he said. "Who else?"

"The NKVD has had this place under constant surveillance," said Natalia Sedova. "They know our every move."

Leon paused. He wrinkled his brow at her. How would she know that?

But she wasn't going to tell him details about Eitingon. "It only makes sense," she said.

"Shields could have disarmed the trip wires with a gun at his neck. I know his father," Leon said.

"Maybe you're too trusting, Old Man," said Hansen.

"Maybe," Leon said.

Natalia Sedova held Leon's arm. "Tomorrow Young and I will redesign the fortifications and warning system," she said. "And then build them. This won't happen again."

In the following weeks she did just that. Sedova added two new guard towers, the ones she'd originally planned, where the men could sit above the house and yard. Young, an electrician, created a more invulnerable warning system that could not be turned off in one spot but had multiple hidden switches. They also shuttered the doors and windows in metal.

But before all that, Salazar found several delayed bombs that failed to go off; if they'd worked, the house would have been blown to smithereens. Then an undercover police agent overheard a man named Hernandez bragging in a bar about taking part in the assassination attempt. When arrested he confessed, pinpointing Siqueiros as the ringleader. He said Shields opened the iron garage gate for them and he named the three other men who left with him and Bobby Shields. Their destination was a farmhouse outside the city in the village of Santa Rosa. There, in a shallow grave in the basement, they found a decaying body. Salazar brought a strand of red hair to Trotsky. Later that day Leon identified Bobby Shields at the morgue and called his father. There was a rumor that Shields had a portrait of Stalin in his New York apartment, but his father said he went there and didn't find one. Leon's support for Bobby Shields remained stolid. "He was a hero," Leon said. "He died for our ideals." Though Salazar, and even Hansen and Cornell, weren't convinced of Bobby Shields' innocence, Trotsky had a plaque placed on the patio wall near the garage entrance: "In memory of Robert Sheldon Harte, 1915–1940. Murdered by Stalin."

Siqueiros had left the country.

LOVE YOU

ONE MORNING A FEW WEEKS LATER a little girl appeared at the gate carrying something in her coat. When she asked to see Trotsky, Leon came down to greet her. She opened her jacket.

"I found your kitty," she said. The kitten squirmed to her shoulder. It was gray, not orange like Lorca; it was a kitten, not a cat; its fur was thicker and it had green eyes, not yellow.

Trotsky touched the girl's hair. "I don't think that's my kitty," he said.

"But your kitty was lost," said the girl.

"How did you know?"

"Everybody knows," she said. She gave him the cat and he took it.

"Thank you," he said.

Sedova was surprised to see him in the garden with the kitten.

"You're going to begin raising cats, too?" she said.

"No," he said. "Besides, this one is male. But I don't want it to outlive me."

"Is it a lottery?" said Sedova. "He won't hurt anything?"

"Nothing bigger than him anyways," he said.

In the coming weeks the kitten followed Leon everywhere. He sat on his books and papers, lay on his lap while he worked the Dictaphone or typewriter. He purred. Trotsky worked with a loaded .25 caliber pistol on his desk and a cat on his lap.

Meanwhile, he was fending off Jacson who, now that Angelof had returned to New York, came by to urge Leon to read an article he was working on. Leon would only see him outside when he was feeding the rabbits.

"For whom are you writing this?" said Leon.

"Maybe you'll be able to tell me," Jacson said.

"That makes no sense," said Trotsky. "You're doing political philosophy? You don't know anything."

"I'm learning," said Jacson.

"As you write? First learn," said Leon. "I'll look at it when you're done."

He got a letter from Van, offering to return, but Leon told him they had things in hand. "It would be too cruel to bring you back to this prison," he wrote.

And Van warned him about Frank Jacson.

"I can handle him," said Leon. "He's one nervous little man. And I have my cat and my gun and my wife to protect me."

Trotsky was more determined than ever to bring Seva into the family. When his Dodge was returned, he bought a second car, a Ford. With two armed guards in the Ford, Young followed in the Dodge, Leon and Seva in the back seat. They drove to Teotihuacan. They had a picnic at the foot of Popocatèpetl, just the two of them, surrounded by three men with guns. He took him to the forest to teach him how to fish. There, with the guards waiting in camp, he could be alone with Seva.

"I don't like baiting the hook," he said to Leon.

"It's a very important metaphor," Leon told him. "Ancient." He showed Seva how to cast out and draw the line in, in tempting jerks that attracted the fish. "I'll bait the hook for now," Leon said. "The important thing is, you can sit quietly and wait."

"Wait for what?"

"For the fish. If it's big enough, we can eat it, and that's a very important feeling. There is no one between you and your food."

"I don't care for it, Grandpa," Seva said.

"Did you think about the sacrifices on the Pyramids?" asked Leon.

"Yes," said Seva, "but I don't care for that either."

"Horseback riding?"

"Horses are big and uncontrollable," said Seva, "and they have their own thoughts."

"And feelings," said Trotsty.

Seva was silent for awhile. The wind moved in the trees. A fish broke water in the pond.

"Why did those men want to kill us Grandpa?" he said. "I thought you were a hero."

"Did Marguerite and Al say that?"

"Yes."

"A hero to one is an enemy of another," Trotsky said. "You know who Stalin is."

"Yes."

"He runs the Soviet Union now and he doesn't want my ideas in the world."

"But your ideas will still be there even if he kills you," Seva said.

Leon smiled, a wry smile. "Did Al and Marguerite tell you about Lenin and the Revolution?"

"That's why I thought you were a hero," Seva said.

"Hate is very hard to understand," Leon said to him.

"Do you hate Stalin?"

"He's killed my friends, my family, my daughters and my sons. He believes that if he kills everyone who can remember he will kill all memory."

Seva was quiet for a time. Finally he said, "I don't want to do politics. I don't want to fight."

Trotsky put his hand on the boy's shoulder. "When I'm dead there will be no reason to hurt you." He remembered his thoughts of suicide. But there was yet work to be done. His biography of Stalin would stand in the world whether he was alive or dead. But he wanted his next assassin to be close and not a threat to Sedova or Seva. The thought came to him again that maybe the greatest gift he might give to them would be his death.

"I love you, Seva," he said, "and for now, this is the best way to protect you."

Seva's line struck and Leon helped him bring in the big brown trout. "A good one," he said. "You must have a good smell."

"I don't want it," said Seva.

"We'll camp tonight," he said, "and eat the fish that we catch."

In Coyoacán, Sedova, with time to herself, was recalling the codes she'd read in Eitingon's dresser. 'O D,' Old man, for Trotsky, even his guards used it now; 'Horse,' for Siqueiros, and thus the assassination attack on the house; 'Duck,' which she now connected to the water attack in Xochimilco; and then 'Mother.' Who was mother if not her? Was that Eitingon's plan, to seduce his way in? Or would it be an attack yet to come?

She found Robins in the guard shed, told him to find a car for them to drive to San Angel, and Diego Rivera. Rivera met her at the lower door with a tequila.

"I'm honored, Natalia Sedova, and happy that you are alive," he said.

"I'm honored that you're honored," said Natalia. She tipped her glass to him. She toasted in Russian.

"Your Mexican has improved yet again," he said, "as well as your Latino etiquette."

"Maybe," she said, "but we needn't dance with words before we talk, Comrade Rivera."

"You are yourself, as always," he said. "With pleasure. But another drink, then we engage."

She took the shot and drank it in two gulps; he downed his in one.

"You do or don't know Eitingon?" she said.

"I don't," he said. "But that's who your friend was?"

"Salazar believes you were involved with Siqueiros," she said.

"And you?"

"Political gossip," she said. "You wouldn't harm us."

"That aside, I know nothing about the layout of your fortress," he said. "I have never been there. More so, you shouldn't have left Casa Azul. You would have been safe there. He wouldn't have dared."

"We're surrounded secret police."

"NKVD."

"They have binoculars, telescopes, they can watch our every move."

"You learned this from Eitingon," he said.

She hesitated. She didn't want to wander too close to the secrets each of them carried, if not lies, then sins of omission for the better good of all. "Yes," she finally said. "But why would he intimate facts to me?"

"To make you look one way and not another?" he said.

"Yet they came as he indicated they would, straight on."

"Someone did." Diego brought her into the foyer where they sat in a patch of diffused sunlight. "The game of misdirection," he said. "Or maybe he liked you. Kings kill kings and marry their wives."

"It won't happen again," she said.

He raised an eyebrow. She hadn't meant it to be ambiguous. *What* wouldn't happen again?

"I've made adjustments to the house."

"So what other way to get to him?" he said.

She let him pour again.

"I'm honored," he said. He took out a cigarette, offered her one, but she turned it down. "Frida and I cannot remain divorced," he said to Sedova. "I can't live without her."

She felt intimate and bold enough with him now. Without doubt, his transparency was part of his charm.

"I can't leave Frida's side. She is unique in the world." He puffed his cigarette. "I've heard a rumor that you and Lev Davidovich never married at all."

"Do you need a priest or a politician to pronounce you're in love?"

"Russian intellectuals may not," he said. "But Mexican peasants do."

"And your affairs?"

"As well," he said, "I am a man. Nonetheless, you would be safer at Casa Azul."

"We've chosen this," she said. "Let us stay loyal, even if not close."

He raised his shot glass. "To your loyalty," he said. "And mine. And to your bravery and fortitude."

"And to Trotsky," she said. "And the revolutions to come."

When Leon got back from the fishing trip she told him about her meeting with Rivera.

"He's volatile," said Leon. "He talks, then thinks, then finds an apologetics for what he said. But he wouldn't hurt us."

"He's smarter than that, Len Davidovich."

"But why did you go to see him?"

"He's our last link to this population," she said. "We're vulnerable here on the right and the left. He is yet our friend."

She went to the kitchen and heated water for tea. At his desk, he fumbled with papers, typed pages about Stalin. The fast-moving events in Europe, particularly Hitler's inevitable advance into Russia, set him back. He couldn't write into that uncertainty. Maybe he should return to his work on Lenin.

Natalia returned with the tea. "I thought he might know something," she said to Trotsky.

"But he doesn't?" said Leon.

"He didn't plot with Siqueiros. He and Frida will re-marry."

"That's a good thing," he said. "For both of them. I'll go to see him tomorrow."

"I think you should keep and eye on Jacson," Natalia said.

"I won't be alone with him, my love. I'll always have someone else there."

But why, she thought, why be with him at all? A man who could persuade a thousand deserters to fight, yet struggled to make a friend—his personal power, his determined vision too much to bear for another being. So he sought to convert some lost soul like Jacson, like Shields? to change the world one person at a time? With trust? Would that confirm his vision?

The next morning, after feeding his rabbits and chickens, collecting eggs, and feeding his new cat, André, he had Olsen and Cornell drive him to San Angel. Rivera was at the door again. Trotsky accepted one shot and a cigarette. They went inside and smoked in silence.

Finally Trotsky said, "Thank you. For everything."

"My betrayal?" said Rivera.

Trotsky smiled. He took in the possibility that the question was double edged—on one edge, Rivera's politics, on the other edge Trotsky's personal betrayal with Frida. But Rivera wasn't the jealous madman he portrayed to the world. "You've wandered off," Leon said. "You never betrayed me."

"You find me emotional, but I'm practical," Rivera said.

"Stalin might say the same?"

"I don't think he has ideals," said Rivera. "He has goals. They could save Russia. They could save the world."

"What world will be saved? A capitalist West, a totalitarian East. Stalin has reoccupied Latvia, Estonia, Lithuania. He's invaded Poland and Finland. Where is the one country that socialism will succeed in? It doesn't exist."

"How can communism survive in Mexico, Leon Trotsky?"

"Resist Stalin," said Leon. "Resist America."

"We've nationalized oil. Soon the railroads."

"American corporations built the wells to drill and the railroads to ship the oil. So now Mexico can pay to ship its own oil to the U.S. American money, American technology, yet runs everything."

"The only ones fighting the Nazis here are Stalin's men," said Rivera. "Cardenas is powerless. The new president will be back in the hands of the *Jefes*, the corporate chieftains."

"We must think of the long run, of history," said Leon Trotsky. "When the current situation ends, where will we land? How will we land?"

Rivera poured a shot and lifted his glass. "You say 'we,' I like that."

Trotsky smiled. He put out his glass and Rivera poured. "We might not meet again," he said.

"Do you think they'll drop a bomb on you from a plane?" said Rivera and they both laughed. "You should have stayed in Casa Azul."

"It only takes one man, one woman, with a weapon."

"Who?" said Diego. "Did you trust Shields? You shouldn't have."

"Stalinists paid Siqueiros," said Trotsky. "Stalin killed Shields."

"After they were done with him?"

"Do you know something?" said Leon.

"No more than anyone," Rivera said.

"Shields could have killed me anytime he wanted."

Rivera drank more. His sigh shook the building. "Maybe he was afraid to die, so he compromised. Siqueiros wasn't paid. He's blind with ideology, blind with rage."

"Ideology as dangerous as a bomb?" said Trotsky.

"He should paint more," Rivera said.

"Like you," Trotsky said. He laughed.

"In fact," said Rivera. "Natalia told you that Frida and I will remarry."

Trotsky nodded.

"I have an illness. The doctors want to solve it by emasculating me," Rivera said.

"That won't happen," said Leon. He raised his glass. "So some things won't change."

"A man must first be a man. Let all else follow that."

"You are a great artist," Leon Trotsky said to him.

"So I needn't be great at anything else?" said Rivera.

Trotsky grimaced. They parted without ceremony.

When he got back to the fortress there was letter waiting for him from André Breton. Jacson was in the guard room, talking with Young who was preparing to leave Coyoacán. He gave Leon the letter.

Jacson stuttered at him. "I need to show you something," he said. He held up some typed pages.

"Is it done?" said Trotksy.

When Jacson didn't respond Leon said, "Finish it." He took the letter into the garden.

My friend and comrade, the letter said in French: I have always been reluctant to tell you how much you intimidated me: the power of your intellect, your will to action, your history of changing the world. So I wish to tell you how much I admire you still, and how important your work was on the essay, though it didn't seem to have much effect in the world. So much for publishing in America where all ideas, good or bad, are equal. Yet, it is the price of being right. Oddly, I think an American said that, not a Frenchman.

I'm writing after hearing of your close call with the assassins. Your survival is beyond the rational, but so it might be with all truth. That sounds French. My thoughts are with you.

Jacqueline has left me finally, inevitably, fed up with me, fed up with Surrealism. My time now is spent planning my escape from France; it has fallen to the Nazis like a house of cards. In this reckless, wrecked world our ideas are pushed like particles in the wind, a Diaspora of ruin, worthless ruminations on the run.

I am sending my love and care to you and Natalia Sedova. May we meet again on the murky plains of existence.

Yours always,

André

Trotsky went to his desk and wrote back to Breton immediately.

Dear comrade:

I am embarrassed by your intimidation. You are the greatest artistic intellectual in the world. You have spoken for art, though history might take it all down now in a tidal wave. But when the bashing of guns and bombs have left us, art shall emerge from the rubble. You have led the world in that transcendence and you will again. I hope to be a part of the crew that sweeps the rubble back. But now, I fear for Europe, caught between the hammer and the anvil. If Hitler takes Russia before the beginning of winter he will turn back to England and who will stop him?

I am sorry about Jacqueline who was strong and beautiful and bright. But you are a man who attracts beauty and brightness, and strength, and you will again. I am lucky that Sedova has taken me back. As for humanity, if no one will wreck us, then we shall wreck ourselves. Freedom is as dangerous as any fire.

Someone who believes in history as I do should believe in the future, as well. Currently, I don't. That is no reason to lower our fists.

Your friend always,

Leon Trotsky

Sedova was not around. Young and Hansen had escorted her to Casa Azul. They walked there. She found Kahlo in her studio.

Frida Kahlo stood up immediately from her wheel chair and limped to Sedova. She offered her hand and Natalia took it.

"I'm sorry," Kahlo said. "I couldn't stop myself." They let go of each other's hands.

"I imagine that you're quite irresistible," said Sedova.

"*He* was irresistible," said Kahlo. "Would you like a sherry?"

Sedova accepted. Frida went to an end table and poured the dry sherry into two small-stemmed glasses.

"Regardless, it is now a footnote," said Sedova.

Frida faked gagging. "Ouch," she said. "I was dreaming of immortality." And she laughed.

"I think that's a Chinese phrase," Sedova said. "Dreaming of immortality."

"A different kind of immortality, I imagine," said Kahlo.

Sedova sipped. "Did you know Bobby Shields?"

"He came by, flirted," Frida said. "He was just a boy."

Whatever Kahlo's tendencies toward promiscuity, her interlopers were men, and women, of artistic and intellectual depth, and if not already famous, at least famous in their fields and on the edge of broader fame. Bobby was too young in many ways besides his youth. More so, she needn't fuck fame; she was famous. But Sedova caught herself in a needless digression.

"No more?" said Natalia Sedova.

"He wanted to see my Stalin portrait," Frida said.

"The police inquiry suggested that he kept a poster of Stalin in his New York apartment," said Sedova. "His father denies it."

"I don't have a Stalin portrait," Frida said.

"You just say you do."

"It gets people excited."

Yes, fuck Leon Trotsky, keep a portrait of Stalin, or pretend to. That was Kahlo. Sedova wondered now if it excited Lev. If it would make him want to fuck her all the more. She tried once again to pull herself away from all that. Likely, it was a mistake for her to come here. Kahlo was enormous and complex, in many ways uncontainably wild. Sedova eyed the canvas propped on the easel behind Kahlo, a self portrait, seated, her chest torn open and her spine exposed from the pelvis to the base of her chin.

"Do you know anything about Jacson?" Sedova said.

"Another baby bird?" said Frida.

"With a gun?"

"Cowards are more dangerous than brave men, no?" Kahlo said.

"Siqueiros?"

"I was there when they met," Frida said. "Lev had a gun, too."

"And would have killed him."

"My point," Kahlo said. "That night he came at 4 a.m. with a small army. And still failed." She poured again for them both, then sat in her chair turning it away from the canvas.

"Do you know Leonid Eitingon?" asked Sedova.

"No," Kahlo said. "Neither Jacson nor Eitingon. Maybe that tells you something."

That they'd both kept hidden enough? But Jacson was now underneath their guard. "I'm worried," Sedova said.

"Leon can live in that shadow. Can you? You came back to him."

"You are re-marrying Diego," Sedova said.

Kahlo spun toward her canvas, then spun away. "Xochimilco changed everything," she said. "After that I thought anything could happen. Why not let it happen?"

"Time is always short?" said Natalia Sedova.

"That's my shadow too," Kahlo said. "A very short time with a lot of pain."

Sedova finished her sherry. In many ways, she felt the visit had accomplished something. The two women stared at each other, Sedova realizing that the two of them had almost nothing in common, nothing but their unexchangeable moments of intimacy with Leon Trotsky.

Young was leaving the Fortress to return home. Bobby Shields was supposed to be his replacement. Young had trained him. They'd be one guard short now. They had dinner for him the night before his departure.

"I'm going home," he said, "to Cleveland, Ohio."

"In terms of the weather, it isn't so different from Moscow, is it?" said Sedova.

"On the belly of Lake Erie," Young said. He laughed. "It's worse." He toasted them. "To stepping out of history."

"You wish," Trotsky said. And the three of them laughed again.

Before wishing each other farewell, he turned to them both. "Keep an eye on Jacson," Young said. "Remember Shields."

"What could have been his motivation?" said Leon.

"Hate for his father might be enough," said Young.

"Freud," said Sedova.

Leon squinted and rolled his head. "Not enough," he said. "Shields was just a boy. Easily twisted and deceived. Older and more savvy men than him were befriended and then murdered by Stalin. The spider waits on the edge of the web. In any case, Stalin killed him."

The next day, Trotsky went to see Kahlo. She was painting furiously now, fed by her successes in New York and Paris she seemed ignited by self-confidence if, as well, pushed by the desire to paint the graphic sources of her physical and psychic pain. She rose from her wheel chair with a cane and limped toward him. She was dressed simply, though her blouse and skirt were yet Mexican, her shoulders covered with a dark rebozo.

"Even yet, I would fuck you now," she said.

"The Old Man?" he said.

"But I never fucked the Old Man," she said. "I fucked the genius, the commander, the statesman." She pointed to his crotch. "I fucked that." She came to him. She touched his cheek and kissed his forehead. "But I'm done with sex. All things end too soon. All but the pain. Where did pain and suffering begin?"

"That's why I'm here to say goodbye," he said. "As the Fortress gets thicker, more profound, my world gets thinner and more brittle."

"Leon Trotsky, there are a thousand worlds. If we are in all of them, we only realize one. But each of those worlds makes a part of the other. You believe in historical circumstance. I believe in spontaneously co-arising worlds. But my world, this world, is shrinking, too. And so I paint it. From the inside out."

"Surrealism?" he said.

She said, "Surrealism is baloney."

"You will change a million lives, Frida Kahlo," said Leon Trotsky.

"And you have changed the history of the planet. You must admit, Stalin wouldn't exist without you."

"So you hang his picture?"

"I have photos of you. They're part of my more essential, private life. Do you want me to destroy them like the letters?"

He hesitated. Finally, he said, "No."

"I told Sedova, I don't have a portrait of Stalin."

"Should you?"

"Sedova is a magnificent woman, but you know that."

"And we somehow made that irrelevant," he said.

"It was," she said. "Do you regret it?"

Did he have an answer to that? No, he did not.

"Sedova called it a footnote," she said. She spun around her cane, her skirts flowing.

Trotsky smiled hard. "Sometimes they are the most important part of the text," he said.

"The story?" she said.

"Whose story?" said Trotsky.

She came to him again. "Do not try to erase my universe, Leon Trotsky. I'm no intellectual. I don't erase."

"We are very different," he said.

"That was the whole point, wasn't it?"

"I spoke with Diego," said Leon.

"Diego is a big, big man," said Frida. "Bigger than he knows. Bigger than any one knows. But me."

"I'm glad," he said.

"And lucky," said Frida Kahlo. "And I'm lucky, too. Though I wish you would have shot Siqueiros." She laughed. "He's back, you know."

"I do."

"The police refused to prosecute him, even though he confessed."

"He didn't kill anybody," said Trotsky. "Innocent on grounds of incompetence."

"He said he only wanted to scare you," said Kahlo.

"He failed at that, too," said Trotsky.

Frida walked away from him, then turned to look him in the eyes. "Leon Trotsky, do you still think I mean what I say?"

"I do," he said. "You just change your mind often."

They both paused in that moment of understanding, in that place where they once met and loved. He walked to her. Lightly and briefly, they touched lips. That was it.

That night, after dinner, Trotsky, Sedova, and Seva sang romantic Russian songs.

"I want to learn the mandolin," Seva said.

"Not the balalaika?" said Natalia Sedova.

"No," said Seva. "A Western instrument."

"I'll buy you one," said Trotsky.

"And I will learn to play it," Seva said.

And afterward, when he went to bed, Leon and Natalia sat and sipped wine.

"What's next?" said Sedova.

"In this moment? In this world?" Leon Trotsky said.

"Tomorrow," said Sedova.

"A blink," he said, "and it will be gone."

"You've changed?" she said.

"For the moment," he said. "For the moment I've changed."

In the coming weeks Sedova worked on the fortifications of the Fortress, a nomenclature they'd succumbed to about their home. Leon tended his rabbits. There were at least a hundred of them now. He didn't eat them or sell them, but built more hutches. He grew to like the chickens, though at times they were cruel to each other, even cannibalistic. He assumed that the species, as a domestic phenomenon, had simply become too successful; they winnowed themselves. Rabbits were the food of the world, the wild world, the civilized world. As for the chickens, he gave eggs, and chickens, too, to his neighbors across the way, thanking them for André. Twice, while he worked in the yard, Jacson appeared.

"I'm trying to understand dialectical materialism," he told Trotsky.

"Another communist who doesn't understand the inevitability of communism," said Trotsky.

"But if communism is inevitable, then everything is inevitable," said Frank Jacson.

"Who have you been talking to?" Trotsky said.

Jacson rubbed his thick short hair. He'd begun carrying a raincoat and a hat over his left forearm. When he saw Trotsky eyeing it, he exposed some typed pages. "Protecting them from the rain," he said.

"What rain?" said Trotsky. "Socio-historical inevitability, psychic over-determination, scientific causality are all different things, comrade Jacson," Leon said. "When the cannonball flies, does it feel free?" He lifted a young rabbit and brushed his lips against its forehead. "I am not a reductionist."

Jacson stared at him, obviously dumbfounded.

He didn't want to discourage Jacson, but the young man needed to understand that intellectuality and social change was built on the minds that came before him. "What are you reading?" said Leon. He presumed that Jacson wasn't reading anything. He said, "Start with Plato and Aristotle. Read Marx. Read about political economy. Leave me alone until you do."

"My essay," said Jacson.

"Read, then finish it," Trotsky said.

As in the days when he lived in the czar's prisons, he found that his new reality, the shadow of threat, his confinement, it was all intellectually liberating. Now, again, he had simple routines. He allowed himself to fall into Sedova's domestic rhythms. He was ready to put his work on Stalin aside and turn back to Lenin. In the evening, as he and Sedova finished eating, he listened to Seva plunk away at his new mandolin.

"Not very good," he said to Sedova.

"Time," Sedova said, though she meant it in broader ways. Trotsky had applied for asylum in France before Hitler marched through it, then the United States, a dead end. He was dangerous enough during the Depression when American workers were in the streets. Stalin, when an enemy of America, was, like Trotsky, a dangerous communist. Now, as an ally of the States, Stalin flipped the same coin to the other side; Trotsky was a traitor and a Nazi sympathizer, a Fascist. Mexican communists were in the streets chanting for his expulsion or death.

"I'm going to take Seva ocean fishing," he said.

"He doesn't like hunting or fishing," she said.

"If he feels a big fish on the end of his line," Leon said.

"If I felt it, would it change me?" said Sedova.

He laughed. He called for the boy. "Come to Veracruz with me," he said to Seva.

Seva stood near the table closer to Sedova, the mandolin hanging from one hand. "Are we looking for a mandolin instructor?" he said.

"You will give me one more try, grandson," said Leon. "If you catch a fish, we'll throw it back. If you still don't like it, we'll study French."

"I speak French," said Seva.

"My point," Trotsky said.

"Day after tomorrow," Leon said.

The next day he readied his office for his return to Lenin, putting aside his books and his manuscripts about Stalin. He reviewed his *History of the Russian Revolution,* surveyed the blank sheets in his notebook, meditated on his Dictaphone. He would start a new chapter of his life when he and Seva returned from Veracruz. He'd let Seva begin his own life. Someone in Mexico City must teach the mandolin.

At dawn, the day before their departure, he fed his rabbits and chickens. The rest of the morning he took down some notes, jotted down some memories, in particular the first night of the revolution when he and Lenin lay on the floor of an unheated office in Petrograd, freezing, their fate and the fate of the revolt both on the cusp of change or death. They looked at each other, their breath floating between them in puffs, and giggled.

He packed for the trip. Then helped Seva pack: rubber boots, a rain jacket, a sweater and gloves. "It will be cold near the ocean no matter what," he told Seva. Then he went to the yard and gazed at his rabbits. He took out a young male, hugged him. "A young buck," he whispered. "I can smell you already." It was evening now, near five o'clock.

Unexpectedly, Frank Jacson appeared, his trench coat hung over his wrist. "I've finished," he said.

Trotsky put the rabbit back inside the hutch. "All right," he said, "let's have a look."

He walked to his office where Sedova stood at the door. "He doesn't come inside," she said. "It's a precaution," she said to Jacson.

Jacson, his elbows tight to his body, spread his hands out, palms up, the raincoat hanging from his left arm.

"You're here," Leon said to her. "It won't take but a moment."

Sedova eyed Jacson suspiciously. He was unshaven and sweating profusely. She stepped aside and let the two men enter. She asked Jacson, "Would you like some tea?"

"Just water," Jacson said in French. "I'm thirsty."

Trotsky was already bent over Jacson's manuscript, his pistol on his desk to his left. The essay was written in French. "You don't know Russian," he said to Jacson. "Best if you put this in English. One of the guards might help you."

When Sedova went to the kitchen, Leon bent over the article again. Jacson's essay was barely articulate and extremely vague. This was the work of an ignorant teenager. Trotsky lifted his head from the manuscript. He was about to speak when Jacson brought an ice pick down on his skull.

Somehow, he'd stupidly swung the flatter end, not the pointed one, and missed his target, Leon's forehead. Jacson had hit the side of Trotsky's head nearer the crown. Leon screamed and lunged at his assassin as the pick dislodged and blood squirted over the two of them. Hearing the commotion, Sedova ran into the room where Trotsky shook Jacson by the throat, Jacson's hands limp and shaking, his right hand holding a gun. She ripped the gun from his hand, but Leon had spun Jacson to the ground and she couldn't get a steady angle on him.

Within minutes, Hansen, Robins, and Cornell burst into the study. The office was scattered with debris, Trotsky's desk chair and Dictaphone broken on the floor. Hansen pulled Trotsky from Jacson and leapt on the assassin, punching him repeatedly on the face and head. Trotsky stood for a moment, blood streaming down his face. "Look what they've done," he said. "The GPU. Stalin." He fell slowly backward, first on his seat, then on his back. "Don't kill him" Trotsky said. "We want his information." Sedova rushed to him, wrapping his jacket around his bleeding head.

"Jacson," he said.

"They made me do it! They made me do it!'" screamed Jacson.

"You're going to be all right," Sedova said to Leon. He was strong, still conscious, still articulate.

"No," whispered Leon Trotsky. "This time it's over."

Sedova applied ice to the wound, then put his head on her lap and when Robins brought her a sheet, she wrapped Leon's bleeding head, the wound now spurting gray matter as well as blood. He took her hand. "I see the gray," Leon said. "But I don't think back there." He closed his eyes. His breathing was suddenly labored. He opened his eyes again and motioned to Hansen to come to him. He said, "Take care of Natalia."

Hansen sent Cornell for the local doctor who arrived quickly and briefly examined the wound and said it was superficial. Trotsky would live. But he closed his eyes and slipped into unconsciousness. Then, in some incalculable amount of time, the police arrived, handcuffing Frank Jacson who screamed, "It's not me! Not me! Them!" Then an ambulance came. At first Sedova refused their help, believing the hospital might be part of the plot, but Hansen assured her that he and the guards would travel with them. The nurses placed Leon on a stretcher bed and put him inside the truck. Sedova stayed with him. She kissed him on the forehead, but he was unresponsive. "I love you, Lev Davidovich," said Natalia Sedova. "You're going to live."

Trotsky opened his eyes and looked at her. He grimaced as he tried to smile. He said, "No." He turned to Hansen. "Take care of her," he said.

"The rabbits and chickens until you're back," said Sedova.

"And André," said Trotsky.

"And Seva," she said.

"He doesn't have any musical talent," said Leon. His chest heaved. "Fishing," he said. "Les lapis." The rabbits. "Because they're too lazy." He coughed. "The world is lazy."

"Now you can be lazy," she said to him, "for the world."

He tried to laugh, but he couldn't. "You're dark," he said. "It's snowing." He whispered, "Rise up. Rise up."

Hansen and the other guards followed the ambulance to the hospital, but Sedova told them to wait outside Trotsky's room. When the nurses began to cut away his clothes with scissors, he awakened enough to stop them from undressing him. "She will do it," he said, pointing to Natalia. Gently, she removed his shoes and socks. He lifted to let her take away his pants, then his shirt.

"You haven't done this for a while," said Trotsky. "I should get hurt more often."

"Less often," she said.

"More often," he whispered.

She placed the hospital gown over him and he lifted himself for her again.

"You're still strong," she said.

Again he grimaced. "Like a train," he said. "The idiot wrote in French."

She said, "Bad French."

His throat rumbled. He said, "I can't laugh."

They rushed him into surgery where they cleaned and dressed the wound. When they brought him back to the room, unconscious, one of the two surgeons said, "I think he could live." The other looked away and said quietly, "There's too much brain damage. The wound is fatal."

There was nothing to think now. She went to his room and held his hand. His features were quiet. He awoke and met her gaze. "My feet," he said. And she uncovered them, kissed each one. They were cold and she massaged them with her hands. He motioned for her forward. "The snow is everywhere. It's beautiful," he said.

"You hate snow," she said.

"It's beautiful in moments," he said. "Then you grow tired of it. Like so much." He closed his eyes, apparently unconscious, but he awakened again. "I'll sleep now," he said to her.

"You shall live my husband," she said. "You will escape death as always." She took his hand and kissed his lips.

"Escape," he said, then closed his eyes.

When she was sure he'd fallen asleep she went into the hallway. The doctor went into the room briefly, returned to her and the guards and said, "He's in a coma." She went back to him and stayed the night. His breath seemed normal and this gave her hope. But in the dawn he began to struggle. He mumbled indiscernibly. She kissed his forehead and lips. "I love you, too, Leon Trotsky" she whispered. He opened his eyes. His lips moved. Silently he mouthed, "I love you," then his breath rattled in his throat and he died.

DENOUEMENT

WHATEVER HIS INFAMY, the news of his death exploded across the world. His funeral cortège was followed through Mexico City by hundreds of thousands. He was cremated and buried beneath a monument in his garden. The rabbit hutches are there to this day, piled against a wall of the Fortress.

Franc Jacson was found to be an NKVD agent, formerly, in Belgium, known as Jacques Mornard, then later, Ramón Mercader, working under Leonid Eitingon. He spent twenty years in prison in Mexico and was released in 1960.

Mark Zborowsky was found dead in the Thames.

Bobby Shields had met with the NKVD in New York City before he flew to Mexico.

Leonid Eitingon was poisoned by the NKVD.

Frida Kahlo rose to international fame, capped by her one woman show in Mexico City where she arrived at the opening in full Tehuana attire, carried in her canopied bed. She painted a portrait of Joseph Stalin and hung it on her bedroom wall.

After she died in 1954, Diego Rivera remarried one year later. He died soon after of penis cancer.

Seva lived in the Fortress for decades as a caretaker. He never learned the mandolin.

Natalia Sedova lived there as a caretaker, too, staying active in the Mexican Trotskyist movement. With Victor Serge she wrote a biography of Trotsky and published it in Paris in 1951. She moved to Paris in 1960 and died two years later. Her ashes were sent to Coyoacán and mixed under the grave with Leon Trotsky's. The two of them lie interred in their garden under the dream, a monument engraved with the hammer and the sickle. ◆

ACKNOWLEDGEMENTS

THE AUTHOR GRATEFULLY ACKNOWLEDGES the assistance of the following sources: *The Prophet: The Life and Death of Trotsky, The Prophet Armed, The Prophet Unarmed, The Prophet Outcast*, Isaac Deutscher; *Frida, A Biography of Frida Kahlo*, Hayden Herrera; *The Diary of Frida Kahlo*, Frida Kahlo; *Stalin*, Stephen Kotkin; *A History of Mexico*, Henry Bamford Parkes; *Trotsky, Downfall of a Revolutionary*, Bertrand M. Patenaude; *The Life and Death of Trotsky*, Robert Payne; *The Man Who Loved Dogs*, Leonardo Pedura; *Tinissima*, Elena Poniatowska; *Frida and Diego*, Catherine Reef; *My Art, My Life, An Autobiography*, Diego Rivera (with Gladys March); *Frida's Fiestas*, Guadalupe Rivera and Marie-Pierre Colle; *The Life And Death of Leon Trotsky*, Victor Serge and Natalia Sedova Trotsky; *Trotsky*, Robert Service; *Trotsky*, Ian D. Thatcher; *The Spanish Civil War*, Hugh Thomas; *Frida by Frida*, Raquel Tibol, ed.; *My Life, An Attempt at an Autobiography, The Revolution Betrayed, The Permanent Revolution*, Leon Trotsky; *Trotsky, The Eternal Revolutionary*, Dimitri Volkogonov.

Personal thanks to: Alicia Partnoy and Antonio Leiva for their politics and friendship, and pointing me to Elena Poniatowska; Sal Velazco for his depthful discussions of Pedura's The Man Who Loved Dogs and Rebeca

Acevedo for her assistance on Mexican culture in the 1930's; to Michael Ventura and Jazmin Aminian Ventura for copious, sympathetic editing, insight, and criticism.

Much thanks to Catherine Segurson and Elizabeth McKenzie at the *Catamaran Literary Reader* and Elizabeth McKenzie and John Blades of the *Chicago Quarterly Review* for publishing adapted excerpts of this novel.

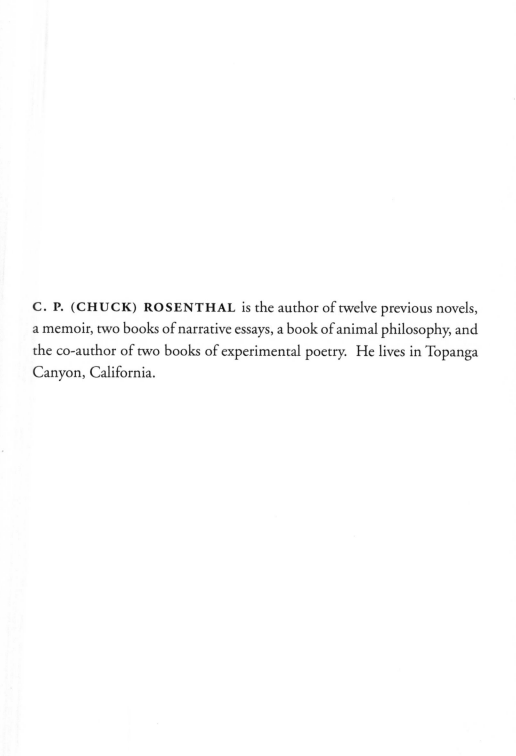

C. P. (CHUCK) ROSENTHAL is the author of twelve previous novels, a memoir, two books of narrative essays, a book of animal philosophy, and the co-author of two books of experimental poetry. He lives in Topanga Canyon, California.

Lightning Source UK Ltd.
Milton Keynes UK
UKHW010703181121
394190UK00002B/379